# The Pulpit Bully

# TINA BAKALAR SPANGLER

iUniverse®

# THE PULPIT BULLY

This is a work of fiction. All of the characters, names, incidents, organizations, and dialogue in this novel are either the products of the author's imagination or are used fictitiously.

iUniverse books may be ordered through booksellers or by contacting:

iUniverse
1663 Liberty Drive
Bloomington, IN 47403
www.iuniverse.com
1-800-Authors (1-800-288-4677)

ISBN: 978-1-4917-6926-3 (sc)
ISBN: 978-1-4917-6925-6 (hc)
ISBN: 978-1-4917-6927-0 (e)

Library of Congress Control Number: 2015910201

Print information available on the last page.

iUniverse rev. date: 07/06/2015

*To*
*Robb, for enduring;*
*Dave, for enduring me;*
*and my mother, who loved to read*

Honesty is a gift we can give to others. It is also a sense of power and an engine of simplicity ... We can simply be ourselves.
—Sam Harris, *Lying*

# *Prologue*

## *Incident*

Seen from across the peaceful lake—cloaked in its splendid green mantle—one wouldn't suspect what was going on inside the whitewashed church that rested on the corner of the block. The 1920s-era stained-glass windows—simple and elegant—would have obstructed the scene had anyone attempted to take a closer look. People accepted it for what it appeared to be or for what they expected it to be.

A local homeless man sat in the park and listened to the inspiring music emanating from within. For a brief moment, he thought about crossing the street and entering the church, but he didn't. He didn't want to risk being hassled by the cops he saw patrolling around the corner. He rested his eyes.

A loud bang, maybe two, followed by what could only be described as shrieking, woke him from his trance, though he paid little attention and drifted off again. A stranger walked by and pressed 911 on his cell phone. Three people inside the church called 911. An observer from a nearby apartment building called 911. The church doors opened, and many fled, though some stayed.

Inside the church in the small sanctuary, people cowered, speculated, and accused. One man, gun in hand, cried. He slowly placed the gun on the pew. No one thought to remove it. Two other men lay twisted and bloody. One stirred.

A woman, ashen, sat frozen beside the bloody mess. Screams pierced the air. Tears poured freely from horrified, fearful, angry faces. Save for the minister's deliberate yet hurried steps, others' movements were chaotic, frantic, tentative, or unfocused.

Police cars arrived within seconds, an ambulance eleven minutes later. The once-quiet neighborhood in this busy city became a hub of activity. People appeared out of nowhere to watch and conjecture.

On any other Sunday, a visitor would have encountered a vastly different scene, perhaps the same cast of characters acting in completely different ways. The church, known vaguely for its outreach to battered women, was respected in the midsized city, although it was not well attended. Growing, but still struggling, the membership worked at building its own community and creating a positive, caring public image. It was an eclectic group that espoused diversity, though one might not realize this upon visiting the church for the first time and encountering the sea of white homogeneity. The minister, who was also the organist, played both rousing melodies and soulful tunes, depending on the day—music that would echo across the lake, occasionally luring in listeners. Likewise, the spirited choir could be heard singing out their joy.

Greeters, friendly and welcoming as newcomers and old-timers alike entered the church doors, would have maintained a quiet, respectful distance. Though guests would be invited to socialize, doing so might not be as easy as they had hoped. The would-be visitor would have observed busy people, happily talking to their church friends and fellow committee members, and would have felt like an outsider.

This Sunday, the newsmongers—buzzards claiming their due—dove into the crowd just moments after the emergency workers. A smartly dressed, perfectly groomed reporter provided a stark contrast to the sufferers she was attempting to reach. She shoved the microphone in onlookers' faces prior to burrowing her way inside. She managed to get the initial impressions of several church members before she was ushered away from the crime scene by the police. Several members sought her out, devastated by what had happened and anxious to explain the horror. The police were in the throes of taking statements, and it seemed everyone had something to say; some of the witnesses were sure they knew what had happened.

# Part 1 Interest

# Chapter 1

*April 9, 2012*

At four o'clock in the morning, Kelly Allen sat at her desk, staring at the various screens around the TV studio for a good five minutes while the news crawl rolled past. Cold, lonely, and seeking motivation, she listened to the ticking of the wall clock, buzzing lights, and someone across the room tapping a keyboard. Around her, there was the usual bustle of the crew making sure the set was ready.

The headlines and jumble of words that she had been half-hearing in the background rose to her consciousness. There had been a shooting at a local church yesterday, something she had entirely missed having done nothing but streamed Netflix all day. The police report had yet to be issued, and the theories had run amok all day Sunday with reporters shaping the story to provide the best possible entertainment. The crawl "broke" and "updated" the same news every five minutes or so. Her station's reporter, Lara Chan, had already given the initial chunk of data to the writers and researchers to make the determination of what and how to air this news. It seemed like something she should pay attention to, yet her heart wasn't in it.

At thirty-seven years old, she was tired of the business. She was both bored and angry with her profession for manipulating the news to generate viewership and ratings. This was not why she had studied journalism, not what she had envisioned nearly fifteen years earlier when she was fresh out of Columbia Journalism School, MA in hand. She had entered the field with all the enthusiasm, idealism, and confidence of a new graduate who believed she would make a difference. She hadn't.

She accepted her assignments, did her homework, and performed as expected. She made good money—more than she had ever expected. Somehow her career had taken on a life of its own. Her long, lean, fit body, her startling blue-green eyes, and attractive toothy smile had not been what she wanted to build her reputation on. About five or six years after following the typical starting career path—newspaper newsroom assistant, researcher, and writer of a few features—she switched to TV. As a research analyst, she was sometimes allowed to contribute to the script for the anchor. A year or two later, someone noticed her. She was handed a script—a news report—and was asked to read it. The reading was taped. The powers that be liked how she looked and how she sounded. Now, as the morning anchor and host of her own morning talk show, she was somewhat of a local celebrity. She was asked to introduce guest speakers at local political luncheons, and she attended charity auctions. She was called on to be the spokesperson for various women's health issues, and she did promos for her own station. She was one of the faces of local TV.

But forty was just around the corner; of late, she had been forced to take stock of her life. What had happened to her dreams? Had she reached the pinnacle of her career? Was it too soon—or, for that matter, too late—to make a change? She was approaching the moment when many women hit their stride and became mentors. But she wasn't done learning. She hadn't accomplished what she thought she would have. She didn't yet know who she was.

Her personal life was a wreck on the order of the *Titanic*, having recently caught her fiancé, the intended father of her nonexistent children, in an affair. The tough cookie she had prided herself on being crumbled, but her behavior said otherwise. She immediately wiped her hands of him and moved on. No looking back, no second-guessing, no forgiving—just moving forward with supreme determination.

Now that her brain was fully booted, she turned her attention to the story at hand. She learned that essentially there were two people who were directly involved in the shooting who allegedly struggled over a gun. One of those people was shot. A third man was collateral damage, or so it appeared, and was killed. At this juncture, there were no verified facts. The stations showed video clips of several church members, along with one of the minister who made a brief comment lamenting the events of the day.

As Kelly listened, something in her was sparked—something visceral, recalling something like a past-life memory, not that she believed in that sort of thing. Deeply entrenched in the event, she made no effort to figure out why the story intrigued her. In fact, she was not even aware that she was so caught up in it until Zack, her producer, spoke.

"Kelly, what on earth are you staring at? I've been trying to get your attention for the last five minutes." His impatience showed as he raised his hand to comb through his ash-blond hair. His usually expressive dark eyes were hidden in a squint, barely seen under his furrowed brow.

She slowed her speech as she regained composure, saying, "Something … happened … yesterday at this church. Something's not right." It was an ambiguous yet obvious reply, incongruous with the usually tailored, articulate, in-charge woman she had become.

Feeling an enormous sense of unease along with a surge of energy and willpower, she announced, "I'm taking this on. This is *my* story."

Zack ignored what she had said and called her to the set. Her morning news show was about to air. By five, the report of the shooting was simmering, waiting for the news writer to add any last-minute updates to yesterday's on-site reporter's copy.

Kelly didn't want to read the script from Lara's reporting on this event, but once the cameras started rolling, she was in performance mode. She read with the appropriate amount of dismay, concern, and titillation to engage the audience. She wasn't altogether putting on an act. She felt it for real, even the need to stir the emotions of the public, which, up until then, had been a maddening part of the job. Now she wanted her viewers to maintain interest in the story. She needed time and fodder to make her case for why she should be the one to follow it. It was whispering to her somewhere deep inside.

# *Chapter 2*

*Late Fall, 2009*

Inhaling the enticing aroma of bread baking, Glenn took a big, exaggerated sniff. "Smells good in here."

"Glenn, could you open the table and get the extra chairs?"

Glenn returned with the chairs and smiled as he watched Amanda preparing a meal for their dinner guests, both of them in the mood for company. Together, they sang along to CDs of old favorites, which Amanda had loaded about ten minutes earlier. Glenn watched as she danced to the beat, moving rhythmically around the well-equipped kitchen, tasting and smiling.

The Corwells' kitchen was not large, so it made the dancing that much more interesting and that much more difficult. Small as it was, they had taken great pride in making it utilitarian. They both liked the great-room concept, which allowed them to visit and talk while preparing food, and to move with ease from kitchen to dining area to their two overstuffed sofas. The living-room area was attractively decorated in deep red and pale, creamy yellows that picked up the colors from the kitchen wallpaper. The window treatments had a thin, subtle stripe that echoed the fabric on the dining-room chairs, although no two patterns were exactly the same. It had a decorator look without being precious. Most of the items had been purchased at separate times. The wall hangings, artwork, and tabletop décor were eclectic, and much of it had been acquired during their travels. They had loved putting their house together. When they moved to Littleton, just two years ago, they wanted the rooms to feel open and to comfortably seat eight at the table—or even more when they used the card table.

Amanda turned off the stove, pleased with the result, and danced over, dutifully, to help Glenn expand the round dining table into an oblong, where she placed, and then replaced, the pretty Italian linen tablecloth they had purchased a few years back.

"Did we get this in Liguria, or was it somewhere else?" she asked.

"I have no idea. Maybe Florence."

"No, I know for sure it wasn't Florence. It was a small town. I can picture the shop. Well, who cares? I love this cloth. Maybe we should use placemats? The linen is hard to clean, and it needs ironing. Claire is coming, and we'll need to set a place for her. She's probably not the sloppy type, though you can't tell with kids. I assume she'll eat with us. She must be used to dining with adults, having older siblings. Kind of like Luke was, I imagine. Bright, mature, serious. Anyway, that's what I think a minister's daughter would be like, and from what I've seen of her, she does seem that way, don't you think?"

"I guess so." Changing the subject, Glenn suggested putting on music that was more sedate.

"Of course—we'll take off this tune when they're here. I'm just in a dancing kind of mood. I'm not sure what to expect of the evening. I really like Steve and Sue, it's always fun to be with Sheila, and Dinny seems so lively. I hope to get to know her better. We've been going to that 'place'"—she air quoted with a cheeky smile—"for a while, but I'm still uncomfortable calling myself a church member. I still feel like an outsider. Maybe I always will. Lately, though, I've been feeling maybe we do belong. I wasn't sure if Steve would accept our invitation. Did your parents ever have your minister to dinner when you were growing up?"

"I don't recall that they did. But if they had, you know it would have been much more formal."

"Well, I don't get a formal feeling from Steve. He's not stuffy. I hope no one thinks we're trying to curry favor or something." She chuckled at herself. "What favor would we possibly get anyway? I hope it's a really fun night for everyone. Too bad Dinny's boyfriend isn't coming—the more the merrier. She said she would bring dessert. I hope it's not fruit. I want chocolate."

"Of course you do. Anyway, you have the cookies just in case, right?"

"Yes, but the cookies aren't vegan. I've had fun making this meal, though I'm sure it won't be of the caliber they're used to."

Amanda brought the centerpiece to the table, a large red pottery bowl filled with artfully arranged artificial fruit, carefully selected to reflect the colors in the room—reds, greens, a splash of yellow, some gold sparkle for the upcoming holidays. She placed the candlesticks on either side.

"We got that bowl in Italy too, didn't we?" Glenn piped in.

"Jeez, Glenn. No, we got it at that shop in Sarasota when we were visiting Mom. But you are right that it is Italian."

As she dressed, Amanda reflected on the past year and how she and Glenn were finally feeling good about being members of TLC.

They had joined the True Liberal Church of Littleton seeking a like-minded community. Amanda had a particularly hard time adapting to rituals, and she even found it difficult to say the word *church*. But she believed in what Unitarian Universalism stood for. She believed in embracing all faiths, as well as no faith at all. She wanted to be part of something organized and bigger than herself that represented some, if not all, of the things she believed to be important.

As she dabbed on a hint of makeup, her mind wandered back to an early occurrence last spring, soon after joining the choir, when she was perched in the musty choir loft along with a dozen or so other singers. She had overheard someone formally—yet facetiously—call Steve "Reverend Dr. Anderson." Steve had grinned and protested, "No, none of that. Just *Steve* is fine." Steve's casual, understated khaki-clad appearance reflected his modesty and cool, laid-back demeanor. His thick, dark, wavy hair, possibly dyed, belied his age, which Amanda took to be around fifty.

At the time, she knew very little about him or how he came to be hired as minister of music. Nevertheless, Amanda was already feeling reasonably comfortable with him, so she had asked if, indeed, he was a minister. Steve quietly acknowledged that it was true, adding that he had been ordained at his previous church, not of the same denomination, a number of years after earning a degree in sacred music. Despite knowing nothing about such a degree, she was rather impressed.

Steve made singing fun. A genuine sense of camaraderie developed in the ensemble. Finding her voice, Amanda was having the time of her life, and Glenn was thoroughly engaged as well.

Around that time, Steve invited everyone to contribute ideas for an upcoming musical service, emphasizing the importance of process. He kidded about how the choir had grown so much that half the congregation would give a beautiful gift to the other half. In the end, the script was entirely Steve's, and everyone loved it. Amanda and Glenn were discovering a new dimension of themselves.

A week or two after the musical production, Reverend Baxter Schmidt announced his imminent departure. The Corwells had been pleased with Baxter's sermons and his leadership on LGBT issues and were sorry to see him go. They felt really proud that they belonged to such an accepting and socially responsible organization. However, fortunately, Steve had the credentials to fill in as reverend, at least on a temporary basis. Amanda later found out that she had not been the first to suggest Steve take the position and was pleased that others felt the same way.

She recalled the conversation she and Glenn had the day of Baxter's announcement. She had wondered aloud why some were so surprised by his departure. He had been there the three years of his contract, and he was young.

Glenn had offered his own thoughts, saying, "People have a way of projecting their hopes and expectations. I don't think they thought much about it logically. They just assumed he'd be here a long time because that's what they wanted."

It had all happened so fast. A few weeks after Steve agreed to help out in the role of consulting minister, he stood in front of the congregation, beaming and speaking humbly as he answered questions posed by the anxious membership.

---

Forty-five minutes later, after a change of both clothes and music, Amanda set out the appetizers. Amanda had initially put on a pair of black slacks and a red silk top, but then she decided that would be too Christmassy and changed to a multicolored print, casual, though still special.

"Mandy, why are you so … antsy? We've had company before. It's not the Duke and Duchess of York."

"I'm not nervous," she protested. "Just … well, maybe I am a little. I want it to go well. But, hey, we are who we are, right?"

"We'll just be ourselves, okay?"

"I don't quite understand why they're bringing Claire. It's not that I mind. She seems like a good kid. Steve said something about not knowing a babysitter. They've been in Littleton over a year. It's hard to believe they don't have a sitter. Anyway, she's eleven or thereabouts, and you'd think she could go to a friend's house for the evening. For that matter, I was babysitting myself at that age and so was Skye—and not just with Luke. I guess times have changed. Remember when we offered the Andersons tickets to the concert?"

"Yeah. They didn't take them."

"Do you remember what Steve said?"

"Not really."

"Neither do I, exactly. But I got the impression that they don't go to concerts very often, which surprised me. I had a feeling it had to do with Claire. You'd think someone with his musical background and interest would have leaped at the chance, even if they had to get an additional ticket to take Claire. Oh well. 'Who am I to judge?' as my mother used to say."

Glenn added, "'Za zeech ziz own'—as your dad would have said." His face glazed over for a minute as he flicked over the fond memories. Amanda became momentarily wistful.

Sheila, the president of the church's board, was the first guest to arrive. Bottle of wine in hand, she threw herself on the couch with the kind of sigh one makes at the end of a very tiring day when ready to party. She promptly stood right back up and offered to pour.

The doorbell rang, and Glenn ushered Dinny in, taking her covered dish and placing it on the counter. "Fruit compote," Dinny announced. "Fruit is the easiest way to be gastronomically correct. I am seriously thinking about becoming vegan myself." Glenn winked at Amanda, preempting her grimace.

It appeared that Dinny, too, had taken extra care with her outfit. She was always well groomed and managed to assemble some beautifully funky outfits, casual like most of the TLC women, though a bit more styled. She took pride in announcing her thrift shop "finds." She had outdone herself tonight. Dinny was one of those innately thin women with high cheekbones, of a "certain age." She never wore makeup, pleased with her natural appearance, although like many women her age, she did color her hair.

Amanda liked clothes and enjoyed dressing up. Sometimes she wished she had friends here to go shopping with, as she did in Monroe before they moved. She didn't know Dinny well, though she thought Sheila's description of her as "charmingly quirky" was fitting. To illustrate, Sheila had told Amanda that at a board meeting, Dinny read a poem as an endorsement of Steve's candidacy for minister; no one grasped her literary vision, but everyone applauded anyway. Dinny had been the first to sign up for choir after Steve was hired. It seemed she felt a special bond with him.

The four of them chatted a bit, primarily about the church. Intermittently, whenever there was a pause, Dinny either thanked them for including her or jumped up to offer help or to pass the tray. A slightly aged Tinker Bell, she sparkled. She flashed her engaging smile and allowed her effervescent personality to bubble over. At times like this, she appeared youthful and delightfully giddy. Other times, in repose or sitting in judgment, the wrinkles around her lips were quite prominent. Amanda imagined that she had probably been a smoker at one time.

When the doorbell rang some fifteen minutes later, Dinny was caught midsentence, animated arms dancing and gesticulating. She continued, "As I was saying, I was at the church earlier when the kids were hanging the decorations. Steve never stopped the music. The kids loved it. I loved it. It was a very special day. And I've been really looking forward to tonight."

Steve entered, sporting a huge grin and carrying a folder. As he walked into the living room, he announced, "Sorry. We got held up at the church. Claire didn't want to leave."

Claire rolled her eyes, mischievously grinned, and said, "You didn't either, Dad."

Steve followed his apology with a flourish of his hand as he proudly, yet with humility, offered his gift. "This is for the Corwells." He ceremoniously handed the folder to Amanda.

In that instant, Amanda felt warm and special, though the sensation was fleeting. The glow immediately dimmed when Steve added, "We always bring our hosts an original piece of music, dedicated to them." Clearly the Corwells were not *so* exceptional. But, she rebounded quickly, brightness returned.

Just the idea that he had composed a piece for them was

mind-boggling. Even if *he* did it all the time, nothing like that had ever been done for them before. They put the folder aside, expressing heartfelt thanks, and once again, wine was offered and poured.

Sheila made a toast and commented that it was too bad Dinny's boyfriend couldn't be there.

Dinny looked straight at Steve, lowered her lashes, covering her softly lit hazel eyes for just a moment, and then she raised her eyelids. With an almost imperceptible glimmer, she said, "Oh, we broke up." Without any additional prompting, she confided, "Aurora is helping me figure out my life. You guys know her, right? She has been such a blessing."

Amanda knew Aurora by sight as a wispy, ethereal sixty- or seventy-year-old ex-hippie type, graceful and airy. She had occasionally shared personal, meandering, and incoherent comments at church during "Sharing Joys and Concerns," a ritual Amanda cynically (sometimes) thought of as "show and tell."

As Amanda got up to refill the plate of hors d'oeuvres, she noticed a rather pouty-faced Claire sitting on the other side of the room. She quietly asked her if she would like a cranberry-splash Sprite, thinking it would make her feel both included and grown-up, especially if it were served in a fancy wine glass. Claire did not light up as expected; instead, she shrugged her shoulders dismissively.

Steve suddenly separated himself from the conversation and interjected on her behalf, "That is a lovely offer, maybe a half glass. She doesn't need more sugar. There were a lot of goodies this afternoon. Say thank you to Amanda."

Claire glared, rolled her eyes again, and said, "Oh, Dad. I didn't eat *that* much."

Steve explained Claire had an early rehearsal that morning, had been up late the night before, and was completely exhausted. The glare remained, as did Steve's smile.

Having been through preteen behavior years before with her own daughter, Amanda suggested that Claire might want to go to the den where there were a few videos she might like, and she wouldn't have to listen to boring adult conversation. Knowing Claire was an avid reader, she offered some books if Claire did not have one with her. Claire told Amanda she had a book and her own video and followed her.

Steve seemed to think this was a reasonable suggestion, and he followed them to the den where he took over, soothing her quietly, and telling her that she could lie down on the daybed, though to be sure to take her shoes off.

Claire said, "I know that."

Steve told Amanda that Claire would not be watching TV, but reading was fine. When Amanda offered the DVD player and a selection of films, Steve reminded Claire that she had brought *March of the Penguins*, an educational documentary, and that one would be permissible.

When Amanda returned to the living room, she was drawn back to the conversation and regretted having missed out on some of it. Apparently Sue had been talking about a political-social topic that she felt particularly strongly about.

Sheila clearly wanted to explore how the church might support the endeavor. "Sue, I had no idea you were interested in today's antiwar movement. I mean, we—that is, I am sure most of us feel the same way, but so far, TLC has not gotten behind it in any organized way. Most of our social justice efforts, like helping with the battered women's shelter, are a result of an individual picking up the ball and running with it. I'd love for us do something in a more cohesive way. Sue, maybe you can give us some ideas to help us get started."

Sue demurred, eyes down. "I would love to get involved if I can. I'd sit in on some meetings, but I'm not much of a leader. Also, I work all week so I don't have a lot of time—"

Dinny interrupted. "Maybe this is an effort that Steve could lead. Baxter did some things ... but I don't know ... I never felt like I could get behind his actions. He just didn't click with me. Maybe he was too into the GLBT stuff for me. I mean I support that and all, but it isn't my passion. Anyway, he was such a loner, too quiet and aloof. Steve, on the other hand, could—"

"Did someone mention my name?" Steve returned from his tête-à-tête with Claire, and Sue shifted her attention to him. She announced proudly that Steve had played piano for a fund-raising event that had been held at their previous church to support the cause.

Steve looked down somewhat uncomfortably as he elaborated, slightly embarrassed, trying to minimize his contribution while emphasizing his dedication to peace.

Although Sheila tried to sound him out about his ideas on the topic, he called her up short by saying that it was probably not the right time and place to talk about it. Everyone agreed.

When dinner was ready, Claire joined the adults. She slumped into a chair, brooding as she picked at her food and played with the veggies. The conversation was lively, and although not completely relaxed, there was plenty of laughter and merriment. Glasses clinked with several toasts. Steve told a couple of jokes, and he and Glenn got on tear with their silly puns.

At different times, someone made an effort to bring Claire into the conversation, but her father succeeded by placing her center stage and talking about her dance performance. At first, she only smiled politely, but her face ignited when she explained some of the highlights. Saturday's performance turned out not to be a recital as Amanda had initially thought; it was a contest. Prompted by her father's questions, while Sue quietly listened, Claire discussed the intricacies of specific dance steps, how challenging it had been to learn them, the music she danced to, and the awards and recognition she was duly accorded. At that point, the conversation dragged. Sheila caught Amanda's eye and tried to gently change the subject at least twice.

Dinny smiled and nodded, feigning interest, interjecting words of praise for Claire along with due credit to her parents. Steve beamed with pride. Sue's smile was more subdued.

Eventually the adults recaptured the conversation. Sue revealed herself to be a witty, deep thinker. Her personal charm, from Amanda's point of view, was her lack of self-awareness about her own talents and abilities. During the course of the evening, Amanda learned about some of Sue's artistic accomplishments and interests, but it was only through sidebars and questions directed to her. Sue worked in a midlevel accounting position for a time-share company, but outside of work, she entered her quilts in craft fairs and had even been in some juried shows with honorable mentions. The rest of the buzz around the table centered on the church, Steve's ideas, and Claire.

The vegan bread did not turn out well at all—Amanda was sure it wasn't supposed to be flatbread—but the guests ate it with good grace. Compliments abounded for everyone's contributions. Before Amanda or Glenn could suggest a move to the more comfortable living room area, Steve announced it was time for them to go. He suggested Claire needed to rest and then joked, "Of course, some of us have to work tomorrow morning."

After the Andersons left, Dinny linked her arm in Amanda's as they walked toward the door. "I'm going to the exhibit at the fine arts museum tomorrow. Come with me! It will be a blast—jazz musicians and an interactive paint-it-yourself event. The flier said to bring something from home to paint. I'm bringing my garden shoes and a toilet seat. Say you'll come! What will you bring?" Before Amanda could say anything, Dinny had it all organized. "We'll go right after service."

Sheila hung back, helping Glenn pick up a few things. She told Amanda she'd call tomorrow, gave her hug, and then left.

Glenn and Amanda reviewed the evening as they cleaned up. Amanda asked, "So what did you think?"

"I'm not sure. What did *you* think?"

"Well, the meal was okay, not my best. The bread was kind of embarrassing, but I thought it tasted all right. Everyone seemed to have a good time. But something was missing. It wasn't exactly what I had hoped. But then again, we really didn't know what to expect."

"I think we got our answer, though."

"What do you mean?"

"About protocol, being friends with the minister and such. It seems to me that Steve was setting some clear boundaries. He was guarded. Now we know."

"Yeah, I guess. I'm a little disappointed, but *que será, será*. Do you think Sue is older than Steve? I really like her. She is really sweet and funny. She's not shy, just quiet. She might not look very fashionable or with it, but she's not the acquiescent, dull minister's wife that she pretends to be. I think she has a lot more going on than what meets the eye. You know what I mean? Well, maybe that's wishful thinking. Truth is I am a little disappointed that she doesn't take a stronger position, especially knowing that she has smarts. In any case, I hope we might be friends. I hope that's possible. I thought it kind of odd that she didn't speak much with Claire. Steve handled everything."

"Maybe they had a fight, and Steve was trying to keep some space between them. You, of all people, know about mothers and daughters."

"Maybe."

"Or maybe Sue was tired, and he was giving her a break."

"It could be that too, I suppose. Let's look at that piece of music."

They opened the folder and read the simple dedication: *To Amanda and Glenn Corwell.* They grinned at each other and took a closer look at the music. Although neither of them was particularly good at sight-reading, they could instantly tell that the piece was somber, heavy with a religious feel, given all the "amens," "hallelujahs," and "blesseds" in the lyrics. They didn't comment on it, but they both knew that if Steve had composed it for them specifically, he surely had not been paying much attention.

Changing the subject while she began loading the dishwasher, Amanda kicked herself for having been coerced into going to the museum with Dinny. "I don't know why I didn't say no."

"Don't go if you don't want to." Glenn was so clear about some things.

"How can I say no now? It's hard for me to lie to make up an excuse. Anyway, maybe it will be good for me to go. I need to be more spontaneous and more adventurous."

"Then go and have a good time."

"It's the kind of thing I hate, though … well, I think I'd hate it."

Glenn allowed his wife to obsess a minute longer before he kissed her on the cheek and said, "Do whatever you want. Just don't make yourself crazy."

After they finished cleaning up, they went upstairs, glad that they extended themselves.

As they got under the covers, Amanda and Glenn resumed their prelovemaking conversation about the evening and about how good they felt being connected. That night, Amanda felt especially connected to Glenn as well.

# Chapter 3

Monday, April 9, 2012, Midmorning

Kelly hadn't felt such vigor in quite some time, and she didn't understand what had awakened it. After the show that morning, she told Zack she wanted to handle the church-shooting story herself, including investigating and writing her own script. She wanted to do everything her way. She was mentally prepared to ask the tough questions and dig.

Unfortunately, Zack denied her request. Kelly was the *face,* the *voice,* and the *personality* of the morning news and *What's Big in Littleton,* not the brains and certainly not the muscle at the station.

In actuality, he was taken aback by Kelly's demand. It was not a request. He was surprised by her reaction when he said no. Kelly was neither a charmer nor a pouter, and Zack had never seen her react angrily before. He actually found it slightly amusing, even refreshing. This project seemed to be personal to her: Kelly, the consummate professional. Kelly, the anchor. Kelly sounded like a righteous warrior princess when she talked about the church shooting. He was puzzled about the change.

Not wanting to speculate, he felt compelled to ask why, which was a question for which Kelly had no answer. She knew it had to do with her life and her career, but for so many years, she had not thought much, if at all, about her future. She had consistently moved forward as positions were offered to her, one step at a time, sometimes two or three steps at a time, however it had happened.

Her anger rapidly turned to frustration, but not one to let anything or anyone hold her back, she brushed off Zack's refusal as well as his question. She knew she had already missed critical opportunities to talk with church members, and she set out to make up for lost time.

Woodward and Bernstein, although still recognizable names in investigative journalism, had mostly faded into the pages of textbooks, Wikipedia entries, and footnotes in a few history books. They had, though, written many books, and there was the Valerie Plame case, some time back, when Woodward was suddenly in the news again. John Wilke, a fellow Columbia graduate—albeit many years before Kelly—was not well known, but was of that same ilk. He had been highly respected in a small circle, covering financial crime. His early death—cancer—was tragic. She had read that the "powers that be" would not allow him to look more deeply into Bernie Madoff when he first got tipped off. Maybe if he had been permitted …

Not at all sure why, Kelly drew a parallel to the importance of this case. The industry either forgot or just simply abandoned that brand of investigative journalism, as the media moved into the blogosphere and Twitter. The current crop of TV commentators had become laughable. Geraldo Rivera, who once broke the story about mental institutions in New York, became a cartoon, in her mind. Then there was the never-ending series of Miss America wannabes who pretended to seriously question pretend pundits, who were nothing more than "Screaming Mimis," with an agenda ranting about one thing or another.

She didn't want to be associated with an industry that was a joke or where everything was polarized versus nuanced. These days, Kelly most enjoyed and respected the news that came in the form of well-written, well-balanced humor and satire that she'd hear on the late-night shows. Jon Stewart was far wiser than the would-be authorities and did a far better job of researching, interviewing, and calling people out than "serious" commentators. Once upon a time, long ago, she had dreams of probing, scrutinizing, and getting the facts lined up before reporting. Sadly, early in her career, she had tacitly accepted that news was simply entertaining and meant to be profitable.

Nevertheless, she wanted—needed—to find out what, if anything, Lara had heard beyond the report Kelly had read on the air. Punctuating each number on her phone pad, she called Lara. Always fashionably tailored and ready to be seen live, Lara was competent as far as it goes, but, like Kelly, she was entrenched in a business that was all about the ratings, little about facts, and next to nothing about teasing out the truth. Kelly doubted Lara had ever even heard of her heroes. Lara wanted to be Kelly.

# Chapter 4

*Spring, 2010*

Upon entering the rehearsal room at the church, Amanda was instantly transported back three years to her mother-in-law's basement the week they had spent cleaning it out of fifty years of items meant to be saved for some unknown purpose. This room, although not in the basement, was dank and smelled of mildew that had made its home for countless years in a carpet that had probably never been cleaned, let alone replaced. The stiff, uncomfortable, and mismatched chairs were discolored with age, but mostly with spilled and dripped coffee. In the center of the room, there was an old, scratched piano that had probably been donated thirty years earlier. It, too, was stained.

The plain white walls hosted old posters, which were hung hastily to cover cracks, holes, and water stains from roof leakage. Someone from another decade must have made an effort to cozy up the room by hanging two pairs of similar but mismatched curtains. They had long since been pulled slightly off-kilter, and the rods were bent. Amanda reminded herself that appearances did not matter, that it was what happened within that had real meaning. Nevertheless, she so wanted the inside and outside to match. She had always felt that way about herself too. If she felt pretty, she wanted to look pretty. She made a mental note to talk to Dinny about what they could do to make this environment more hospitable and harmonious with the emotions and music being generated.

Although the room itself was not inviting, Steve cheerfully made a point of welcoming new choir members. On that evening, Carol was being ushered in and introduced. Amanda did not especially like the way Steve did it. He said, "Let's welcome Carol and thank her for joining our motley group."

Everyone, en masse, said, "Welcome!" and "Thank you!" It was meant to be funny, but Amanda no longer thought it was. It felt contrived and childish, especially since she had heard virtually the same words several times since joining the choir, including her own welcoming. Nevertheless, the choir was developing into a cohesive subset of the church community.

Though Carol had been a TLC member for some time, she was an infrequent attendee. When she did attend, she was impeccably dressed. Amanda had always envied Carol's sense of style. Though usually informal, she was always classy. When she dressed for an occasion, her outfits, though not fancy, were elegantly understated. Tonight she wore ponte knit black slacks and a simple ivory silk sweater accented with a colorful print scarf, gracefully draped. Aside from appearance, Amanda liked the way Carol presented herself with soft humor, a ready and genuine smile, and a straightforward, no-nonsense manner. Carol seemed like a genuinely good person, someone who was fun to be around, and Amanda was glad she had joined the choir.

Amanda whispered to Dinny that she wanted to talk after rehearsal about redecorating the room. Dinny scrunched her face in a way that Amanda interpreted as "a monumental undertaking."

Every week, Steve put the rehearsal agenda on the whiteboard. The routine quickly became familiar to any newcomer. It included a warm-up—singing the easier hymns—then feedback about last Sunday before tackling the more difficult pieces. The rehearsal was relaxed with a fair amount of kidding around, which Steve sometimes initiated, but he tolerated it from the choir for only just so long. There was a hint of formality behind the casualness. People were polite and offered feedback carefully, mostly positive. If there were a criticism, it was always tactfully said and included the word "we" to make sure no one felt blamed. But in truth, the criticisms were relatively minor and amusing, such as "We botched that high note again" or "We need to learn how to clap." Occasionally, someone would say they didn't like a particular piece, but, generally, there was no griping.

Everyone was always invited to join in an after-rehearsal gathering at a local pub for wine, beer, and good conversation. Not everyone came every week, though there were a few regulars that attended, including Amanda, Glenn, and Steve. When Will joined the choir, he became one of the regulars, and the pub group coalesced, often around him. Will was a stout, muscular guy who looked like a man who had played sports in his youth but allowed beer and good food to take precedent.

Carol became one of the tribe, beginning that very first evening she joined the choir. Sam, a longtime choir member, made an effort to get there when he didn't have to run home to help out with the kids. Dinny came less frequently. Jonah was among those who showed up fairly often, when he could get a ride and had money for a drink or when someone offered to treat him. Some others came once in a while. Although Sue was a choir member, she never went to the pub; she always left practice early to pick up her daughter, or if Claire happened to be hanging around the church, to take her home.

Amanda had hoped to socialize more with Sue, and the pub outings seemed the perfect situation for it. A couple of times, she had enthusiastically tried to coax Sue into coming, but Sue always declined with a smile. She'd say, "You know how it is. I have to take Claire home. It's a school night." Once, Amanda had been in a particularly feisty mood and suggested that Sue could come out and Steve could take Claire home. Sue lit up for an instant, but then her brow furrowed. She said she would ask Steve if it would be okay. She took him aside and returned beaming. She seemed so happy to be able to join the grown-ups.

The night that Sue joined them, Amanda learned a good deal more about the Anderson family than she ever had with Steve. Sue was forthcoming and guileless, cute in her own way, though not a beauty. Steve and Sue had not been married as long as Amanda had initially thought, and their other kids were significantly older than Claire. Some were married, and all but one lived on their own and had been for at least the last eight or nine years. Amanda wished she could spend more time with Sue, having been exposed to scintillating conversation and enjoying the rather vivacious personality that had once again emerged that evening.

But on this particular spring evening, after being beckoned with a flick of his finger to plant a kiss on Steve's cheek, Sue went home with Claire. Steve joined the group at the pub. Eight people squeezed into a large booth and chatted noisily with Carol. Steve joined the conversation when he heard something that interested him, but he tended to listen more than talk. Having begun his tenure as consulting minister the previous September, and with new people frequently joining the church or choir, Steve was often asked questions about himself.

As things settled, Carol turned to Steve and asked about what he had done prior to coming to Littleton.

Dinny supplied the answer. "Steve ran an ice cream business after leaving his last church. He has great business experience."

Carol said, "An interesting diversion from ministry. What led to that career move?"

Steve shrugged and grinned. "Money. A guy has to earn a living and support his family. And who doesn't love ice cream?"

"What brought you to Littleton, specifically?"

"My wife was looking for a job here. Her parents were beginning to need our help." In the absence of another question, he added, "Her mother was developing a tendency to wander off."

The conversation took some twists and turns away from Steve. There were lots of questions directed at Sam. He and his wife had recently had a baby girl. Amanda asked him about Tommy's behavior with his new sister and how he and Rachel were doing. Sam was his usual good-natured self. As he whipped his glasses off, Clark Kent style, and puffed out his thin chest, his alter ego emerged and he announced, "We are super!" He then deflated slightly, and with a shrug, he added, "Rachel does everything, and I pitch in as much as I can. Tommy is adjusting. Actually, he has been great helper with Lena."

Sam was unassumingly brilliant. There was not much that he couldn't do—or, for that matter, that he didn't do. He volunteered countless hours to develop and manage the web page for TLC. He showed up for every church event with Rachel, Tommy, and Lena. Tommy, their five-year-old, was one of the politest kids anyone would ever encounter. He was bright and had a sense of humor that, although hidden most of the time, appeared when the connection was sparked. But, essentially, he was as shy and understated as his father. This was a child who had been given lots of attention, opportunities, education, and love, but he was no showoff. There was never a tantrum and not a bratty, entitled bone in his body. He listened—just like his parents did.

"You guys are such a sweet family. You can't be that perfect all the time, can you?" Amanda joked. Sam smiled sweetly and shrugged.

Steve supplied a knowing nod, suggesting he was familiar with all the joys and challenges of raising children. Someone asked, "How many do you have?" He laughed as he raised his fingers, showing six digits. "When our little 'oops' danced into our lives, she was such an unexpected delight. The older kids had to adjust, but everyone loves Claire. She became the older kids' mascot. She was talented from the get-go and thoroughly enjoys entertaining the family."

Carol interjected. "You had built-in babysitters, lucky you!"

For a second, Steve looked blank and then said, "Oh, yes, but we didn't want to take advantage of the kids. We never had the money, the energy, or the time to go out much anyway." Carol looked puzzled. Sam smiled sweetly and said nothing. Neither did anyone else.

More wine and beer were consumed, and as usual, Will burst out in song. Dinny and Jonah joined in, and then more hesitantly, but still happily, Amanda and Glenn did too. Sam held back, even though he enjoyed every minute. Steve grimaced with good humor and announced it was time for him to leave. Sam, too, left, and everyone wished him well.

Jonah had tried to get Steve's ear throughout the evening and asked Steve to stay a while longer.

Steve said, "As much as I would like to, I have to take Claire to school in the morning, and, of course, I am a working guy you know!"

Jonah sighed his disappointment but quickly recovered and joined in the merriment, sharing his knowledge of just about everything.

On the way out, Steve passed Will's wife, Sheryl, who had just arrived. He nodded politely with no sign of recognition.

The rest of the group stayed on. Carol turned quietly to Dinny after Steve left. "I didn't want to press it, so I didn't ask Steve why he had left his previous church, but I am curious."

Dinny recited, "A more junior person was hired as head minister. Steve knew it wouldn't work well for the new guy to have someone experienced working under him. It's normal to do housecleaning at such a time, so it was expected that Steve and others would leave. Knowing it was the right thing to do for the church to allow the young minister to make his own mark, Steve was fine with it."

Amanda listened to this sidebar with one ear, even as she tried to join in the conversation with Will, Jonah, and Sheryl.

Carol attempted to ask another question of Dinny, but it became obvious that Dinny wanted to do something more fun than answer questions. Dinny turned her head in another direction and started singing another cheery bar song with Will.

Amanda turned to Carol and said, "You started to ask about Sue.

She is really delightful, though she's pretty quiet. She has a beautiful singing voice."

"I noticed that tonight. Why didn't Steve ask her to do that little solo?"

"I've asked the same thing. I told Sue she should volunteer, but she just smiled and said, 'No thank you.' So I made the suggestion to Steve, you know, to let him know that we wouldn't be offended if Sue soloed. He simply said he can't do that for obvious reasons." Amanda shrugged.

"How did they meet?"

"Well, as far as I know, they met at their former church. Sue was in the choir; they both had been recently divorced, their eyes met across a crowded room, and ... voila!" They laughed.

"I thought maybe their first marriages were very brief, a long time ago. So all the kids are not both of theirs. The way he talked, I thought they were."

"Yeah, I thought so too at first. He always jokes about 'his, hers and ours, à la *The Brady Bunch*.' He has mentioned the challenges of raising such a brood, but I think at least some of them were out of the house by the time he met Sue. One of his sons lives nearby. The others, besides Claire of course, live someplace back in Tennessee."

Carol said, "I know this is gossipy, but—"

"Yes, of course," Amanda said. "But that's what we do sometimes, right? We can't always be perfect! Anyway, it seems normal to me to want to get to know more about the minister."

"Okay, so on that note ... any idea why the divorces?"

"Well, in fact I do, though I am not sure how this came up, when this was said, or really why. I'm sure Glenn didn't ask. Steve revealed once that his wife left him for a lesbian lover. When Glenn and I discussed it, I said that must have been really hard for him. But Glenn said maybe it was easier than for another man."

"He has a point."

"I don't know about the circumstances of Sue's divorce, other than

29

apparently both spouses left around the same time. They were both lonely. The timing was right."

Suddenly the noise tapered off. Will ordered another beer, so Glenn ordered another as well, while Amanda nursed her wine. Will announced, "I have this group of guys who sing together on my back porch every so often. Would you like to join us this Friday? Anyone play an instrument? Bring it along!"

All agreed it sounded like great fun.

Before the evening came to a close, Amanda remembered that she had wanted to ask Dinny about redecorating the music room.

Dinny was peremptory. "We have other priorities. Steve doesn't care about it. No one does. So let's focus on other things."

Amanda thought it could have been redone at virtually no cost, with some cooperative labor and a few donations of leftovers that people wanted to be rid of. But Dinny passed on the idea, and that was that.

Always happy to socialize and sing, Amanda and Glenn looked forward to joining Will and his friends for folk singing on the porch. When they confirmed the time, Will said he had asked Sam as well. It would be a big old sing-along.

When Amanda and Glenn arrived on Friday evening, Amanda saw Sheryl and a couple of other women she didn't know sitting on the lawn, far from the men. On the steps of the sagging, gray porch, Will was tuning up and entertaining the guys with some bawdy ditty.

Amanda initially sat near the women, but in short order, jovial Will asked, "What are you doing over there? Aren't you going to sing with us?" She was delighted to be so explicitly invited, and she moved her seat immediately. Carol arrived a little while later. The evening was raucous good fun for all.

When Amanda and Glenn arrived home, Amanda said, "I had such a good time! I really like Carol. And Sheryl. I wonder why she stayed on the sidelines."

"I think those women just don't sing. They are listeners."

"I hope it becomes a regular gathering, like the pub group. For the first time that I can remember, I feel like I have a crowd. Don't you?"

"Sure."

"I love being part of a group that we can pull together for an impromptu party or sing-along. It was great. Singing with people makes me feel so good. Something is emitted in the air when singing, and everyone catches it."

"Yeah, like germs. Give me a break, Mandy. I agree, though. It was a good time."

"Was Will serious when he told you he wanted to form a real singing group, with rehearsals and performing?"

"I don't know. We'll see what happens."

---

A few weeks later, The New Littleton Minstrels was born. This had been a dream of Will's ever since his college days. He invited Glenn, Amanda, Carol, Sam, and Jonah to be part of it.

A couple of weeks after its inception, Dinny, who had not come that Friday night, heard about the new group and asked Amanda if she could join. The group discussed it, and no one objected. The New Littleton Minstrels was now comprised of four men and three women. Not everyone came to every rehearsal, but Will, Glenn, Amanda, and Carol were the core group members. Dinny and Sam came most of the time, and Jonah was less consistent.

Rehearsals were switched from the church to Glenn and Amanda's home, and it became their habit to go out for a beer and burgers afterward; Sheryl often joined them.

Will, always the first to arrive, bounded in one evening, guitar slung on his back and announced to the Corwells, "I got us a gig! I'll wait for everyone to get here to explain." Too excited to wait, he went on to tell Amanda and Glenn about what happened. He could not stop grinning. Amanda outwardly tempered her enthusiasm, though inwardly, she was aglow. She worried out loud to Will, asking, "Do you really think we are ready for prime time?"

"Hell no!" Will laughed. "But we'll do this anyway. Assuming everyone wants to."

"I can't speak for everyone, but we sure want to. I can speak for you, Glenn, can't I?"

"You often do, honey pie."

Will guffawed. Amanda wrinkled her nose, twisted her mouth, and uttered, "Ha ha."

As the others arrived, Will burst out about the gig, unable to contain himself. Carol was on board immediately. Dinny had a slew of suggestions and mentioned some potential obstacles, but she agreed in spirit. Sam was delighted, but he pointed out he might have some difficulty getting to more rehearsals than they already had scheduled, considering his newborn.

Dinny latched on to that as well, asking hysterically, "Are we going to have to rehearse even more? It's hard enough finding a time each week that works for all of us. I don't know. I want to do it. I think we should, but maybe we need more time." She whipped out her calendar and started listing all her commitments. "Monday is bridge, garden club. We're already rehearsing on Tuesday. I reserve Wednesday for meetings. Choir on Thursday … I need to leave time to schedule doctor's appointments and see Aurora … Fridays are out …"

Will ignored her and said, "We'll work it out. Let's talk about a song list."

"How about 'Solidarity Forever' and 'Octopus's Garden.' We know those real well," Carol suggested to an enthusiastic response from most.

"I don't know about 'Octopus's Garden.' Don't we need permission to use that song?" Dinny asked.

"We're not getting paid," Will replied tersely.

"But people are paying to get in. I think that's the same," Dinny protested.

"It's a donation to cover costs, not an admission fee." Will's thick hand went to his forehead, making little attempt at hiding his irritation.

Dinny abruptly switched to a cheery tone, throwing out another song title as though it was an imperative. No one objected. Sam made another suggestion that also resonated. Will beamed and thanked him for his great suggestion, thinking he should have thought of it himself. Sam grinned, embarrassed but pleased.

Will went on to name several songs that he had been thinking about, including two new ones.

Dinny frowned. "I don't think we should add new ones. We need to stick with what we know."

"Let's hear the songs and then decide," Glenn said.

Will gladly picked up the guitar and said, "I thought you'd never ask." He began to sing, a grin spreading across his wide face, and the others, except for Dinny, tried to pick up the tune and join in the chorus. Eventually, she joined in as well.

Jonah rang the doorbell close to forty-five minutes after they had begun. "Sorry. Had to beg a ride," was all he offered upon entering. He flashed a smile, assuming all would be forgiven.

Will scowled though he didn't confront Jonah. Dinny filled Jonah in about the gig and rehashed the discussion of the song list. There were more digressions as Jonah added his opinions about the song list, which prompted Dinny to revisit the solos. No one wanted to argue, but this bit of petulance put everyone in a bit of a sulk, albeit briefly.

Carol swung the group around to a better mood when she chimed in, literally, with a horrendous rendition of one of their favorites and said she would be willing to solo.

Will suggested that Dinny and Amanda try harmonizing. Dinny continued to sing the melody. Later, when they took a bathroom and water break, Amanda tried to replicate the harmony and collaborate with Dinny. Dinny made a concerted effort and seemed to get it.

After another hour of serious music time, Will raised the notion of getting professional help with their harmonies. "We do okay improvising, but maybe we need some actual notes. I think Steve would be willing to write for us."

Jonah leaped on this idea. "If we are going to perform professionally, we need professional leadership and arrangements. I'd love to work with Steve."

Will quickly replied, "Oh ho! Hang on, Jonah. I didn't say anything about becoming professional! We are not getting paid, but we still need help."

Dinny also liked the idea of bringing Steve into the mix and announced, "I'll see him tomorrow. I'll ask him then."

Will noticed that the others hadn't said anything, so he asked what they thought. Glenn tactfully offered a different viewpoint. "I agree we could use written harmonies—I know I could—but I'm not so sure that Steve will want to do it."

Will countered, "What makes you say that? He's always been a supporter. He has already committed to giving us the main song for some Sunday services. He's asked me to perform a solo for the service next week. He likes us."

This was news to everyone. Glenn positioned his reply. "Maybe so. I'm just not sure he likes our kind of music."

Amanda offered another thought. "He has a lot on his plate, so even if he said yes, I'm not sure he has the time."

Carol agreed and Sam quietly nodded.

This seemed to ring true with Dinny as well and she quickly changed her tune. "Amanda's right. He is terribly busy. We need to find ways to help him with his current obligations, not add more. We don't want to burn him out."

Everyone concurred that it would be awful for the congregation if Steve became so overworked that he left. Jonah added, "We need to protect him."

Dinny said, "You know that he's composing songs for the choir.

Whenever I'm there, he's either composing or practicing. Such a talent. Carol, you might not know this, but he was considered a prodigy."

Jonah grinned contentedly and said, "He is the best. How did we get so lucky?"

Carol asked if the board were considering Steve for a permanent ministerial position. With a distant, dreamy air, Dinny responded, "We would love it. Steve promised he would work on becoming fellowshipped with a shortcut so he doesn't have to go back to school or start all over. You know he wasn't ordained in a UU church, and it would be much too hard on him to start all over again."

Amanda recalled Steve's reply that day last spring to a question about how long he would stay at their church. Nerves were raw then, and skepticism was rampant after Baxter left unexpectedly. Steve had responded perfectly, saying, "I love this amazing place. It's our church home. I will stay as long as I am wanted." Everyone had been so relieved to hear it.

"Well, I don't know how he does it all." Carol shook her head incredulously.

The board, together with Steve, had crafted a dual role that satisfied everyone, or nearly everyone. Dinny had let it be known that Kyle Whitman was not immediately in favor of the hire, though no one understood his objection. In any case, he had been outvoted. Amanda didn't know Kyle; it seemed that few did. Kyle and his husband had arranged some social outings for church members. Amanda and Glenn had gone to one but didn't talk to either of them. When Kyle had introduced himself as a board candidate, Amanda remembered hearing that he had been on church boards elsewhere and had professional financial expertise. He had been a TLC member for quite some time. She thought she might have voted for him at the time—he seemed capable—but couldn't remember for sure. Maybe she and Glenn had split their vote.

"Where does this leave us then?" Will asked.

Before anyone replied, Sam turned his laptop around to show Will a site he had found during the debate about Steve. Replacing his look of consternation, Will's smile returned as he studied the entry describing how to create simple vocal harmonies for amateurs. Sam offered, "I'll figure something out using this. A lot of it can be done digitally, mathematically. I think we can make it work." Sam often found simple, elegant solutions to problems that eluded others.

After everyone left, Amanda commented, "Thank our lucky stars for Sam. I'm glad in the end they agreed not to involve Steve. I'd hate for him to say yes, and then we'd be left waiting with no music."

"Or say no and disappoint everyone," Glenn countered.

"I don't think he would ever say no. It's not his style."

"You're right. I'm not sure what made Will think he would enjoy helping us. It's apparent that he hates folk songs and our brand of silliness at the pub. He winces every time someone bursts out in song."

"People think Steve is just being funny when he does that."

Glenn mused, "Maybe he is."

"Hard to tell, though. I didn't know he and Will were so chummy, did you?"

"Will gets around. He's so affable. And, he generally gets what he wants."

"Do you think he asked Steve to have the stage next Sunday or vice versa?"

"I think it's a mutually advantageous relationship. Does it matter?"

"No, just wondering. As long as everyone is happy …"

# Chapter 5

*Summer, 2010*

Amanda showed the bride-to-be and her groom around the church, explaining, hands in motion, all the various possibilities for personalizing the space. She ran up the steps to the chancel to demonstrate with her gestures how it might be arranged to suit their needs. She exuded confidence in what TLC could provide, and the couple immediately wanted to sign the rental agreement. They asked about the minister and, once again, Amanda's face glowed with pride. "You'll love him! He's really terrific. I'll make arrangements for you to meet with him so you can get to know each other. He'll take great care of you. He has several different services that can be tailored to your needs. Would you like me to arrange a conference?"

Sheila overheard the tail end of the conversation. After the couple left, she teased, "So you're here again?"

"Almost as often as you are!"

"Is Dinny around too?"

"Actually I don't really know. She might have come in when I was showing that couple around. I've been getting so many calls. It's pretty exciting."

"It's a lot to keep up with, I imagine."

"I enjoy it."

"How do you know about Steve's wedding services? He's never done one here before."

"I know, but when I volunteered for this role, I asked him. He told me he's done hundreds and made sure I understood he didn't just mean the music."

Amanda threw herself into life at TLC with gusto and a deep sense of commitment. In the early spring, she had agreed to cochair the annual pledge drive with Dinny and later accepted a position on the board of trustees. Though neither commitment excited her, she felt a responsibility to give back to TLC. She had been pleased that Steve had encouraged and supported her as a board candidate. Around the same time, he chose Glenn to be on the minister's advisory council.

Amanda and Glenn attended almost every church event and helped with various projects, enjoying every minute of it. Steve had announced that the upcoming year's community-building theme would be "home," and he had already been composing and selecting music.

Amanda had just barely begun her official term on the board. She was astonished when the first disagreement arose at the first meeting. While she had not expected meetings to be a bed of roses, she had expected open, honest discussion that was friendly and loving.

Sheila raised the issue of a financial review, stating that it was time for it according to the bylaws, and asked how the board wanted to proceed.

Kyle appeared to be put off. "This has never been done properly." He sounded accusatory.

Sheila took Kyle's response in stride, but Dinny took offense, saying, "It's always done the same way."

Kyle pushed back, "It hasn't been done correctly. We've had problems before, including with ministers."

Other board members were silent. Amanda had no point of reference. Sheila took the reins and plowed forward with no comment or judgment. "So, how should we handle this?"

Kyle offered to do the review, though only if the treasurer and Sheila were present so that there would be no doubts about anyone's integrity. No one objected, and a vote was taken. Sheila tried to move on to the next agenda item, but Kyle, after a long pause, interjected, "Point of order. I did not hear a second to the motion before the vote was taken."

Meg said she thought someone had seconded it. Sheila asked the clerk to read back the minutes, and a second had not been recorded. The process was repeated with the correct procedure. The air was stale.

Meg introduced a fund-raiser, the brainchild of one influential member. Two board members expressed that they had "concerns," but those concerns were not openly discussed. Others wanted to approve it right away. To Amanda, the fund-raiser—something to do with selling religious figures—did not seem to be in keeping with the church's values of accepting all, not just selected, beliefs and of using one's own critical thinking processes rather than seeking answers from an "authority." But she was not asked her opinion and hesitated to say anything negative.

Dinny asked Steve for his judgment.

Steve thought for a minute before responding. "In my experience, issues around money can be sensitive. Something similar came up at Ridgecrest Road Church when I was there." He did not actually make a point or tell what had happened, but Dinny and Meg nodded as if they had heard what they needed to hear.

In the pause that followed, Sheila filled the gap by saying, "It is *our* responsibility. Let's think about it and table it for now."

Amanda had no idea what Kyle's bugaboo was, but it was evident he was not Mr. Popularity, and maybe with good reason. Nevertheless, despite his manner, it appeared to her that he was usually right.

People didn't ask questions or try to understand different viewpoints; and on the flip side, no one tried to clarify or explain nuances. A lot of assumptions were made. Everyone *acted* nice, polite, and no one wanted to hurt anyone's feelings.

It was evident some individuals had their own agendas, pet projects, or favored programs. Amanda tried to think about what her agenda was and couldn't come up with anything that meant a lot to her. She had no particular ties to any procedure, policy, committee, or program—with the exception of the choir.

Steve was one of the first to leave the building, mentioning his long day and long ride home. Lagging behind on the way out, Amanda approached Sheila, hoping for an explanation of Kyle's behavior. Sheila told her that there had been unresolved questions around finances with Baxter and implied that Kyle had encountered similar issues at a previous church he attended. She neither defended Kyle nor made judgments about anyone else. When Amanda pressed about the obvious tension, Sheila simply said, "It's just the way Kyle is." He didn't seem to bother Sheila, and she didn't let on if she was bothered by anyone's reactions or behavior.

In the parking lot, they saw Kyle, briefly thanked him for offering his services, and watched as Blake greeted him with a quick kiss and a big, warm loving smile. Kyle then turned right around and asked the two women if they would like to join them for a quick snack and a glass of wine. They looked at each other with nary a hesitation and enthusiastically nodded.

In his car, Steve stared as Blake kissed Kyle. For an instant, he took on the face of a four-year-old who wanted to steal a cookie and then thought better of it. The look of apprehension—just as quickly as it had appeared—vanished. He started the engine, smiled and waved to whomever might have noticed him.

# Chapter 6

The New Littleton Minstrel's first gig was part of a folk song fest held in a small park about an hour's drive from Littleton. Attendees and performers were mostly old-time folkies with a few young singer-songwriters itching to try out some of their own tunes on what would likely be an accepting and appreciative crowd.

Jonah had begged a ride with Amanda and Glenn, and practically the whole way there, he talked about Steve and how much he admired him. Glenn wanted to practice in the car to be ready for Will's four-thirty rehearsal, but Jonah was having none of it. "We're fine," he said authoritatively. "Will is making more of it than he needs to. And, by the way, we need to change the way we do that first number. It should start as a solo and then build to the other voices. I checked with Steve. He agreed."

Will misplaced, looked for, and found the program list three times and was pacing in the parking lot when the Corwells and Jonah arrived.

Once he saw the others, his demeanor changed to good humor and smiles.

It was Dinny, not Jonah, who brought up changes in the first number. Will bristled but did not lose his temper. With his usual chortle, he simply said, "Let's keep it the way we did it at rehearsal."

Prompted by Dinny's command to "have fun," Carol threw off her jacket, showed off her New Littleton Minstrels T-shirt, did a brief jig, and announced she was ready!

Sam's eyes sparkled, and he was smiling as usual, but he said little. Some of the Minstrels were more anxious than others. Even though this was a casual sing-along, the Minstrels wanted to sound good, hoping they would be asked to return.

At 4:35 p.m., Will pulled out his guitar and started strumming. They all joined in a warm-up song, not anything they were performing. No one knew the words, but they started making up verses, really silly ones, singing until everyone was relaxed and thoroughly enjoying themselves.

Carol was particularly boisterous, improvising and playing around with some rather bawdy lyrics that had everyone in hysterics. Glenn, clever as always, managed to throw in some delightful double entendres that made everyone think twice.

They went through the song list, made lots of mistakes, and promised they would do better when it was "for real." They had a grand time for an hour. Dinny asked Amanda to go over the harmony one more time on the number she had trouble with and then recanted. "Never mind. I'm just going to sing what I want when the time comes." Amanda held back a snort and said nothing. Dinny was ... well, Dinny was Dinny.

Will, not surprisingly, suggested they have a beer, and no one objected. They gathered at a nearby dive bar, ordered drinks and burgers, and migrated to other topics besides church and singing. In another group, politics might have been an ugly subject, but, luckily, with the Minstrels, they were all pretty much in agreement, so the playful criticism and jokes did not offend anyone. The dominant sound was laughter, but the sound of clapping and backslapping also emanated from their cozy corner table. Others at the bar stared at the group on occasion, but the Minstrels paid no heed, having such a good time in one another's company.

With fun and beer as their backdrop, they put on a great show, at least that's how they felt. After the performance, a few audience members commented about what a good time they had and how they could see how much the group enjoyed one another. That was reward enough.

Before everyone parted ways, Carol found a moment alone with Amanda, making a point of telling her how good she felt around her and the rest of the group, how much she valued her insights and her singing, and how close she felt to the group. Nothing could have delighted Amanda more. She felt exactly the same way.

Dinny traveled back with Glenn, Amanda, and Jonah. Glenn and Amanda listened while Dinny and Jonah talked in the backseat. Dinny mentioned how much time Steve spent at the church and how often she ran into him there. She talked to Jonah about all that Steve had taken on, how he raised his daughter, etc.

Jonah needed no convincing of Steve's greatness. Apparently, Steve had been offering Jonah counsel, and while he never revealed why he needed the one-on-one time, he praised Steve for being incredibly intelligent and saying all the right things, always making him feel better.

When they talked about Steve's musical talent, Amanda echoed some of their sentiments, though when she mentioned there was a certain type of heavy, overly religious music he sometimes selected that she didn't particularly care for, Jonah seemed to take personal offense and challenged her.

"I'm just stating a preference," Amanda began. "I'm not arguing that the music isn't great. I just don't like it. But that doesn't mean he shouldn't choose the music." That warranted a harrumph from Dinny.

In a flash, Dinny suggested to Jonah he might want to talk with

Aurora. Jonah had no idea who she was so Dinny launched into a colorful description of her first glimpse of Aurora's house.

"I drove up to her funky, somewhat dilapidated, though quaintly and colorfully painted cottage and instantly felt at home on her front porch. There was a comfortable old Adirondack chair and a torn wicker rocker, as well as a Buddha statue, several incense holders, and candles surrounding two wooden birdcages, one with a parakeet and the other with a flying fish and pig mobile. After deeply inhaling, I instinctively knew that I was going to get all the answers I wanted. I'm sure you will too."

"You should write that one down, Dinny," Jonah responded. "You have a way with words."

"I did! I'm taking a writing class. Actually, it's supposed to be a poetry class. But if I want to write prose rather than poetry, I just do."

Not to be outdone, Jonah continued, "I dabble a little myself. In fact, that's one of the things I have talked to Steve about—putting some of my words to music."

Dinny waited a few seconds, and then she suggested the three of them could collaborate. With her usual inability to perch on anything for very long, she noted that, although she still visited Aurora every now and then when she felt guidance was needed, she was currently speaking and studying with a local yogi. "It is really about the meditation and getting in touch with my inner being," Dinny explained. "I'm working on that. Everyone should do it. It's relaxing. We all need less stress. Amanda, you should come with me next week. Glenn, you could do it too."

Amanda had tried yoga and had ambivalent feelings. She was perfectly happy with her current exercise routine. She turned to face the backseat and said, "I'm sure yoga is wonderful. When I did it before, I liked the stretching. My instructor wasn't a yogi; he just did it for fun and exercise, which is what I like. I don't really feel a need to meditate, and frankly, I have little to no stress in my life. But thanks. I hope you continue to enjoy it."

Dinny stared blankly, not fully comprehending why anyone would not want to be more spiritual. Lack of stress was completely foreign to her. She pursued the issue. "But, like Steve says, we're all on a journey. Don't you want to move forward on yours and discover what it's all about, who you are, where you are meant to be? It's what we should all be doing. Well, I am." Amanda's reply was brief. "It's not on my to-do list." The subject was changed. Glenn said nothing.

Later that evening, Amanda said, "Glenn, if I hear one more thing about spiritual practice, finding myself, or being on a journey, I think I'll puke."

"I know what you mean."

"I'm not sure what others mean by spiritual, though I think I am sufficiently spiritual in my own way. TLC is supposed to be open to all, accepting and nonprescriptive. I don't want to work toward anything at this point of my life! At this point, for me, journey means traveling on vacation. One of the things I love about Will and Sheryl is that they're so relaxed, grounded, and in the moment."

Glenn added, "They do seem to have settled and accepted life. No angst. Straight shooters. They know what they want, and they do it. They don't judge anyone by some vague notion or measure of spirituality. I don't think spirituality has ever come up in conversation."

Shifting the topic slightly, Amanda commented, "I want to talk to Steve about some new ideas for the service to vary his procedure. His sermons are good—people like them—but rather than talking about our journeys, maybe there are different ways to *show* how UUs can experience spirituality. I mean in addition to music of course."

"One would think he'd welcome some new ideas," Glenn flatly stated.

"Well, I'd like to think so. I know he's not always receptive in choir when someone makes a suggestion. He's determined to do his best on his own. Have you noticed that we never have a group review of the last week's service anymore?"

"It is still on the agenda. It's possible he just forgets."

Amanda went to the bedroom to read—and think. She thought about how Steve might react when she suggested variety. Even though he was technically off for the summer, he expected it of himself to attend board meetings. She thought about the future of the church and all the possibilities. She thought about the life she and Glenn were building and of the many friends they had made. She reflected on how content she was.

---

Amanda and Dinny spent more and more time together and became good friends, despite their differences. People got used to seeing them together. They were having fun and doing some good work as well.

One afternoon, sitting in one of the open rooms at the church, they were trying to plan a cleanup effort when they got to gossiping and sharing stories. Leslie walked by, which brought a scowl to Dinny's face. This then led to her complaining about an incident where she had ended up in a shouting match with Leslie.

Dinny jumped from her chair to pick up a candy wrapper that she had eyed in a corner of the room, and she told another story, a confrontation between Kyle and Leslie that had occurred a year or two before. Amanda made an unsuccessful attempt to keep up with Dinny, who was in her whirling dervish mode. Their planning session was clearly being sidetracked by gossip, but Amanda, nevertheless, enjoyed the stories. It was all news to her. She was just beginning to get a feel for how the board worked and who was who, aside from Dinny and Sheila.

The conversation suddenly turned to Rachel Winters when Dinny caught sight of one of Tommy's drawings on the bulletin board. Seemingly out of the blue, Dinny commented that Rachel and Sam had had difficulty conceiving their second child, Lena. An abrupt change of topic by Dinny no longer surprised Amanda, though she was astonished at the apparent level of intimacy that Dinny had with Rachel. She hadn't ever seen them talk to each other. Given the difference in their ages, and that Rachel had a full-time job, Amanda hadn't even thought that they would be friends and had no idea where or when they would find the time to talk. Rachel never came to the pub and had only once come to a Minstrels' sing-along. Dinny was always startling her with what she knew about the people in the congregation.

"She talked to Steve about it last year before he officially began as minister. He must have been so warm and encouraging and really empathetic, given what he and Sue went through to conceive Claire."

"What do you mean?"

"Oh, he told Rachel about the difficulty they had had. And you know how well that all turned out for Steve. Claire is the apple of his eye, to use a cliché. And look how it turned out for Rachel and Sam."

"Don't you find that odd?"

"Odd? What?"

"I mean, considering how often he has described Claire as a 'happy accident.'"

"I never heard him say that."

"Really? Any number of times when people first meet him and ask about his family, he says, 'mine, hers, and our little oops.'"

"Well, I never heard that. Maybe they had tried for a long time and had given up trying, so she was a surprise."

Amanda took that as a plausible explanation even though it still seemed weird to her. In any case, she imagined that Claire had been born fairly soon after they married, given other things that had been said. But since it was really not important one way or the other, she dismissed the thoughts.

They settled down for a brief period. Amanda tried to steer Dinny back to the task at hand, but even as they began to work through some details of how to engage more people in the cleanup effort, the conversation took various twists and turns, including a quick mention of Carol looking terrible at the last rehearsal and Dinny telling Amanda she had been the obvious choice for board VP. The pair ended up talking and laughing about high school experiences.

It got a little more serious when Amanda confessed, "I was not very happy in high school. I had some fun, but I just wanted to grow up and get out fast. I'm sorry that I missed my chance to enjoy my youth. I'm making up for lost time now."

"Well, *I* had a blast," said Dinny. "I loved high school."

"Where did you grow up?"

"Cos Cob, Connecticut."

Amanda had had no idea, given the ex-hippie persona that Dinny projected. Amanda knew Cos Cob was in one of the wealthiest counties in the country. "How long did you live there?"

"Oh, practically my whole life. I went to Wesleyan for a year, though it didn't suit me, and things have a way of happening. I got married, had a kid and then another one. Then a divorce and then another marriage. You might not know how that goes."

"I got married young too. We have that much in common. You stayed in Cos Cob?"

"Actually I moved to New Canaan with my second husband." She seemed both a little embarrassed and little scornful when she said, "He was an investment banker."

Dinny stood up and followed Jennifer Michelli to the kitchen. "I need to talk to Jen about something," she called as she scampered away, not even looking over shoulder.

Amanda began to revise her picture of Dinny. She had seen her as bubbly and energetic, definitely not grounded. Dinny filled her days with various activities, joining this or that group, getting together with people. She emanated a sense of commitment and genuine caring, even if the projects turned out to be short-lived. To Amanda, Dinny was a free spirit who enjoyed life and who threw herself into Ping-Pong and Tai Chi with equal intensity as her latest civil rights cause. She had not pictured Dinny as part of the country club set.

She reimagined a different version of Dinny. The club-joining junkie with a penchant for the arts morphed with her volunteer docent work at the Bruce in Greenwich. Her ethereal, sprite image merged with that of a more classic, traditional aristocrat. She could envision Dinny's thrift store clothes replaced with Lilly Pulitzer or St. John's. She saw the evolution from donating to or volunteering in the thrift store to shopping in it. She could picture her chatting and sitting in judgment at a charity luncheon at Neiman Marcus, high cheekbones, blonde coifed hair, pursed lips flashing into a smile for the society-page camera, sitting with friends who looked the same. At this thought, Amanda laughed inwardly. "Sitting in judgment" was exactly what she was doing.

Dinny returned. "Where were we?" She shuffled some papers without looking at them. Amanda's attempt to refocus was thwarted again when Dinny unexpectedly picked up their conversation about high school and began to reminisce about her cheerleader days, being voted the class wit, and dating. Swiftly she added, "It wasn't perfect, though."

Amanda had to ask, "What happened?"

"There was one problem that persisted. But eventually I blew it off and just went on doing what I enjoyed anyway."

"Was it serious?"

"No. Well, maybe. No, not really. Some girl—and I know who it was—started a rumor about me. Probably jealous. But it stuck. I didn't really let it bother me. But I got a reputation, if you know what I mean. It was hurtful. Yet, kind of funny really."

Amanda knew what having a "reputation" meant, and she did not understand what was funny about it, although it did explain some of the comments on Dinny's Facebook page that cropped up fairly often. She felt sorry for Dinny but imagined, as this happened so long ago, she was probably long past whatever pain it had caused. She also thought that the first marriage might have been "rushed." No one cares anymore, but back then, it was something.

That afternoon, Amanda learned a lot more about Dinny than Dinny learned about Amanda. Dinny's second ex had an affair with his much younger assistant. Apparently, several of her friends knew the assistant was not the first of his outside dalliances. At least one of her friends had *firsthand* knowledge. A bigger picture emerged as Amanda realized that Dinny, who was constantly searching, although bright and creative, had never really landed. In any case, Guy, her second ex, had been a "real catch" as Dinny expressed it. They had been madly in love, and she had her share of envious friends and acquaintances. It was also a second marriage, or maybe a third, for Guy. They had met when he was still married, and she was newly divorced.

Then Guy left her some years later. To his credit, he did not leave her without a means of support. But he did leave her without an identity.

Like Alice's white rabbit, Dinny looked at the clock, scrambled in her purse for her calendar, and immediately started for the door, saying she totally forgot another appointment, and she needed to be downtown in five minutes. She told Amanda to finish up and called out, "Namaste," just before the door closed behind her. Amanda looked at the array of paperwork and incomplete plans, feeling somewhat like the prince left holding a shoe, only more captured than captivated. She packed up everything and left the building, questioning if the cleanup project would ever get organized.

---

Dinny and Amanda's cleanup event was a moderate success. Although it was not a large group—and there were some no-shows among those who said they would help—a good number of the "old reliables" were there. Even Steve worked just as hard as anyone else for a few hours, lifting, toting, painting, cleaning, and fixing. It all felt right—one happy family, reflecting Steve's familiar phrase, "our church home."

A few days later, Amanda walked into the church to tie up some loose ends and pick up some material related to her new role as board vice president. Claire was reading in the front office, and Steve was talking to someone in his office. Claire was sitting with her back to the door.

Amanda asked, "Reading anything good?"

Without bothering to turn around, Claire dramatically lifted the book so the book jacket could be seen. It was the final Harry Potter book.

With a degree of enthusiasm, combined with a hint of impatience, Amanda said, "Of course! I should have known. On every kid's summer reading list."

"It's not on a list. I just wanted to read it."

"You are quite the reader. You always have a book, right?"

With a smirk and a nod, Claire went back to reading, and she looked up when she heard children singing in the other room.

Realizing that the children's drama, song, and dance class started that week, Amanda made another attempt to reach the tween. "Claire, would you like to participate in the class? We can still get you in. It's right up your alley. I hear you've been in a play or two. It would give you something to do with other kids." She thought the cost might be an issue for Steve, but she had already looked into waiving fees in certain cases.

Claire wrinkled her nose and snorted softly. "Oh no! I'm fine. I'm beyond that." The kicker came with Claire's next comment. "My dad and I groan every time we hear them singing." She giggled and added, "They're *so* bad." The accompanying innocent grin and twinkle in her eyes made it clear to Amanda that Claire was mimicking what she had heard, rather than being genuinely nasty and obnoxious.

Amanda let the comment pass without responding, asking herself whether Steve had said this to his daughter because he couldn't afford the camp tuition. Then again, Amanda remembered the numerous dance and singing lessons that Claire had on her schedule. There was enough money for those. Maybe he did think she was beyond this level.

Amanda finished up her business quickly and was about to leave when Dinny exited Steve's office.

"Hey, are you free for lunch?" Dinny asked.

They left Dinny's car in the lot and drove in Amanda's to the Klatch 'n' Kounters, a favorite coffee shop. Over bites of cranberry-walnut curried chicken salad and iced coffee for Amanda, and a vegetarian sandwich and green tea for Dinny, they talked about what event they'd work on next. She knew it was none of her business, but Amanda wondered what Dinny had been discussing with Steve in his office. She waited to see if Dinny would supply an explanation. She didn't.

Inevitably, the talk did turn to Steve. Dinny started singing his praises yet again. Amanda liked him well enough too and thought he had provided some important things for the church, though she wasn't as enamored of him as Dinny was. When she commented that she had been trying to figure out how to raise the topic of varying the service, Dinny pursed her lips. Her eyes narrowed and she said, "You're the only one who feels that way, Amanda. Everyone loves his services."

Amanda explained that she liked his services as well. She only wanted to suggest that there might be ways to add diversity and be less predictable—not to actually tell him how to do it.

Dinny sniffed, clearly offended. She pointedly asked Amanda if she was displeased with Steve.

"No. I just said that I think he's fine. There are just a few things that I find a little annoying …"

"Like what?" Dinny challenged.

"Well, for one thing, I get tired of his jokes."

"They're what make him who he is. I'm telling you everyone else loves the jokes and all of his music. I see you laughing too."

"Okay. Yes, I do. I wish he, and maybe all of us, would be a little more receptive to different ideas, and be more collaborative. We're supposed to have a joint ministry. Dinny, do you remember when you suggested we change the words of a song to fit better to the rhythm, and he said it was not the time to discuss it?"

"I was annoyed. I admit that. But I could see he was too busy to deal with it. He has his own way of doing things, and it is his job to make those decisions after all."

"The point is that he *says* he wants to hear from us, but it seems like he really doesn't. Sometimes. Sometimes, he says the right things. But then it seems so—I don't know—pro forma."

"If he gets frustrated with us, well, he's only human. He recovers quickly and always says thank you to us. Where is this going, Amanda? It's not a big deal."

"I never said it was. You asked me if I was unhappy with him. I said no. But that doesn't mean I think he's perfect."

"No one is perfect. You're too picky. It's not right to criticize the minister. He's as perfect as it's going to get—for us."

They ended the meal by sharing a lemon bar. Amanda drove Dinny back to the church. As she dropped her off, she noticed Steve's car was still there and got a glimpse of Dinny heading back inside.

Part 2
Intuition

# Chapter 7

*Monday, April 9, 2012, Late Morning*

During the ten minutes of talking with Lara, Kelly got a little more information. She learned the name of the deceased was Sam Winters. She learned the identities of the two men who tussled: Jonah Spencer was one, and the one seriously wounded was Kyle Whitman. She discovered that there had been ongoing animosity, anger, and threats at the church. It was still undetermined if the violence had been planned.

Questions started popping into her head: *Why would anyone bring a gun to church? What were the threats and who made them? Anyone else involved? There had to be a backstory. Why were the police there so quickly?*

Lara told her that Sam had a wife and two young children. He presumably was a well liked, quiet member of the congregation, someone who helped out mostly behind the scene: gentle, positive, responsive, and responsible. As far as anyone knew, he had no enemies and had not ever irritated anyone. He didn't sound like a target. But stranger things had happened.

A dramatically different story emerged about the other victim. Mr. Whitman was a known troublemaker who had often touched nerves, an apparent agitator. Many people suggested he was emotionally disturbed. He certainly was a thorn in everyone's side. Speculation was that he had brought the gun. Some said he had threatened the minister. At this point, it was widely believed that Jonah had wrested the gun from Kyle and, in the process, shot him. It was unclear how Sam was killed; ballistic experts were working on it. The reports were mixed about how many shots were fired. There was little known about Jonah. He was a big, soft-spoken, gentle guy who seemed sensitive and smart. That was all Lara had gleaned.

More questions percolated: *Who was Jonah? Why was he in a position to get the gun from Kyle, if that was what happened? Why didn't anyone know much about him?* The shooting had appeared fairly cut and dried from initial accounts by witnesses, as well as online and cable news commentary and conjecture. In the end, Jonah held a gun, cried, and then put it down. *Why would someone threaten the minister?*

She wanted to see the videotape that had run earlier, including the random comments, shots of people crying, and the minister's statement.

Kelly set to work. She investigated on the sly, so she juggled the profile of a local celebrity chef and the theft of a family pet as well. But she was on her game. She could do it.

In rapid-thinking, multitasking mode, she sent a quick e-mail to her parents to let them know all was well and that she would call over the weekend. While she loved her parents, she had been avoiding lengthy conversations ever since her breakup with Ray. What was it her mother always said about love? "Respect supersedes and underlies love." Kelly chose not to give that aphorism much thought when dreaming of shooting bullets into Ray.

Her mom, stepmom actually, would periodically tell her that she admired her hard work and was proud of her career, though she'd point out other things are important too. Really? Who had time for "other" things? And when she did make the time, look how poorly it turned out. Better to work harder. Mom said, "Love was work too." Not only did it take work to keep it going, but love was also about sacrifices. One would do things for the sake of their loved one that he or she would rather not be doing. Though Kelly recalled these words, she had not absorbed what they meant.

She had thought about finding and talking to her birth mother once. She hadn't said anything to anyone, not knowing how her stepmother and father, both of whom she loved more than anything, would react. But in the end, she didn't think it worth her while. The woman had abandoned her; what use would it serve?

*What's done is done.* Kelly was fourteen when Dad and Mom thought she was old enough to know her story. She respected them for telling her, that they thought her capable of understanding, and that they recognized her maturity. So she was loath to admit that she wanted to stick her fingers in her ears and say, "Don't tell me. I don't want to know. I am not going to deal with it." Instead, she let them talk. She didn't ask questions or probe any deeper. It entered the part of her brain—or was it the heart?—where she locked it up. There were secrets hidden in there: her eleven-year-old self being nasty and teasing a friend, Mom's subsequent scolding and lecture, Dad confronting her when she lied about drinking and watering down the vodka, insults about being awkward and skinny, and past boyfriends and lovers. It was the place where she stored the hurts. She didn't talk about these things.

Over time, although unconscious of it, Kelly had built up a seemingly impenetrable fortress around those feelings. The problem was, unbeknown to Kelly, if walls were built to keep hurts from coming in, those same walls prevented their escape. So they stayed buried. Inevitably, there are some chinks in the armor, and sooner or later, another hurt would get thrown in. Kelly never listened to her inner noise. She chose to move forward. Kelly would take anyone on—anyone other than herself.

She would make the call on the weekend.

The next morning, having done as much thinking and preliminary research as she could, Kelly's initial hunch—that there was a far more intriguing story here than a simple whack-a-doodle church shooting—became even stronger. But all the pieces were not in place by a long shot. She had not even talked to anyone directly.

Working late is definitely not good for someone who has to get up at three and be TV-ready by five. Luckily, she had the kind of hair—thick, glossy, straight—that, thanks to her two-hundred-dollar haircuts, fell into place with little fussing.

However, without hesitation, she called her makeup guy as soon as she arrived at the station, knowing he would have to perform some magic. Manny was a delight, always confident about his ability to perform theatrical transformations. Sadly, poor Manny was not confident he would ever find true love. He was always fretting over some unrequited infatuation. She adored him. In addition to doing good work, with his frequent compliments, he was good for her recently diminished ego. She looked forward to his enthusiasm and some light conversation.

Unexpectedly, Manny offered a new piece of information about the church shooting. It turned out, according to him, although he did not know Kyle personally, he had a bit of a reputation and had pissed off more than a few people in their circles, but no one believed he would bring a gun to his church. Everyone said he *really* loved that church. Not that Manny understood why anyone would love church. He referred to himself as a very lapsed Catholic, for somewhat obvious reasons. He called himself "forbidden fruit." But, as he put it, he had "no friggin' idea" what Kyle's church believed. Manny mentioned another guy who, apparently, attended the church once in a while and had been there on Sunday. Kelly tried to figure out what to do with the new information as she went on the air with—again—a prepared script that was largely a repeat of yesterday's news, with the addendum that "an arrest was expected soon" and the ubiquitous "stay tuned for breaking news" followed by "more at noon."

She had to get permission to move forward with the story, and Kelly was prepared to make her case.

---

Later that morning, Zack caved. In his mind, it was not so much caving as having his own curiosity piqued. He thought he understood Kelly Allen pretty well, but apparently he didn't. Maybe there was another Kelly buried beneath the stony, hard-driving, fun but serious, emotionally invulnerable exterior. For him, it was not so much the story of the gun in church but the story of Kelly that he hoped would be revealed. Truth be told, she did have some interesting thoughts about the church incident, and he thought it could make a good magazine piece, maybe a pilot for an ongoing series. If nothing else, assuming she found something of substance, more viewers would tune in for the short run. Her passion for getting at the truth would far outweigh Lara's workaday approach. He remembered Kelly from grad school as the relentless student who never stopped asking questions—really good questions. They were not friends, but they had been in a couple of classes together, one of which was a seminar on journalistic ethics. He had been impressed with her then, as he still was.

Now he had to pitch the idea to the station execs. He had, in fact, never failed to sell an idea, so he was not especially worried. He gave her the go-ahead and made arrangements for other newscasters to cover some of her off-air responsibilities. She was free to spend more time interviewing, doing what she did best—at least what she believed she did best. Others might still prefer her on-air skills and striking, unparalleled beauty. For Zack, it was a toss-up.

# Chapter 8

*Fall, 2010*

After receiving Glenn's call, Will's face turned ashen as he sunk farther into his well-worn reading chair. Carol was dead. It was completely unexpected. While she had missed the last few rehearsals and had seemed a little tired at times, no one had known that she had been diagnosed with terminal ovarian cancer—except, as it turned out, Steve.

Sheryl and Will showed up at Glenn and Amanda's to mourn, cry, and process what had happened. A close bond had formed among the Minstrels, though most especially among the four of them and Carol. This sad afternoon, they ate, drank some beer, drank some wine, and found a way, as sometimes happens, to have a laugh or two as well.

Steve and the Votarini family planned the memorial service for the following Saturday, and choir practice hadn't been canceled. They marveled at how Steve could hold it together and get so much done. He had to prepare sermons for both the Saturday and Sunday services and had to help the Votarinis organize the event.

The next day, Will, devastated by the loss of Carol, called Steve and asked to meet at the Klatch for coffee and for solace.

Steve arrived first. He fidgeted in his chair uncomfortably, but when Will sat down, he opened the conversation without hesitation. Never had they had such a serious exchange. Prior, Will had met with Steve on occasion to discuss playing and singing musical interludes for a service. Steve had asked Will for his advice on a church matter at the same time and a bond had developed.

This day, the tone was very different. Will openly shed tears, while Steve gulped and swallowed hard, demonstrating that he would remain strong. They talked about Carol and the memorial service.

Will lamented, "Carol was an integral part of our singing group. Although we had not known one another for very long, we all have become close. We had a lot in common, really enjoyed one another's company. I am not sure I ... or the group ... will ever feel the same without her. I'm worried."

Setting his mouth just so and turning his gaze downward, Steve said, "Thank you for sharing that. I understand. You know, she died in my arms." He paused, waiting for a reaction.

"I had no idea. You amaze me sometimes." Will reached his pudgy hand across the table in a gentle gesture of appreciation.

"When she told me about her diagnosis some time ago, I immediately rushed to her home to visit. Sue made her one of her lovely quilts. Her family called me to her side when it was evident that she had reached the end. We had all become quite close."

Will was surprised to hear this, having heard nothing before, but it was just like Steve to have connected so deeply and to maintain confidentiality. "That must have been awful, both emotionally and ..."

"It comes with the job. This time, it was peaceful. It isn't always. I've been through those last minutes before. It wasn't the first time I've cleaned up," he said somberly.

"Wasn't hospice there? Are you sure you'll be all right for Saturday? I'm worried about you."

"What I need from you is your support to help keep me and the choir from falling apart. I count on you, Will. You've become very important to me. You're a trusted advisor, a mentor, as well as a friend."

Will smiled, put a hand to his heart, and completely shifted his position so that he could place a protective arm around Steve's shoulder and give him a warm hug. "You got it. But really, how are you doing, personally?"

"No, no. It's not your job to worry about me."

Will was pleased that Steve had shown his vulnerable side with him and had asked for his help. He felt fatherly. He enjoyed being needed and at the same time he was proud of Steve. Will knew their bond was mutual.

The next day at choir rehearsal, Steve broke from the usual pattern to have a solemn talk with his group. Tears were shed. Although there wasn't a soul who hadn't been through the death of a loved one or a battle with cancer or some other illness, they grappled with their emotions. The silence was palpable. Steve provided reassurance. He knew just what to say—and the right way to say it.

As a group, the choir promised Steve that they would hold it together. Steve wanted them to be role models for the rest of the congregation in respect for, and in deference to, Carol's family. Steve had suggested that it would help him too since he was so deeply affected, saddened, and in need of support.

After rehearsal, Steve did not join the gathering at the pub. Only a small group went, not to party but to commiserate and have something to do other than think about death by themselves.

"I'm having trouble dealing with this," Will said. "It really is fortunate that Steve is so steady and in control. It's good for all of us. Not sure about him, though."

"What do you mean?" Sam asked.

"As I understand it, Steve was there for her from the beginning, and even when she died, he was with her. He and I have gotten pretty close.

He puts up a good front. He stoically mentioned that this was not the first time for him. Even so, it can't be easy. He's human after all."

The group talked about how they could sustain Steve and support one another. Carol had been a dear friend to everyone. Sam, usually so reserved, could not hold back his tears. He quietly began singing "Danny Boy" with his soft, sweet tenor. It was almost a whisper.

As Sam drifted toward an indefinite ending to the song, Dinny offered, "I think it's useful to focus on the singing and the music. It will help. I only hope I can refrain from crying when the Minstrels sing 'Amazing Grace.'"

"I don't think anyone will be able to hold back their emotions," Will replied. "But we have to try for Steve."

"I wonder what it was like … to be there … I mean, when she … died." Amanda did not really expect an answer or explanation.

To her surprise, Will gave her one. "No one talks about what actually happens, physically. You only hear about the one who's dying being at peace or of the soul lifting, but it ain't all that pretty. I mean, she was in his arms, for God's sake. He said he cleaned up while the family went for a walk."

Again Amanda considered this, softly musing, "No hospice? And this wasn't the first time for him? I never thought of that aspect of the job."

The subject was dropped when Will spontaneously started another song with that big, old smile of his spreading across his face. It was one of the silly songs that The New Littleton Minstrels often sang together, one they knew well and enjoyed. They all sang, much to the dismay of some patrons and much to the joy of others.

That Saturday, The New Littleton Minstrels breathed both their last farewell to Carol and a sigh of relief when Steve quietly mouthed, "Thank you," after the final note of "Amazing Grace" drifted into the air, hanging in sorrow.

After the service was over, during the subdued coffee and cookies gathering, there was a good deal of quiet discussion as people scanned the many photos of Carol. Individually, several people sought out different members of The New Littleton Minstrels to express their appreciation, in particular for the song they contributed. Several Votarini family members specifically said it was the best part of the service for them, more meaningful even than the sermon. Carol's sister, Wendy, approached Amanda gingerly.

"Thank you so much for being Carol's friend. She talked about you." Amanda could feel the redness creep into her face, not even knowing her friend had been ill, but she nodded as Wendy continued. "She was so disappointed that Steve never visited after the first time. She hoped he would be more of a resource to her." Thankfully, Wendy moved on quickly as Amanda was at a loss for words. Confused about what Wendy said, she unconsciously filed the comment in the back of her mind.

Few noticed that Steve shed his robe and left very quickly after the service. Everyone marveled at the thoughtfulness and sensitivity he provided to help loved ones move on with grace and acceptance, although he did not appear to be able to do that. All agreed that Steve did not look well. There were many comments about the toll Carol's death had taken on him. The board offered him some time off, but he valiantly declined, stating he had much to do and needed to be present for others.

Driving back from the service, Amanda said, "I feel depleted. But also, in a strange way, I feel good about how the funeral came together. Is that sick? I mean … shouldn't I be depressed?"

Glenn responded, "Give it a break, Mandy. You feel what you feel. Each of us mourns in our own ways. You and I have a certain capacity for processing and intellectualizing our feelings, but that doesn't mean we don't have them."

"I suppose. Steve left early. Did you notice?"

"Actually, I didn't. But I'm not surprised."

"Really, Glenn?"

"He's had a lot on his plate. It does take its toll. And, anyway, I don't think schmoozing is his thing."

"You're kidding me, right? He's a talented raconteur! He socializes, tells stories, and makes jokes. He always makes a point of talking to visitors and newcomers."

"Mandy, that's true, but I don't think he especially wants to be social or is completely comfortable with it. He allots a certain amount of time to it, though—like at the pub."

"You have a point. The membership made such a fuss about Baxter not extending himself. I guess Steve is trying to make sure he does it right. Maybe he's trying too hard."

"Well, yes, that's what I'm saying. It seems like he works at it, purposefully. I think he's good at it, don't get me wrong, but he always makes a point of telling Sheila about his conversations with guests and how he's building relationships."

"Well, I don't see anything wrong with that, Glenn. She *is* the board president. But I get what you mean. He's gregarious and completely charming, but there's that distance we felt when he came to dinner. Maybe he's a little shy. Funny thing is I got the impression that Baxter was a little shy, even though I got to know him pretty well from his sermons. Steve is different."

"I don't think Steve is shy at all."

Amanda thought about that observation before replying, "No. I'm not sure why I said that."

"It's like he's learned how he's supposed to act."

"Well, everyone has 'issues,' I guess. As long as he performs well, and he's doing good stuff here, it's okay with me."

Steve had pulled it together heroically and delivered the "sermon of his life" or so it seemed, given the congregation only knew the ones delivered at TLC. In any case, there was not a dry eye at the church or any complaints about anything. At the next choir rehearsal, later that week, Steve humbly revealed that Carol's family told him it was a wonderful service and had personally thanked him for his role in making it all work as well as the sermon. He then, purposefully, shared that "credit" with the choir. "I couldn't have done it without your understanding and assistance. Thank you."

A month later, greeting each other in the parking lot outside the Klatch, Sheila and Amanda briefly hugged and then went inside, directly to a booth in the back to make sure they were not interrupted or overheard. Despite its actual size, Littleton had a small-town feel.

Still standing, Sheila launched in with a resigned smile. "Someone sent me an anonymous letter complaining about Steve's sermon last week, saying that it crossed 'separation of church and state' lines when Steve talked about specific candidates. Though visitors attended on Sunday, the letter could just as well have come from a member. Doesn't matter. I had to check with our attorney. We could be vulnerable. I want you to know the matter will be brought up at the board meeting this week, and we'll have to have an executive session so we can discuss it without Steve there. I've told him already."

Not minding Sheila's direct style, Amanda got right into it as well. "How did Steve react when you told him about the letter?"

Hanging her suit jacket on the hook, Sheila shrugged before she slid into the booth. "He didn't say anything. His face froze for a minute. I'm sure he wasn't happy, but he'll be fine. I think."

Amanda sat down and sighed. "I hope nothing bad happens as a result. He's pretty sensitive. This can't be the first time this sort of thing has come up. He's been around the block. I would think given his propensity to research, his smarts, and his experience, he probably knew he was going up to a line and knew when to stop. He must be used to these hysterical reactions and know how to respond. I'm sure everyone will support Steve."

"I'm not that sure, but we'll see."

Amanda guessed at what Sheila meant. They ordered their lunch and chatted about several other church matters as well as some personal stuff. From time to time, they came back to the subject of Steve's sermon. It was a relatively brief lunch since Sheila had an appointment with a client.

Later that week, Sheila explained to the board that their attorney advised discussing the issue with Steve and putting a note in his file, a fairly simple CYA solution. Kyle vocalized that he agreed with what the attorney suggested. The rest thought putting something in his file was unnecessary and would hurt Steve's feelings. Eventually, the board voted and agreed to have only a verbal discussion with Steve, a kind of a wink-wink, slap-on-the-wrist, don't-do-it-again sort of thing.

Kyle made a detached comment, saying, "I don't like the way Steve handled himself around Carol's death."

The group stared at him in disbelief and annoyance.

Sheila tried to smooth it over. "I think Kyle means Steve was overwrought. He seemed to be broken up by Carol's death. The ordeal was hard on him."

Kyle neither confirmed nor clarified the statement.

The majority agreed that the past few weeks had taken its toll, and no one wanted to be onerous to Steve, adding any more burdens or worries. Again, Kyle neither agreed nor disagreed.

The consensus about the sermon seemed to be that even if he had gone a little too far, it was still a good one, and no harm was done. When the final vote was taken by ballot, there were two people in favor of inserting the official memo in the file, and five opposed.

Steve returned to the room, his face pinched with apprehension. Sheila delivered the message that he needed to be careful, but there was not going to be any official action taken.

With a red face and teeth gritted in a compressed smile, Steve said nothing. Some of the others elaborated and yakked over each other, some trying to make him feel better and others filling the uncomfortable silence that hung there.

When Steve had still not said a word, Amanda finally asked, "How do you feel, Steve? What's your reaction?"

What he said next stunned Amanda momentarily, and later she found out Sheila was taken aback as well.

"I'm disappointed in this board," Steve said. "I would have hoped you would have respected my experience and would come to me immediately if there were a problem—and that it would not have come to this."

Amanda carefully, and with empathy, explained the board's decision once again, believing that Steve must have misunderstood.

Steve's face did not show any sign of softening.

No one else reacted. They certainly didn't say anything then or at any other time. It appeared that they felt properly chastised and somewhat ashamed or embarrassed. Perhaps everyone did—except Kyle who was always difficult to read.

After the meeting, Amanda approached Sheila and said, "I didn't know what to make of it. It was not what I was expecting at all. He seemed angry and a little defensive. He actually went on the offensive."

Sheila agreed and added, "I think he implied I was at fault, and I *had* talked to him—had given him a heads-up—although I couldn't say anything officially to him. He turned it around. It seemed like he didn't understand how easy we were on him and how everyone tried to be sensitive to him while covering ourselves legally. He never even said he was sorry for causing a problem or potentially creating a big one. He didn't seem to realize the risk to the church itself."

Amanda changed the subject, remarking on Kyle's behavior. "I don't know Kyle very well, but he seemed kind of removed, a bit distant, almost angry. It didn't bother me, but a couple of others seemed to react badly to him. Meg visibly flinches every time he opens his mouth. Am I missing something?"

Sheila was circumspect. "Kyle has his own way of doing things. There have been some issues in the past—actually only one that I know of. But people do not always respond well to him. As far as I know, if he was angry, it was because he likes things done by the letter of the law. I guess it bothered him that the majority did not follow legal counsel. I think he was bothered by the sermon too. And there was Carol and the memorial."

"I know. I'm not sure what his objection was. I thought everyone was pleased and admired Steve. We all saw the toll it took. We tried to help and support him. The board even offered to give him time off."

"Well, in the end, the man is an adult. We have to accept his stoicism or independence or whatever. He didn't accept our help."

Nothing more came of it.

# Chapter 9

*Wednesday, April 11, 2012*

Armed with her on-air charm and fully charged, Kelly began to set up interviews. Zack had okayed a cameraman so she could capture the interviews on video, either for review or to be broadcast on the show. Even if it was just going to be a news story, her primary objective was to find the absolute truth, but she had to be strategic about it.

She was pleased, though not altogether surprised, by the receptivity. Everyone liked to claim their fifteen minutes of fame, and everyone wanted to tell their story. Almost everyone. She could not get to Jonah Spencer because he was still under investigation. Kyle Whitman was also under scrutiny, and he was sedated in the hospital. Steve Anderson, the minister, said he was too upset and too busy to talk; he had a congregation to attend to. After she had left a couple of voice-mail messages, she finally caught him, apparently by surprise, when he answered the church phone. He ended the call very abruptly with no commitment to meet.

She thought about the video clip of Reverend Anderson that had been shown on the news on Sunday. Her first viewing of it had netted nothing significant. Somewhat attributable to a full head of dark hair and unencumbered movement, he was youthful in appearance despite crinkling around the eyes. He was wearing a clerical robe, but it did not hide his slight frame. He was average height. He had a classically symmetrical face that was neither exceptionally handsome nor homely, a son of Middle America. Watching it the second time, something bothered her and impelled her to watch the same twenty-second clip a third time. It was then that she became conscious of her initial visceral reaction. She chalked it up to her distaste for "men of the cloth" and even allowed that she did not feel an immediate connection or affinity to him. And yet, she was drawn to him.

Packing up their gear, she and Rick, the cameraman, went to the church for the first scheduled meeting. The yellow crime scene tape kept people from the sanctuary, but the rest of the church was abuzz with activity. Reporters were still trying to get a story on the fly and making the most they could out of the mess.

Sitting in a remote upstairs room of the old building, Kelly began with Sheila, the board president. She asked some warm-up questions, which she quickly perceived was an unnecessary accommodation. She got to the point quickly. "So, Sheila, what happened on Sunday?"

"I really don't know. I'm waiting for the police investigation."

Kelly was not going to accept that. "Come on, Sheila. Let's have the background context here."

Intending to be circumspect, but wanting to be helpful as well, given all that she knew, Sheila said, "Everything started to change when Steve filed a formal complaint against Kyle. Steve was having trouble coping with Kyle's hostility. The board had to deal with it, protecting Steve and his position, as well as Kyle, as a member of the congregation. But Steve didn't see it that way—and neither did most of the board. The argument proffered was that Kyle should not be allowed to behave as he had been. Steve felt Kyle should not be on the board. No one wanted to lose Steve."

"So relationships were strained."

"Ha! To say the least. Essentially we were in a war. People were assigning and taking sides.

"How did you feel?"

"I wanted no part of it. It's not how we operate at this church. We don't kick people out or off the board. Others were fed up with Kyle and thought he was dangerous."

"Did you?"

"Only to himself, really. I mean not physically, except insofar as the tension he created might have affected his health."

"Why do you think he brought a gun to church?"

"I don't know that he did."

"That seems to be the common understanding."

"Common understandings can be deceptive."

"Indeed." Kelly considered this only for a minute, knowing it to be true. "So what do you think really happened?"

"I'm not going to speculate on that. I don't have the facts."

"But you must have an opinion, a feeling …"

Sheila shook her head.

Kelly said, "Okay, so give me more of the unofficial goings-on. What was happening here in the last few months?"

"Certainly in the last two months, anger and hostility heightened. I don't think Kyle could take more of it. He was at the end of his rope."

This comment puzzled Kelly, considering what Sheila had just said about not thinking Kyle was violent. She let it sit while Sheila went on.

"Steve had his own issues. Let's just say there was no love lost between them … plenty of love here for Steve, though."

Kelly saw another opening to get to some underlying stuff. "Tell me more."

"People are in love with Steve … in all different kinds of ways. Some quite literally, maybe. He has that kind of charisma."

Kelly seized the opportunity to lighten the discussion. With Kelly's wink and a smile, along with assurances that what was said at this point would be off the record, Sheila was willing to share that she had an unexpected encounter with someone in Steve's office that had made her think it possible that something improper was going on. Kelly turned off the recorder, and the cameraman left the room.

Sheila described the episode, telling Kelly that she had seen a pocketbook hanging on a chair that she recognized, but no one answered when she called out. As she started to go about her business, she thought she heard sounds in a back room. Steve emerged from the copy room. As he rushed out, he said he had to get Claire from her dance class. But someone else was in the copy room. Sheila did not say who it was.

Sheila told Kelly that she thought it was funny and was never sure what was going on, if anything. Kelly pressed to find out who the person was, but Sheila declined to say more. Instead, she asked Sheila when this happened and what she did following the awkward incident.

Sheila responded, "It happened some time last year. I let it go. I had deeper concerns at the time and needed to wrestle with what to do about the brewing conflict. It was on that very day that I had received Steve's formal complaint."

"What was the nature of the complaint? On the record." Kelly signaled to Rick, and recording resumed.

"At first, Steve accused Kyle of being disrespectful, yelling at him for no apparent reason. Steve had been expressing concerns for a while and felt attacked, but then he put it in writing."

"Wait, you said 'at first.' Did the complaint change? Escalate?"

"Oh yeah. He made a formal complaint and then another one maybe a month later, using the word *bullying*. Initially, he told the board that Kyle had 'anger management' issues and implied he should be on medication."

Kelly stopped Sheila to summarize. "He talked about the condition that he suspected caused Kyle's anger issues. At some point after that, Steve made another complaint, saying he was being bullied."

Sheila nodded, letting Kelly draw her own conclusions and added, "The accusations continued to be disturbing. He stressed that he was working in a 'hostile workplace environment,' and that he was being 'harassed.' I had to handle it."

"What did you do?"

Sheila summarized all the efforts made to settle the dispute in a grown-up fashion. Then Kelly turned the discussion back to Kyle. "How did Kyle react to all that?"

Sheila revealed that Kyle was her friend and that she kept her friendship separate. "He didn't like Steve. But his behavior had to be dealt with. I had to take Steve's concerns seriously and do the right thing. Kyle volunteered to avoid contact with Steve. You'll have to ask him about his feelings. I'm not going to answer for him. And I am not going to guess at what happened Sunday."

Closing out the discussion with Sheila had been easy, although Kelly was sure there would be a follow-up conversation. Sheila was a bright, attractive woman, the kind of leader she would have voted for if she ran for public office. Her fortitude and strength of character were admirable, and she was fair, yet not without compassion and humor. It did not appear to Kelly that Sheila would "play" politics, yet she knew how to hold her cards and was able to maintain both decorum and a sense of justice.

After that initial interview, she knew there was so much going on that if she didn't limit her focus to the perception of *what* happened on Sunday versus the *why* for now at least, she could easily be there hours with each person. She wanted to establish justification to go back in more depth later. Kelly sent Rick back to the studio. Audio would be sufficient until later.

As she waited for the next interviewee, Kelly overcame a momentary feeling of regret at having started this endeavor. She wasn't at all sure it would be worth the effort. While she enjoyed talking and learning about others, a group of churchgoers was not as interesting to her as a group of political activists, intellectuals, or even farmworkers might be.

Will Marlborough was next, followed by Amanda Corwell, and then Denise Vanderhoven—Dinny. While Sheila's story had begun to shape her view, she worked hard at maintaining distance and objectivity, knowing full well that the truth of what happened was not likely to come from a single source but from putting all the pieces together. In between the scheduled meetings, she would try to get some impressions from some of those who were still hanging around.

Kelly struggled to resist the natural temptation to allow her initial judgments to color her questioning and listening skills. Neutrality and openness were prerequisites in her profession; to ensure that position, Kelly had to deliberately set aside her known biases and suspicions. While she always mused about whether she would like an interview subject, *liking* a person was not of concern. At the outset, she had to trust and believe everyone. She had no reason not to.

She wanted these people to be comfortable and relaxed; to ensure that they were, she had to listen without prejudice. She knew well enough that the analysis would occur sooner or later, and she needed to hold off forming conclusions for as long as she possibly could.

Dinny, the last one for the day, was scheduled after a late lunch. Around noon, though, Sheila called to say that Kyle was willing to make a statement—but only to Kelly. That interview could take place at the hospital early that evening. Kelly knew that had taken a bit of finagling since Kyle was being closely watched both by the police and doctors, and he probably had legal representation too. But apparently he was well enough to be questioned and had welcomed the opportunity to tell his side of the story. Kelly appreciated her good fortune at getting an exclusive.

# Chapter 10

*Winter–Spring, 2011*

About two months after the infamous "political" sermon, Sheila scheduled an off-site planning meeting to begin discussing the next fiscal year.

The board and Steve sat in a comfortable living room atmosphere and discussed modifications to the agenda. There were fundamental procedures and policies that *Kyle* wanted addressed. However, Sheila and others felt it critical that the board make some broader decisions and gain consensus on what direction to take for the long term. Members had started to worry about whether Steve would be there another year to help them move forward.

Sheila put it to Steve as tactfully as she could, saying, "We hope you will be with us next year and for the long-term. We'd like to understand what your intentions are. If you don't plan on staying, we need to let the congregation know so we can begin a search for another minister." No one knew what progress had been made toward the goal of becoming "fellowshipped" as he had promised to do since the beginning.

Steve thought for a moment before he responded. He stiffened, set his mouth, and reiterated much of what he had said before. "As you know, this is my church home, and my dear wife became an official member last year. We made a substantial pledge, beyond what we could afford, but in keeping with 'per-member' expenses. We want to stay here as long as we are needed and welcome."

Sheila had no choice but to be more direct. "We can continue hiring you as a consultant, but this congregation might want a 'called minister' soon. And while we would love that person to be you, we need to know if you are eligible. Have you made any progress in finding out about applying your previous ordination and training to the UU fellowshipping process? Is there a shortcut from the usual procedure?"

Kyle bit his tongue.

Steve swallowed hard, fixed his smile, and said, "I have met with my mentor and with our esteemed district bishop. They have been advising me. But as you know, with my experience and two advanced degrees, I have no intention of spending more time studying. And I won't leave my family. At my age—and with my family obligations—it simply is not feasible."

It appeared that the topic was put to rest with an assumption that he was working on it. A minute or so later, however, Kyle quietly asked, "What is your master's degree in?"

Steve glared and responded, "Sacred music."

Kyle said, "Oh."

No one else paid much attention to the digression, and an animated discussion ensued.

Kyle later told Sheila he was put off by Steve's use of the term "bishop"—a title not used in the faith—and he wondered who his mentor was. More than that, though he kept it to himself, he was quite sure that only a handful of universities offered a degree in sacred music. It was a highly specialized field, sometimes taking five or six years of study. It didn't sit right with him, not because a master's in sacred music was impossible, but because it seemed improbable.

Several months later, in April, some board members talked before their regular meeting was called to order. Neither Kyle nor Steve was present. Amanda's mouth dropped as she learned about the complaint filed against Kyle, although no one else seemed to be especially surprised or bothered.

Dinny said, "I don't blame Steve one bit. Enough is enough. We have seen how Kyle treats Steve. He's intimidating. We all know that some people witnessed Kyle yelling at Steve and then bad-mouthing him publicly."

Not being aware of the particulars, Amanda said, "It doesn't sound nice, I agree. But why couldn't Steve just handle it and discuss it privately with Kyle? Lots of people yell at one time or another—ask my kids or Glenn."

Amanda's question must have been naïve or self-evident to others, and she dropped it. Everyone else seemed to completely understand—or at least accept—Steve's need to file a formal complaint.

Earlier in the day, Sheila had told Kyle and Steve that they would be invited in to talk, individually, to the board, but they were to wait in other areas of the church. Sheila called the meeting to order and then called for an executive session. This was the second of such meetings. Although no one was aware of it at the time, there would be more to come.

Once the nature of the complaint was explained formally in the executive session, Steve was the first to be invited in. He walked into the boardroom, head bowed, sat stiffly in his seat, and looked around the table. "I need you to know how personally distressful this is for me. I never imagined someone would do this to me. But just as importantly, I need you to know I'm very concerned about Kyle." As he went on, his tone became increasingly grave, and he changed his posture from upright to a slight slump.

He stood up as if to provide more credibility and strength and continued purposefully, somewhat heroically. "I am very upset by Kyle's actions. I never wanted it to come to this, but it has gone on long enough. I have never encountered anything like this before in my long career." He abruptly sat, and once again, appeared tired and profoundly disturbed. "I am terribly worried about Kyle's health, though I'm worried even more about the well-being of this congregation. There is no telling who his next target will be. It is clearly random." He shrugged, suggesting he could not see any reason he would have been victimized. "I need to point out that this is not the first time Kyle has attacked someone. You all remember when he verbally assaulted Leslie. I was afraid, at the time, that it might happen again, but I never expected it would be me." He sighed heavily and asked forgiveness for showing his agitation and fear.

Everyone listened in respectful silence, nodding in sympathy.

Amanda recalled something Dinny had told her about an incident with Kyle and Leslie, but it had occurred long ago. She also remembered Dinny mentioning a screaming match—was it Dinny who had screamed? Or Kyle? Were those the same incident or two separate ones? She had heard Dinny raise her voice. She had observed her commanding people; some might have said she sounded shrill or bossy. Amanda had never heard Kyle yell, although she had seen his frustration and his perseverance when trying to get the board and Steve to comply with policies and procedures. To be sure, those efforts and the way he presented things did annoy many on the board, as well as Steve. She took in what she heard, trying to process the information as fairly as possible.

Steve continued, "I trust this board, and I think it is important for you to know Kyle was diagnosed with early-onset Alzheimer's and has gone off his medication without his doctor's approval. This could account for the anger. I only found out recently when I was sharing my fears with a friend of Kyle's and searching for a plausible explanation for his behavior." He stated earnestly that he felt Kyle needed professional help, emphasizing that they needed to support Kyle, but felt they could not ignore the behavior. It was potentially harmful to everyone.

This disclosure was met with stunned silence. The board members had not been aware of Kyle's condition.

Amanda's eyes widened imperceptibly. She was troubled for different reasons. The very fact that Steve would reveal this confidential piece of information was shocking in its own right, but Amanda was especially alarmed because she was quite sure it was simply not true. That one of Kyle's *supposed* friends would share this with Steve was also disturbing. Amanda had hit an emotional trifecta, feeling astonishment, dismay, and apprehension. She remained speechless along with the others.

No one questioned Steve about this information. Everyone appeared to understand why he felt he needed to share it. No one asked for specifics about the accusations either.

When Kyle came in, he sat stonily, eyes staring outward at nothing in particular. He quietly admitted he had lost his temper with Steve at a regional conference, though he never offered any explanation or described what had occurred. He voluntarily offered to stay away from Steve, avoid e-mail and phone contact, and take a month's leave from the board. Neither his facial expression nor tone of voice ever changed. His face turned red when he apologized for the difficulties this was causing the board. He appeared genuinely humbled and contrite. The board breathed a collective sigh of relief.

Despite the thoughts reeling through her head, Amanda changed the topic as she walked out of the church with Sheila and Dinny. "On another note, what's going on with the AIDS dinner? Don't we get a group together every year?"

Dinny echoed the question, having forgotten about it, but also surprised she hadn't heard anything about the dinner yet.

Sheila replied, "Kyle and Blake handle that. I don't know what the current status is."

The next day, Amanda approached Steve when he was at his desk. "Can we talk for a minute?"

He pushed away his paperwork and turned his chair to face her with a welcoming smile.

She continued, "I realize that what happened with Kyle must have been difficult for you. I want you to know I'm upset by all of this too. I also think you should know that what you were told about Kyle is not true. He does not have early-onset Alzheimer's or anything like that, and when the *mis*diagnosis was discovered, he went off the medication carefully—with a doctor's supervision. Kyle told us about his medical situation, and I just reconfirmed it with Blake."

"Oh."

Amanda, self-consciously and awkwardly, left Steve's office.

# Chapter 11

The core group, including Steve, was at the pub after choir practice later that week. Sheryl arrived a couple of minutes after everyone else. They maneuvered and shuffled around, trying to settle themselves onto the cracked leather bench. Extra chairs were hauled over to accommodate Jonah and Will.

Kitty, the server, wiped the table and tested her memory with a grin. "IPAs for Will and Sam; Sierra Nevada for Glenn; Malbec for Amanda; Pinot Noir for Steve. And you?" she asked, looking at Jonah. He ordered Red Bull. "And do you want a beer too?" she asked Sheryl.

Some time later, Will faced away from Steve, slightly blocking him with his broad frame. In a stage whisper, with a tiny smile, Will asked, "What's this I hear about someone bullying our minister?"

Watching Steve smile and start to say something, Amanda cut the conversation short, saying, "Not to worry, it's all fine."

Steve took the cue and thought better about saying anything.

Will also picked up on it, realizing he should not have spoken. "Well, I trust it will be handled appropriately," he said.

At home that night, Amanda said, "How did Will get wind of the problems between Steve and Kyle? There haven't been any non–board members at our meetings. There are no minutes from executive sessions, not that anyone ever reads minutes anyway—except Kyle. Glenn, you're on the minister's council. Has anything been said there?"

"Not a word."

"I really don't like that suddenly Will's getting involved. As far as I know, Will doesn't know Kyle."

"He didn't mention Kyle by name."

"True."

"It could have been Dinny who gossiped or ..." He thought for a moment that Steve could have said something, but as that would have been extremely inappropriate, he dismissed the thought and moved on. "I hope we can keep up the momentum of the Minstrels. It's always hard during the summer when people go away."

"Me too. I feel so energized by our singing, even with Carol gone. I really miss her, though. Still, I'm so happy belonging to TLC too. Have you noticed I can now use the word *church*?"

They laughed and almost simultaneously burst into "Amazing Place" sung to the tune of "Amazing Grace." With Glenn creatively ad-libbing and improvising, a new anthem was created.

Glenn said, "Maybe we should give this to Steve for the next time he says, 'We're going to rewrite some of the old tunes with new words.' Remember that?"

"We did *one*! Then poof! Not done again. Maybe he hated what we did or just forgot about it ... or maybe not enough people paid attention."

Several weeks later, The New Littleton Minstrels led another songfest at a local seafood dive. They had finally found someone to take Carol's place, vocally, although they all agreed no one ever really could replace her. Nevertheless, they had a wonderful time in one another's company, exercising their voices. After paying the bar bill, Amanda and Glenn caught up with Will and Dinny in the parking lot.

They were welcomed over, and Amanda heard them harping about Kyle. She said, "I know that Kyle has not been easy to deal with, and he does scowl a lot, but I don't think he's a bad person—"

"You saw what he did to Steve at the last board meeting," Dinny challenged. "You could have cut the tension with a knife. You even said that yourself. Kyle is a bully."

Amanda gritted her teeth, wanting to stop Dinny from saying more about what had occurred, given that Will was not on the board. However, given that Will knew something anyway—and the board meeting was public even if no one else was there—she made an effort to reconstruct events accurately in order to reshape perception. "A bully?" Amanda said. "I don't see that. Yes, there is tension. But it takes two to make something of it. Kyle might look at Steve a certain way and ask pointed questions, but that's it. Why doesn't Steve say something to Kyle if he's uncomfortable? He just sits there. No one confronts Kyle's behavior."

Will calmly replied, "When a person says he is bullied, you have to take it seriously. Bullying is never the victim's fault. By definition, if Steve feels bullied, then he is a victim, and you take care of the victim. He's our minister. He deserves respect. We need to keep him here and protect him from being harassed. Steve is not cut out to let bullying roll off his back—and he shouldn't. He's very sensitive. He had issues with bullies when he was young. It's not something he deals well with, as if anyone could. How to deal with this problem is up to the board, and I hope you do the right thing."

"Kyle doesn't express himself well when he disagrees, but I don't *think* he means to be malicious." Amanda found herself defending Kyle when she only wanted to be objective and nip the burgeoning conflict in the bud.

Dinny shot back. "He disagrees with everything! How can you excuse him and defend him like that? He's been harassing Steve for months now. The phone calls and e-mails were incessant. It's evident that he does not like Steve and is looking to get something on him. It's intentional. He's just mean."

Amanda countered, "He might not like him, and he's entitled to his opinion. I've seen Kyle in meetings, and I would say he's nitpicky, not menacing. If he makes a pointed statement or asks a question, why isn't it just addressed? If you think by asking a question, he's implying something, then say so. Ask him. Call him on it. I'll try talking to Kyle about how he can make his points without being contentious and ask questions in a way that does not seem hostile. But from what I see, this is how he behaves with everyone when he has a concern—not just Steve."

Dinny took the next swing. "So that proves Steve's point. He's a danger to us. We need Steve, and we can't risk losing him. We cannot have that kind of behavior here. This is a loving community. If Kyle randomly targeted Steve, there is no telling who might be next. We have to protect everyone."

Will nodded in agreement.

The conversation continued a bit longer with the two of them defending and sheltering Steve. Suddenly, Dinny asked Amanda, "Are *you* against Steve too?"

"How did you get that from what I said? I love Steve and what he has brought to the church. As I've said before to you, I don't think he's perfect. He certainly isn't handling this well, in my opinion. I would have expected a minister to be better equipped to handle this kind of behavior. Seems like every church must have someone who's a little ornery."

"A little ornery? Ha! That's what you call it? Steve told me he had never in his adult life encountered such behavior."

Though he had remained silent up to that point, Glenn gently changed the subject to something more pleasant and everyone acquiesced.

Amanda kept her mouth shut and puffed out a soft grunt, but they left one another on a positive note. As she got into the car, she said, "Glenn, I'm really tired of this pussyfooting around and then talking behind people's backs. Why can't we get these people to talk to each other?"

"It's not what they do."

"Well, I am going to make it happen at the first opportunity I see. There is no reason this can't be resolved reasonably, if not amicably."

---

The following week, standing behind the pulpit in chinos and polo shirt, Steve delivered a sermon that the congregation appreciated even more than usual. Although the assembled group had previously heard only a little about his past, that day they learned more. Steve included a reference to a boyhood encounter with bullying and how deeply the boy had been affected. The story was more of an allegory than a precise memoir, and he embedded information about how he had worked to help support his family by playing the organ and piano in churches of all denominations, as well as the local Jewish synagogues. These experiences inspired his calling and appreciation of different faiths.

With the title, "Living One's Values," he also included a snippet about how he came to be a vegetarian and then a vegan, which was a rather interesting and tender story. Steve mentioned his visit to his uncle's farm where chickens were slaughtered. He was a young, sensitive child and had never been aware of how the fried chicken that was served to him for dinner actually came from a live animal that had been held captive, nurtured, and fed with the express purpose of being killed. He found it nauseating in principle, as well as literally, and had been preoccupied with it for weeks. That was when he decided he would never eat meat again, and later, he eliminated all animal products from his life.

# Chapter 12

Dinny waltzed into the church office with a cheery hello to anyone who might be around. Hearing no response, she went about her business, scanned the mail, and went outside to do some gardening.

Coming back into the building for a drink of water, she ran smack into Steve. "Oh my Lord, I am so sorry. I had no idea anyone was here! I was running in for some water and to do a few chores. I need to get cleaned up. But since you're here, do you have a minute? There's something I want to ask you. I think you might have some insight that could be of help to me."

"Sure, Dinny. I'll be here for another hour or so."

After a cool drink, she changed her clothes and freshened up, making herself presentable. Having changed out of her jeans, dirty T-shirt, and sun hat, Dinny walked out of the ladies' room, wearing a sporty red dress that traced the slender curves of her body and showed off her tanned and freshly shaved legs. She credited "staying busy" more than anything else for her slenderness, though she did, indeed, watch her diet. She had also recently experimented with eliminating meat and dairy.

She gently knocked on Steve's door, and without waiting for him to answer, she walked in. "Oh, Steve. I wanted to show you this new brochure for the Bartlett Concert Hall. I have recently gotten involved with some of the people on their board. This is a draft for next season. I *know* you will be interested." She leaned in casually, close enough for him to catch her very lightly lavender-scented body—no perfume, just lotion.

Steve quickly replaced his initial frozen stare with a carefully crafted grin. He brushed his hand through his hair as he subtly pushed his chair a little farther from Dinny. "Thank you for thinking of me. I'll take a closer look a little later."

"I want to go to the committee with a review from an unbiased expert and potential subscriber—that would be *you*. Do you think this is a good program? Would it appeal to a wide variety of concert attendees? How about the layout?"

She tried to prolong the conversation, and although Steve was not altogether interested in pursuing it, he played his part well enough. Dinny was an influential church member, and he didn't want to let her down or displease her. Although he maintained his distance, she didn't notice.

Turning to his computer, he said, "Oh, look at that. I need to respond to something right away, and then I need to pick up Claire from her rehearsal. Thank you for thinking of me."

"No problem! I'll be in on Thursday morning. Let me know then." She hung around, busying herself in the outer office, until she caught a glimpse of Steve heading into the copy room. She quietly followed him in.

Very shortly after, at around five o'clock, Dinny heard the door chime signaling that someone with a key was entering the building. Steve escaped first, with a cheery good-bye. Minutes later, Dinny sidled passed Sheila with her own chirpy good-bye. For an instant, she fretted she might look foolish having been there with Steve, though she was following her heart and that was what mattered—another piece of sage advice from Aurora.

# Part 3
## Investigation

# Chapter 13

*Wednesday, April 11, 2012*

Pleased that the first interviews were finished, Kelly breathed in deeply and let out a big whoosh.

Her meeting with Will had been positive. He was a good-humored man, as much as circumstances allowed anyway, thoughtful, and clearly biased. Will was one of those people who made a fabulous first impression, and she could understand why he was popular.

Dinny had a rather narrow and tinted viewpoint. She was all over the place, and Kelly did not quite know what to make of her. She thought about some things Amanda had said about Dinny, and she drifted back to something that had happened a few years earlier. There was a girl named Sandra Edelman in her high school who was popular, outgoing, and very attractive. Kelly had never met her. Sandra was a year behind in school, but it was well known that Sandra was "easy." At her fifteenth reunion, Kelly had been talking to one of her classmates. Brian Reznik was one of the brainiacs, a nice guy, very interesting, and well on his way toward making a fortune in a new technology start-up.

A woman walked past their table and said hi to him, flashing a big smile. When Kelly asked who that was, he told her it was Sandra Edelman. The first thing that popped into her mind and out of her mouth was, "Sandra Edelman? Boy, she had quite the reputation! What is she doing here?"

Brian told her she was there because she had married someone from their class. "But," he added, "that wasn't only a rumor. Ask anyone who was on the football team. She came on to me once, a couple of years ago—after she was married. They have an open marriage."

At the time, Kelly didn't think more about it, though much later, she began to think about whether facts preceded a reputation or vice versa. Maybe Brian projected that she was coming on to him because he already *knew* about her and was predisposed to thinking of her as seductive: taking off a scarf, leaning a certain way, a friendly hug, or even just being as smiley and sociable as she was when she passed them. Or maybe she really did.

She kicked herself for automatically associating Sandra's name with her reputation, which got her thinking even more broadly about how reputations can be formed: a little truth, a little embellishment, a little wishful thinking, a little deliberate malice. And, reputations tended to stick.

Refocusing, she continued to assess the interviews. Amanda was wordy and difficult to restrain. Kelly could easily see why people would lose patience with her. While animated, she was also intense. It had taken a great deal of effort to limit her to talking about Sunday so intent was she on providing too many details and nuances. She was so annoyingly comprehensive that she would probably never be the most popular person around. On the other hand, she had some insights about Kyle, Steve, and the board dynamics that were worth pursuing.

Kelly sensed that there was a lot more to the story that Amanda was itching to get out, but she could not determine whether all or any of it was important or if she had an ax to grind. Overall, it was clear that Sheila had not been all that successful in reducing friction, and a lot of people did not react well to how she had managed things. Kelly would start pulling more together after talking with Kyle.

Later that afternoon, she sat on an uncomfortable chair next to Kyle's hospital bed. It didn't take long for Kelly to realize that Kyle was not an easy person to figure out—and a really difficult interviewee—and the whole bloody mess was extremely complex. She knew she would have to speak more with Kyle and others to get it untangled. He had not fully recovered, which added to the challenge.

At the start, she limited her questions to gathering information rather than asking directly about the shooting. Both Sheila and Amanda had given her a little background. Dinny mentioned that he was raised Mormon. Kyle confirmed a few things others had said about him, though he laughed at her assumption that he had been Mormon.

"No," he drawled patiently as though he had heard this before. "I was never a Mormon. My sister is one though! We were raised Presbyterian. Regular WASPs. However, I *was* born in Utah!"

As she learned more, Kelly got the impression that if one read Kyle's résumé, it would not accurately or adequately reflect who he was or his various talents. On the face of it, it appeared that he was unsure of what career he wanted. He had tried a lot of different ones: the ministry, computer technology, psychiatric nursing, finance, chef, baker, and more. However, it was not so much that he was a job hopper but a career adventurer. Everything he tried, he did well—and he accumulated a lot of information and contacts along the way.

Kyle was not like many people Kelly had known. He defied being easily characterized, though she guessed that others did try to brand him. They probably found him difficult since he was different, and they couldn't identify with him. Yet, he was not a loner or weirdo; in fact, he was quite sociable. Nevertheless, people tend to like people who make them feel good. Kyle was no smoothie.

Talking about his past, Kyle revealed, "I was board president at a church in Kansas when I discovered that the minister did some rather tricky things with the accounts. It is never beyond the realm of possibility."

"Oh, did you suspect Steve of foul play?"

"Not at first. Not with the finances."

"Later then?"

"That was after."

"I don't understand—after what?"

"After I found out about the degree."

"I'm not following, Kyle. I'm sure you're exhausted, and with the medication, this has to be tiring for you. Maybe I should come back?"

"No, please don't go. I'm fine."

"So continue. You said something about a degree."

"You don't know about that?"

At that point, the nurse came in to take his blood pressure, and Kelly stepped out of the room.

What she had gleaned so far was that, above all else, Kyle held himself up as a proper steward of the church and was not going to let anything untoward happen on his watch. But so far, the central questions about Sunday had not been addressed. When she asked about his relationship with Jonah, all he said was, "There is none. I don't know him."

He knew he pissed people off, and they were not appreciative of his efforts. He had a blunt way of speaking. His short sentences sometimes sounded like non sequiturs. Also, telling people that they are not doing things right certainly can cause them to take offense or feel embarrassed.

On the other hand, Kelly had gathered that Kyle was not well known by many. Will had never talked to him. Dinny had made a lot of assumptions, so her assessment was in question. Clearly, Amanda and Sheila had been able to get under the surface of Kyle more than the others, and they were friends. They had fun with him and had gone out socially. And then there was Blake, sitting in the waiting room, periodically checking on his mate, prepared to advocate as needed.

Kelly had no idea about the fun part, but she was finding him attractive in an inexplicable way. Handsome, to be sure. His gruffness had its own charm. Maybe it was his depth and intelligence. Or the steel blue eyes. In any case, she knew deciphering the enigma that was Kyle would be hard work.

She was allowed back in the room after the nurse had finished with him, and Kyle seemed to have a lot more energy than before. She had been assured he was on nothing that would drastically alter his behavior or mood. Maybe the oxygen and blood transfusion were kicking in.

Kelly continued getting to know Kyle better.

"I don't like to lead. I get things done," Kyle said in response to a question. "I attended various committee meetings, though. I think that's a board member's responsibility. Not everyone does."

"Do you mean 'not everyone does' as in attends meetings or not everyone thinks a board member should attend meetings?"

"Both."

There was a long pause. Then Kyle blurted out, "Everyone loves Blake. And everyone loves Steve."

She had heard a little about Blake's gift of giving; he was frequently described as "compassionate" and "a gentle soul." As with many couples, there appeared to be a yin and yang but—also as with many people—appearances often belie what actually is. Not that she doubted Blake was a warm person.

"You're not crazy about Steve, are you?"

"Not one bit. You could say I despise him."

"Did you attack him? Did you want to shoot him?" The minute she blurted out the questions, Kelly regretted it and knew it could mark the end of the interview.

"Depends on what you mean."

The man had saved her. She recovered. "How would you interpret that?"

"I didn't harass him. I did want to shoot him, though. I was mad. I was determined to set it straight."

"You didn't want him as a minister, did you?" She was gently probing and challenging.

"No. I didn't. I know others did."

"You were on the board when he was hired?"

"Yes. I voted against hiring him."

"So, you never wanted him there and were working to get him out?"

"I didn't know him. We hadn't gone through a proper process—vetting. I was outvoted. I went along with the outcome." He shrugged his acceptance.

"Were you suspicious of him for some reason?"

"I had no reason to be then."

"Later?"

"He made mistakes."

"What kind of mistakes?"

"Not just mistakes. There are different ways to run a service. He should know about them. I didn't check into plagiarism. That's possible, I suppose."

Kelly had no idea what he was referencing. She sighed. Kyle really tried her patience, though she plowed on and pushed through with an intuitive sense that there was a lot more going on than appeared on the surface. She was still struggling with his admission that he wanted to shoot Steve. At a loss, she said, "Tell me more."

"He screwed up a sermon last fall. We could have lost tax-exempt status. Sheila never did find out who wrote the letter. None of us did. Then there was Carol Votarini's death. He didn't handle that the way he should have."

Before she could follow up, he was onto something else. His mouth turned down and his voice was angry and mean. "I wasn't going to take the blame anymore. I tried to keep quiet for the sake of the church. I was boiling mad."

Kelly still had no idea what he was talking about and wondered if he had momentarily snapped. She sat silently to see what he'd say next.

"I suppose you heard I was inundating Steve with letters and phone calls. He accused me of bullying."

Kelly had yet to hear of any examples of actual bullying behavior, though she had heard the label used when others mentioned Kyle. She allowed him to continue in his own way.

"That bastard didn't return my calls or answer e-mails. I needed to hear from him." He spoke as though antecedents and context were understood.

"When was this? All the time?"

"After a while, it seemed like all the time." He sighed deeply. "I tried to get hold of him about the AIDS dinner. I wanted his support as our minister. I needed him to agree to change choir practice since the dinner is a public event held every year on the same day. Steve knew that." He grunted.

"So, what happened?"

"I yelled at him. I got frustrated. I tried for more than two weeks to meet with him and get an answer."

"When was that exactly?"

"Last April."

She gathered that was about the time of Steve's first formal complaint.

As she ruminated, Kyle switched gears again. "They didn't like it when I questioned Leslie's committee either." Without knowing what it might take to get the full story, Kelly risked asking him to explain.

Through a series of fits and starts, she was given enough to understand that Kyle had thought Leslie's committee had done something, or was about to do something, that was possibly in violation of city regulations, and he did not want the church to get into trouble for it. He wasn't accusing anyone of misconduct as much as he was checking to be sure the t's were crossed and i's dotted. It didn't go over well, and there was some yelling. Someone ended up crying. Steve had been asked to help resolve the issue. This was a couple of years back, and there had been no further altercations. However, this past year, people started talking about the incident again.

Some of this was beginning to make sense. She had heard Leslie mentioned before, but she was far from connecting all the dots.

The next thing she heard from Kyle helped close another gap. "That church has no checks and balances."

Suddenly Kelly had an a-ha moment. "That's why you worry about the finances."

Kyle raised his eyebrows, surprised that she had not understood this all along, but he nodded patiently. "That's what happened in Kansas. And I was ultimately responsible. I had to figure out what to do to unravel that mess. They blamed me."

"So you have been trying to prevent that from happening here. You're on guard?"

"I try. Obviously I'm not that good at it." He looked at himself wrapped up and hooked to a machine in a hospital bed to make his point. His self-deprecating humor did not go unnoticed. Suddenly, he started to cry, and with a catch in his throat, he whispered, "Sam."

Kelly allowed him a moment of grief.

"So, Kyle, tell me what happened with the finances."

"There was some trouble with reimbursement. Policy needed to be clear."

Again, Kelly needed clarification. "The board or Steve?"

"Both." Pause. "Steve got reimbursed for some expenses that were illegal. Tax laws don't allow it. We had to get money back from him. It took hours and hours of our time to correct the books and deal with the IRS. I was not happy."

"Did you have trouble getting the money from Steve?"

"No. That wasn't the issue."

She thought she understood. Kyle presumed Steve had improperly used church funds intentionally. Another reporter would have moved on, but something compelled her to ask one more question about the money. "What *was* the issue for you?"

Again, Kyle seemed stunned that she had not figured it out. "Two things: he didn't apologize, and he should have known."

Something in his tone prompted Kelly to cycle back to one of Kyle's first comments. How could she have almost forgotten about the degree?

"Kyle, what do you mean he should have known?"

"Ministry isn't only about spiritual knowledge and leadership. There are a lot of practical aspects one learns in school, like finances. And they teach you and help you learn how to deal with the emotional stuff that comes up in most churches."

Quickly integrating these pieces, Kelly combined them with Kyle's concern about how Steve managed Carol's death. She drew some conclusions. "So you think he should have been better able to work through his own discomfort and that he should have known about the boundaries between church and state." As Kyle nodded, she said, "Tell me about the degree."

Kyle's mouth formed a crooked, angry half-smile, half-grimace and declared, "He's a liar."

On the verge of pressing for more information, they were interrupted again. This time, Kelly had to leave since Kyle was to go for a procedure. She thanked him and tried to speak to Blake, but Blake was busy following the gurney.

⸻

At the end of a very long day and a stint at the gym, while soaking in the tub Kelly mentally replayed what she had heard. There was an interesting mix of perceptions among church members and suppositions about what had occurred, not to mention a variety of emotions. But what was coming to light, although had not yet crystallized, was that the precipitating events were more complicated than a simple feud or difference of opinion. The very passion with which people spoke about Steve Anderson—that he came up as a topic more than Kyle or Jonah— was enough for Kelly to conclude there was a lot more to the story.

Giving her heels a good scrubbing with the pumice stone, her back the loofah rub it sorely needed, and one last luxurious minute in the bubbles, she climbed out of the tub and dried off. What she could not shake off, however, was a persistent inner voice that was demanding to be heard: *This is important.*

Grabbing her robe and glasses, she opened her laptop to visit the church website, thinking she could already have done that. Staring at the picture of the minister, something stirred. It was not something she could identify—just a flicker of a feeling.

She was struck by the congenial tone of his biography. It was friendly and folksy, and it managed to convey a sense that he was special. *We were so very fortunate to have found this wunderkind, Steve Anderson."* She put aside her own skepticism about organized religion so she would lessen the likelihood of missing something critical. She wondered who wrote the copy. When she had been asked for a bio, she wrote her own, though someone might enhance it for PR purposes. But this was a small church. Surely, they did not have a PR person. So if Reverend Anderson had written most, if not all, of it, why would he describe *himself* as a wunderkind? *Who really uses that word, especially on himself?* The man was over fifty. There was only one broad statement about his previous employment. *He comes to us from Ridgecrest Road Church in Knoxville, Tennessee, where he was ordained.* There was no mention of any degrees. Tired, she wrote a note to herself: *Look up Ridgecrest Road Church, find out what schools Steve Anderson attended, check out degrees.*

Although the various past accounts were potentially important, she thought she should be focusing on what had occurred on Sunday. While she believed that Steve was not just an incidental player in the conflict at the church, she had to remind herself that he was not involved with the shooting.

She shifted her focus back to Kyle. Despite finding him somewhat irritating, he grew on her. Even in his hospital bed, she could tell how large and muscular he was. His jaw was set, firm, squared, and prominent, but it was in balance with the rest of his face. She observed a slight dimple with his rare smile. His eyes were penetrating and hardened much of the time when he spoke about what had happened, though she had also witnessed his tears. *Too bad, such a loss for our gender.* She conceded that he had found the love of his life, and that was fine with her. As difficult a subject as Kyle was, Kelly was pleased with how it went overall. She had learned one great big new fact: Kyle thought Steve was a liar. *But* that was still tangential to the shooting, as far as she knew.

She had hoped the interview would offer an insight into either Kyle or Jonah's possible motives. He and Jonah didn't know each other. So far, there was not much to go on, other than hating Steve, presumably for his dishonesty. Is that enough motivation to want to kill? Some people thought so or thought there was more to it. There was a hell of a lot of anger all around. Kyle was a known bully. He could have been at his wit's end, as Sheila had intimated, which could account for his rage. But what was he trying to accomplish by bringing a gun to the church? It didn't click with the image of the man she interviewed in the hospital.

She let her mind wander. The first place it went, unbidden, was to Ray. She was not about to let her thoughts, let alone her emotions, loose with that one. She deliberately switched gears, thinking about how she was able to convince Zack to give her the story and how her prep work last night had paid off.

As she tried to sleep, she completely abandoned control—something she seldom did. Trying not to think about Ray, she recalled happier times. What began as a happy memory of a birthday party with Dad playing Marvello the Magicman led to thinking more deeply about her parents. Dad had once been married to her birth mother. Something happened to her, but Kelly didn't know what. She had no idea how they met in the first place, and she had never asked, perhaps afraid of the answer. She worried that it could have been possible Dad hurt her mother the way Ray hurt her. But Dad married Mom after meeting her in some group they both belonged to—or maybe they were taking a graduate class. She had not paid much attention. She recalled Mom telling her that Dad had been scared of raising his girl by himself. Mom was stable, grounded. Dad had always kidded, saying Mom had saved his life, but Kelly knew there was truth to it. She didn't need the details of what happened between Mom and Dad. All she needed to know was her birth mother didn't want her—and Mom did.

As her mind drifted, she began to feel more discomfort but also more fatigued. Eventually, she fell asleep, only to be awakened a few hours later by a disturbing dream. She was walking from room to room in a never-ending house, never getting back to the front door, and never having a clear idea of what the whole house looked like. It left her feeling unsettled.

Remembering her project, and seeing it was almost time to go to work anyway, she got up and attacked the day with a newfound energy.

That morning, with the first six hours of her day under her belt and *What's Big in Littleton* off the air, Kelly made a quick call to Rick. She thought it might be good to shoot more video as she conducted the interviews. She mentally prepared to meet with the first of her appointments for the day. There were a couple of follow-up interviews and some new faces. However, after jumping out of her chair and taking a few steps toward the exit, Zack stopped her.

Not particularly adept at hiding her annoyance and with a propensity to move forward, Kelly asked, "What is it?" But then she sheepishly grinned, quickly apologized, and made a crude remark about needing to pee.

Zack laughed at the typical off-camera, intentionally unrefined Kelly and called her out on her excuse. "The restrooms are over there," he said, pointing in the opposite direction. "I would think you would know that by now."

"Okay, you got me. I was heading out. Is that all right?"

"Of course it is. I just thought you would want to know I got clearance. In fact, they thought it might make a good in-depth program, not just a news story. They want more details. If it's going to be an exposé, we need to figure out how we distinguish ourselves from *20/20* and *Dateline*. You know, the angle."

"Hold on. Now it's *we* and *our*. I thought this was *my* baby." As that last word came out of her mouth, she winced. "I want full credit. I am the writer, director, and producer, right? We have an agreement."

"Kelly, take it easy. I'm on your side. We're not enemies here. I only meant *we* in the most benign way, as in we're in it together—support, you know. And if you need assistance, I'm there to help. But let's be clear: you do need me to get this thing aired. Don't go getting high and mighty with me."

Kelly grinned inwardly while scoffing outwardly. "And you are not my mother. So watch how you speak to me."

"But I *am* your boss. Don't forget it." It was Zack's turn to grin inwardly.

"Okay, it's a draw. Can we move on now? Is there anything else you want?"

"Well, uh, not really, I guess. I just want to be sure you know I am in your corner on this—and I'm interested … in *your* story."

"Got it. Gotta go. See ya later."

Zack was not one to be shaken, confident as he was, but he occasionally became nonplussed in Kelly's presence. She put him off his game. He didn't think he had ever known anyone quite as brash and direct. Kelly had numerous oxymoronic qualities. She was guileless, sophisticated, self-absorbed, and sensitive to others. She didn't waste her time on whiners and self-made victims, but she did not lack compassion. No one crossed Kelly, though she was not unpleasant. Despite having strong positions and her own agenda, she was a team player. In many ways, she was a model employee. She always followed through and was dedicated to her work. Plus, she was a terrific on-air personality: beauty, unbiased presentation, and an authoritative voice. She could have been a prima donna, but she wasn't. However, she certainly was demanding. With such an interesting combination of traits, Kelly Allen fascinated him.

# Chapter 14

*Late Spring and Summer, 2011*

One Wednesday morning, after her exercise class at the church, Amanda saw Steve in the sanctuary just as she was about to leave. Having heard that he had asked for the upcoming Sunday off due to the death of a dear friend, Amanda walked in to pay her respects.

"Steve, I am so sorry to hear about the death of your friend. The funeral is this weekend?"

Steve looked up, thought for a second, and responded, "Oh, thank you. I appreciate that. Yes, I have been asked to be there. I feel it's not only my obligation to help, but I want to for myself and for the family. We were quite close. She took me under her wing when my mother died."

"Oh wow. I didn't know. I assume you will be conducting the service then. That must be really tough."

"Hmmm. Yes, it is difficult. But, as you know all too well, I've done it before." He frowned and reminded Amanda about Carol. Then he said, "Fran was very dear to me. I was only in college when my mother died.

She was really like a surrogate mother to me and grandmother to my boys. I don't know what the boys and I would have done without her."

Feeling empathy and pleased about getting to know something more personal about Steve, Amanda left after repeating how sad she felt for him. She briefly mentioned the conversation to Glenn and thought no more about it.

As it happened, she and Glenn began to feel that Steve and Sue were drawing closer to them when Sue invited them to one of Claire's recitals two weeks later. "We're asking some of our church friends to come as part of our extended family. We thought you'd enjoy it."

It sounded like a fun get-together to Amanda and Glenn, and they looked forward to spending time with other church members. They felt good about supporting the Anderson family, and Amanda did enjoy watching kids perform.

When they arrived at the auditorium the following Sunday afternoon, Steve greeted them and told them where to sit. He excused himself and left to join Sue and Claire backstage. In his absence, they found the only other person in their party was Claire's half-brother. Craig, Steve's older son, was about twenty-five. They felt slightly awkward, not knowing him, and the conversation was stilted at best. Mostly, there was silence. Trying to fill the void, Amanda said, "I'm so sorry about the loss of your family friend." She wasn't quite sure how to say "surrogate grandma."

Craig looked blank.

Amanda said, "Fran? I know your father was upset. I'm sure the funeral was terrible, though also well done, with your dad being there. Did you go?"

After a few seconds, Craig responded, "Oh! You mean the funeral he went to a few weeks ago? No, I didn't go. She was really just my father's friend." The lights dimmed, and the show started.

Following the performance, as they left together, Steve invited Glenn and Amanda back to their house for a light supper. Craig did not join them. During supper, Sue busied herself with serving and only contributed to the conversation with minor interjections, mostly about food choices. Claire had hidden herself away, presumably doing homework or reading. The conversation meandered from one topic to the next, quite pleasantly.

Steve mentioned that since he and Sue were renting, they would begin to house hunt in the area, intending to put down more permanent roots. They were also looking for the right school for Claire. The Corwells got the impression that Steve was letting them know that he anticipated a long tenure in Littleton and at TLC.

Glenn mentioned that he saw Paul Goldberg at the last service, a man he knew to be an activist and a philanthropist, a like-minded person who would fit well with TLC.

Steve arched his brow and leaned in. He asked to hear more.

Glenn added, "Well, aside from being a platinum or gold circle donator to both the Bartlett Hall and the arts museum, I'm pretty sure he's involved with some humanitarian efforts overseas, as well as here. I heard he attended antiwar demonstrations that some of our members went to." Glenn hoped that might stimulate a reaction, given this was an area that Sue and Steve had expressed interest in.

Steve nodded, but he did not comment on becoming more active in peace work at the church. He said, "I have a lot of experience talking with that type. I'll be sure to look for him."

A wink and a smile left no doubt in Amanda's mind that Steve would purposefully schmooze Paul Goldberg, something she personally found abhorrent, but she understood it was expected of a minister.

As the evening neared an end and conversation came to a standstill, Steve introduced a new topic, somewhat out of the blue. "Tomorrow's a big day!"

Glenn and Amanda didn't know what he meant.

With a grimace, Steve added, "The powwow with Kyle."

Glenn nodded.

Shortly after, they said their good-byes and walked to the car. Before Glenn started the engine, he said, "Powwow?"

Amanda echoed his vexation. "Did you hear that Craig barely knew who that woman was ... Fran?"

Glenn did not put two and two together, but he noted that Steve had invited them to schmooze *them.*

"Why us?" she asked.

"I am on the mediation team, or whatever we're calling it. I think he wants to get me on his side."

"Why would he do that? Who does that? There are no sides. He would surely want this settled in a way that no one is hurt, wouldn't he? Glenn, I don't think that's what he's doing. But I will say I am disappointed that more people weren't there tonight. I'm thinking about who else they asked, and why they didn't come. No one mentioned the event to me, but then neither did we to anyone else."

Glenn said, "I don't think anyone else was invited."

―――――――――

Late the next month, Glenn and Amanda prepared to go to Atlanta to attend their very first General Assembly, a national UU event where UUs from across the country develop agendas and build community. With a mix of excitement and trepidation, they surveyed the offerings and selected which programs they wanted to attend—some together and some separately.

Amanda looked forward to the social aspects of the event, and the singing, having heard great things, especially from Will and Sheryl, about GA. A contingent from TLC would be there, including Will, Sheryl, Dinny, Sheila, and a few others. Steve told them that he planned to stay with one of his grown daughters who lived nearby.

When they arrived, they felt overwhelmed by nice people everywhere and so many options for what to do! With crowds, food, singing, workshops, and shopping, there was not much time to relax, unless one did not participate. Amanda was determined not to waste a minute and intended to attend a workshop whenever possible.

The TLC members ran into friends throughout the course of the day. At one point, Sheila told them that she had received a call from Steve who said he would not be coming.

"Why?" Amanda and Glenn asked at the same time, clearly unhappy. Glenn added, "Did something happen?"

"Apparently Claire had a last-minute dance competition."

The three of them looked at one another and shrugged.

Amanda and Glenn attended the last workshop of the day. At "Creating a Just Society," Glenn caught sight of Paul and Linda Goldberg. As they exited, Glenn noticed they were wearing TLC badges. He reintroduced himself, having met Paul several years before.

Paul seemed genuinely delighted and immediately asked about Steve, saying that he had expected to see him there. "Steve suggested we attend, that we would probably like it. We are very impressed."

That caught the Corwells by surprise, though they were pleased that Steve had remembered to approach Paul and that he had followed through so quickly.

Trying to save face for Steve and TLC, Glenn tactfully told them that Steve had been unable to come due to a last-minute family thing. Expressing her concern, Linda said, "I hope everything is okay."

Not wanting them to worry and feeling embarrassed by Steve's excuse, Glenn and Amanda reassured them it was not a life-threatening emergency and told them Steve would be back in the pulpit the following week, as far as they knew. The Goldbergs expressed some additional words of disappointment, and the two couples parted.

Amanda was pleased that the TLC group chose a quiet cafe that night. Glenn mentioned the encounter with the Goldbergs. Not one of the people at the table knew of the Goldbergs or their new connection to TLC and Steve. This added to Amanda's annoyance that Steve had not come to the event, which had been planned years in advance.

Not three weeks later, when Glenn attended a minister's council meeting, he found Steve alone and said, "We ran into the Goldbergs at GA. They were disappointed not to see you there. You must have made quite a good impression on them!"

Without hesitation, Steve said, "Yes, Sheila and I recommended that they attend GA. I'm glad they did."

Glenn drove home with a degree of confusion. When he walked in the door Glenn called to Amanda in the living room, "I mentioned seeing the Goldbergs to Steve, and he said he and Sheila had talked to them."

"But Sheila had no idea who they were when we mentioned them to her over dinner."

"Exactly."

By that time, Glenn and Amanda were becoming more than a little disillusioned with Steve, not as a minister—although they saw some room for improvement there—but as a person. Little things, which in and of themselves didn't portend much, took on a greater significance when combined. That night, they tried to understand why Steve would not have expressed any regrets that he had not attended the conference and why he had felt it necessary to tell Amanda about the "surrogate grandmother."

They kept their personal disappointment and reservations separate from their work at the church. They didn't want to upset others unduly or gossip, so they said nothing to anyone.

It was not until one evening in July when Amanda got off the phone with Kyle that the doubts really began to rise and itch, not unlike the sensation of an ant crawling up a leg. One ant was bad enough, but she was afraid of an army of them.

"Holy crap!"

"Who was on the phone?"

"It was Kyle. You are not going to believe what he said. I'm not sure I believe it. I trust him, and he always does his research. *Thorough* is his middle name. But it just can't be true. There has to be an explanation."

"Okay. You have my attention. What?"

"You know the disturbing feelings we've been having about Steve? Well, maybe this sheds some light. Kyle thinks that Steve lied about his degree. He has suspected this for some time."

"How so?"

"Kyle had an inkling that degrees in sacred music are pretty rare and only a few schools confer them. So he checked it out."

"And?"

"University of Tennessee doesn't offer it, and according to Kyle, it never did. Kyle is sending me the documentation, including some letters he received from the university's administration. Why would Steve say he has this degree if he doesn't? It's not like it's a job requirement."

"There has to be an explanation. Does anyone else know?"

"Kyle told Sheila. He doesn't trust anyone else. He doesn't want it to get out—doesn't want to upset everyone at church."

"Well, did Sheila say anything to Steve?"

"I guess not. From what Kyle said, it seems they agreed to wait to see if it comes up when he signs his contract, which he has yet to do. It's been almost a month. The contract has a specific deadline for making application to be fellowshipped. To apply, he will have to submit official documents. It's bound to come out then."

"There has to be another explanation."

"That's not the whole of it. It seems that when Sheila checked the personnel files at the church, no diplomas were there, and she asked Steve to bring them to her. There were some pieces missing from other people's files as well. That explains why Kyle had harped on making sure personnel files were complete, which is one of the things he irritated the board with. It seemed like he was just hassling needlessly."

Steve's résumé was on file. It didn't state that his master's degree was in sacred music, as he had told so many people. Amanda and Glenn as well as Sheila surmised that the miscommunication might have been a matter of semantics, so it was best to wait to get both of his advanced degree diplomas before jumping to any conclusion. However, Steve had told Sheila that he didn't know where they were.

Sheila phoned Steve's prior church in Knoxville, where he had been ordained. She had a hard time getting through to anyone who would or could answer her question. Whoever she talked to each time she called did not know Steve. Eventually, someone told her they found a notice of some sort that indicated Steve was ordained as minister of music, but they could not supply any information about his degrees.

Amanda did a little more searching on the UT site. She found a listing of all past dissertations and authors. Steve's theses—his master's and doctorate—stressed composition and performance. There was nothing about religion or ministry or anything sacred. Furthermore, UT was a state school, and although classes in comparative religions were offered, it was unlikely, Glenn surmised, that ministry would be taught.

━━━━━━━━━━

Amanda and Glenn spent the rest of the summer dealing with the Kyle/Steve issue, as well as continuing to sing with The New Littleton Minstrels. The latter gave them both respite and joy.

Despite their personal doubts about Steve's integrity, they were still ascribing to the notion that the discrepancy with the degree was not particularly harmful to the congregation, and it was not reason enough to disrupt the overall happiness and stability of the congregation. Steve was wildly popular and had done a great deal to instill energy into the community.

In the middle of July, Sheila and Amanda agreed they needed to discuss the unsigned contract with Steve, highlighting the requirement that he file an application for being fellowshipped. They needed to be informed if he didn't want to move forward. *If* he had not told the truth about his degree—and that was the reason he had not signed the contract—they'd be giving him the perfect opportunity to come clean.

Sitting in his office, Sheila began the discussion with Steve by asking him if there were any problems or obstacles to signing the contract.

Steve paused and replied, "As you know, with my experience and training, I do not want to spend time away from my family or a lot of time studying."

The two women avoided eye contact with each other, both having lost patience with this oft-repeated refrain that they viewed now as a song and dance.

Calmly, Amanda responded, "Steve, you know we completely understand. I know I wouldn't want to undertake a new course of study at my age. Since we don't know what you would be required to do, all we are asking is that you look into it—if you still want to."

Sheila added, "You don't have to be fellowshipped to stay on. We have leeway to do what we want here."

Steve maintained a stiff sideways smile, head tilted to the left. He did not breathe the expected sigh of relief.

Amanda asked, "Is there anything that would stand in the way of your completing the application? We're not asking if there is anything that would stand in the way of you becoming a settled minister. We need to take step one before we can determine step two."

Steve simply said, "No."

The meeting ended. Shortly thereafter, he signed the contract. He had until November to apply. The two women felt they had given him ample opportunity to tell the truth.

A few weeks later, Sheila found a large envelope in her inbox at the church. Attached was a note in Steve's handwriting, "Found under a box of sweaters." Next to the note was his personal version of a smiley face. Needing time to think about what to do, she didn't tell anyone right away that she had the diplomas. However, a few days later, she felt the need to discuss it with someone. She wanted to tell Kyle, but she was afraid of his reaction, and she called Amanda first.

"What is his degree in?" Amanda asked.

"It says sacred music, summa cum laude."

116

"But we know that's not possible."

"Right."

"Did you tell Kyle? What did he say?"

"Not yet, but I will. It won't come as a surprise to him that Steve would falsify the diploma. But he'll be furious. We have to keep the lid on this, and we have to keep the lid on Kyle. If he steams over, it will not be good for anyone—most of all him."

Amanda quickly offered, "I'll call him. I've always found him to be someone who listens to reason. I have to say I'm with him on this. I mean, I might have said that I have a degree in history when it's an education degree with a *specialization* in history, but when you submit a diploma as part of your record ... and it isn't real ... that's a whole other story. Is it even legal?"

"He doesn't have any theological/seminary type training that would even go toward that degree, so your example is too generous. It's more like if he said he had a degree in history when the degree is in acting, but he played an historian on a TV drama series."

Amanda did some research and discovered that it was *not* legal to submit a fraudulent diploma. Ironically, one of the specific examples she found about why it was illegal was that someone "such as a minister or counselor" with a counterfeit diploma could represent himself or herself as a professional who has specific training, and others might put their faith, confidence, and trust in him or her because of that training.

Nevertheless, when she pointed out this particular statute and article to Kyle, he told her he had already checked, but unfortunately, the law was never enforced, even though it was still on the books. Precedents had been set at the state Supreme Court level, so it was not worth pursuing.

What they all had hoped—that Steve would be man enough to admit his lie so they could move on and lead the church forward in a positive direction—apparently was a pipe dream.

# Chapter 15

Thursday, April 12, 2012

Late in the afternoon, Kelly returned to the station to catch up on her work and let everything she had heard that day settle to the back of her mind. She ruminated in her leather swivel chair, eyes closed. While it was never quiet at the station, Kelly had always found a way of tuning out the noise to concentrate.

"How is it going, Kel? Did you find what you're looking for?"

Kelly automatically squirmed at being called "Kel." She raised her eyes for a second, thought interrupted. *Zack is still at the studio, which is not unusual, but since when had he made a habit of chatting?* "Hmmm. Oh, yeah, fine, good ... some weird people, some weird church."

"Kelly, do you have a story or not? Any good material here?"

Hearing his direct tone, she sat up. "Why? Is there a problem?"

"No problem. Yet. But upstairs will want updates on progress. They are paying you to produce something and want to be assured of a return on their investment."

"Yeah, I know. Is there entertainment value? That's all they're interested in. Will it make money? Well, Zack, what about the truth? Doesn't anyone care about that anymore? I have to check to see if an arrest has been made and if the DA has filed a charge. Last I heard, they were holding Jonah for questioning, and of course, holding Kyle—in the hospital."

The desk phone rang, and she excused herself. She picked up the phone and spoke briefly before hanging up.

"So?" Zack asked.

"Well, *some* people are going to be shocked and angry. Seems they arrested Jonah Spencer and let Kyle Whitman off. Many of those church members insist that Kyle started the dispute, brought the gun, and had a motive: to shoot the minister. Turns out the bullet that claimed Sam's life and injured Kyle came from a gun registered to Jonah Spencer's brother-in-law."

"Whoa. What's the charge? More importantly, Kelly, where is the human-interest angle? What's the edge here?"

"Lay off, Zack. I'm looking for something else, something that exposes truth … about …" Unsure how to complete the thought, she said, "As I said before, who the f**k cares if the story's entertaining or sexy? I want to know what happened. I've heard enough to know there is more. The thing is …" Kelly stopped short of telling Zack about her hunch about Reverend Anderson. He would never understand intuition. Neither did Kelly, for that matter. Only at that very moment had she become explicitly aware that, at least in part, she was operating with her gut. This was foreign to her, and she found it somewhat frightening. She backed off.

Zack pursued, "Yeah? The thing is … what?"

"Nothing. Never mind. Forget it. I don't know. I don't want to talk about it." She turned back to her computer.

For her part, Kelly did what she had to do for the next day's *What's Big* program and then went home and had a glass of wine. Little by little, pieces of the last few days started to assemble in her mind. *Who is right? Are they all right? Is no one right? What else is there that I don't know?*

She started to review, writing notes as she went. Some of the TLC folks she interviewed were clearly more emotionally involved than others. Some were more rational, and some were almost irrational. Some had a lot of information, and some had bits, but each bit could prove important. Of course, personal bias always existed. She needed more facts. Sheila and Amanda had alluded to information they were not at liberty to discuss due to legal ramifications. And then she still had nothing on Jonah.

She reflected on Steve. *What was going on with Reverend Anderson that he would ignore my calls and tell me he was too busy? He certainly seemed to hold himself in high regard. Was he indispensible to his congregation 24-7?*

She realized how arrogant she was to assume her own importance. Of course he was busy. He was a minister at a church that had just had a shooting. Tomorrow would be a research day. Phone calls, Internet searches. Interviews would be on hold, except for the reverend—if he should become suddenly available. She was not about to dismiss what Kyle said about Steve Anderson being a liar, but she had yet to find if it was true. If so, what had he lied about.

Getting ready for bed, a nagging thought wormed its way into her consciousness. *What had Dinny said about Steve?* That he was a vegan. *Why is that important?* She reached for her notepad. Thinking how old-fashioned it was that she *wrote* notes, she began to flip through pages of handwriting. There was kinesthetic memory and visual memory. She found it! Someone else had mentioned it as well. Ah, yes, he was a principled vegan—no ingesting or using animal products at all. *Yet he sold ice cream?*

# Chapter 16

*Fall, 2011*

Sheila put her hand to her head to ward off an emerging headache. Now Kyle had implied that Steve had defrauded the church by getting reimbursed for nonqualified expenses.

Without evidence that Steve's actions were deliberate, there was nothing that Sheila could do except allow Kyle to bring up the issue at the next board meeting. The reimbursements had been going on for more than a year and had IRS implications, as well as just being a royal pain in the ass and a complex problem to unravel.

Sheila had spoken to Amanda earlier in the evening, saying, "Kyle is furious—again or still. He thinks—and I guess I have to agree— that given his history, Steve should have known church and IRS rules, despite not having the sacred degree he claims he has."

At the board meeting, Kyle insisted on getting this issue into the official minutes.

Steve looked down at his hands during most of the discussion.

Kyle looked directly at Steve with an accusing, angry glare, which was not missed by anyone in the room. No one wanted to witness, let alone confront, Kyle's display of bitterness and hostility. Kyle spoke in a monotone; he sounded rigid and gritty.

Steve quietly seethed but maintained an even, almost pleasant tone when he replied, "I said I would give the money back."

Sheila confirmed that she had talked to Steve and that they would get it straightened out.

Kyle persisted, "This is going to take hours. Several of us need to be involved. It's an IRS matter as well as a church matter. We need to make sure it doesn't happen again."

"What more do you want of him?" Dinny asked.

Kyle remained silent. Everyone looked to Steve for an explanation, solace, or a plan.

Steve's fixed expression and set jaw were an indication of his mood. Suddenly, he looked at Kyle. His eyes squinted, and his lip curled for a second. In a flash, Steve looked down again, presumably remorseful, possibly embarrassed, possibly neither.

Some of the board members registered their discomfort and irritation by shifting their positions and looking at one another. Everyone wanted to move on.

But, in addition to rectifying the problem, Kyle pressed to examine the reimbursement policy, as painful and bothersome as it was to everyone. Originally, he wanted to include a consequence for violating the policy in the future. However, thinking better of it, he never presented that aspect of the proposal in the meeting.

Steve had seen the original copy, taking great personal offense, and said so in the midst of the discussion. Sheila pointed out to him, several times, that it was off the table—in fact, never on it—and would not be included in the revision of the policy.

Others reassured him that even if a punishment were included in the revised policy, it would not be retroactive. His fears and pain made no sense to Amanda.

Sheila was out of town when two e-mails hit about a week later. Prior to her departure, Sheila had told Amanda that she needed a rest and therefore would not be looking at or responding to church e-mails all week.

When Amanda saw the e-mail, she yelled loud enough to be heard downstairs. "Yikes! I think all hell is going to break loose."

Without looking up from his book, Glenn asked, "Now what?"

Laptop in hand, she ran downstairs. "Look at this e-mail. Then look at Steve's reaction."

Somewhat reluctantly, Glenn got up and looked over Amanda's shoulder. They studied the memo sent by Kyle to board members. It was a reminder of the newly rewritten reimbursement policy. He had sent it in reference to a request from Steve to attend a choir directors' conference. Kyle informed the board that although the request had not been made in the requisite time frame to get full board approval per the policy, it was still within guidelines since Sheila had granted approval. Ostensibly, he sent the e-mail to remind the other board members about the policy. Although he was not explicit, possibly he wanted to imply that Steve's expense report should be reviewed. He had requested that someone else let Steve know that his expenses would be reimbursed using the new policy.

Glenn looked at it and said, "So? What's the big deal?"

"Well, the big deal is that Steve got the memo—a mistake in a group e-mail account I am guessing."

"But really? So what? It's just a review of the policy."

"Look at what Steve wrote."

Glenn read the reply where Steve said, "I've had enough. This is the last straw. I will not be harassed and bullied anymore." They observed three important things: first, it was evident that Kyle had not intended Steve to see the e-mail; second, even if he had, there was nothing that constituted harassment in Kyle's letter; and third, in his reply, Steve had cc'd several people, including Will, Jonah, and Leslie, who were not on the board, and he did not include Kyle.

"What is he thinking?" Glenn said. "Now I *know* Steve's behavior goes beyond misrepresenting his degree. His comments at the outset of the mediation suggested that he might not have wanted to come to terms with Kyle."

Amanda tried to be objective and fair. "I'm not certain. He might have no idea what bullying really is. He's truly offended, for some reason—overly sensitive, in my opinion. Close to paranoid maybe. It would be so easy for a mature, grounded person to deal with this in a totally different way. He has good people skills. I just don't get it. Anyway, what did he say that made you feel he doesn't want to work out an understanding with Kyle—that he didn't want it to end well?"

"It was his attitude. Steve shrugged off the mediation, as though he felt we were going through the motions, and then he said, 'We all know this isn't going to work, but thanks for trying.' At the time, we took it to mean he didn't think Kyle would change. Now I'm pretty sure that's not what he meant."

"I didn't know. You never said anything."

"No, it's confidential. I didn't mean to say anything now. Donna and I were really being neutral."

"No one else can know this."

Amanda went to the bedroom, and Glenn went to the TV room. Unbeknown to each other, each wrote a response to Steve. When they reconnected later, they laughed and shared what they had written. The notes were different but had a similar theme. Both were trying to provide context to help Steve get past his anger by explaining how they viewed Kyle's intent and clarifying what he had said in the note.

Both, in different ways, pointed to the inappropriateness of bringing other people into the discussion. Both made sure that Steve understood their responses were not official responses. Amanda had hoped to end it that evening. Both notes were sensitively worded to reflect empathy for Steve's point of view while expressing a different interpretation of Kyle's e-mail.

In short order, they received a joint, ingratiating letter back from Steve with a lengthy explanation and long defense countering each thing they had said. It began, "You are both so very near and dear to me ..."

Unhappy with his reaction, they did nothing else that night. But the next morning, before service, Amanda spied Dinny about the same time that Dinny saw Amanda enter the crowded social hall.

"I've had it! I'm livid." Dinny stomped across the room, willfully indifferent to anyone else.

Amanda caught Dinny's eye when she heard the fury rising from fifteen feet away and rushed forward, meeting her halfway to try to temper her before the entire church was in an uproar, asking questions and demanding to know what was going on.

Amanda whispered, "Dinny, hold on. Did you read Kyle's memo? He didn't mean for Steve to get it."

"It doesn't matter what Kyle wrote or what he intended. It's Steve's reaction that counts. Subconsciously, Kyle wanted Steve to get it. Freud says there are no accidents."

"Shhh. Even if that were the case, there was nothing—"

"Don't tell me to be quiet. I don't care! I don't want Steve upset! No one does."

"Dinny, this isn't the place to be talking about it. People are listening."

In a loud whisper, not quite under her breath, Dinny said, "I don't care. This bullying is not going to continue."

Feeling an enormous sense of urgency to control the damage, Amanda knew she had to speak to every board member she could that morning, as well as to Steve and Kyle. She needed Glenn's help to speak to some other board members after the service while she got hold of Kyle. The last thing they needed was for Kyle to explode.

After the service, Amanda quietly ushered Kyle to a private room. His face was grave, although he had no inkling about the furor that his memo had created. The first thing Amanda did was to verify that Kyle had not intended for Steve to get the memo.

"I didn't send it to him," Kyle stated definitively. "What's going on now?"

"Kyle, it was a group e-mail list, and his name was in the group."

"No, I deleted it. I specifically wrote that 'someone other than me' should pass along the information to Steve. I had agreed not to contact him."

"I know. But, apparently, it was an old list. It was an accident."

"Ah." Kyle winced at his error.

"I need to let you know that Steve did not react well. We are going to try to talk with him as soon as we can."

"What did he say? Will you show me the e-mail?"

"I don't want to do that. It will only upset you more—"

"I have a right to see it."

"I can't argue that, but it should not be me who gives it to you. It should be Steve. This is between the two of you. He should let you know directly, but—"

"Since he won't, why won't you tell me what he said?"

"When you are in a better frame of mind, I'll show it to you. I'm worried about you. You've been through a lot already. Trust us."

Kyle sat in sullen silence, red in the face and near tears. Amanda could not discern whether the source was anger, hurt, or remorse. She felt caught between deep concern for Kyle and deep concern for the church constituency. She did not want Kyle to blow his cool. It would only further damage his credibility and reputation. She didn't want him to reveal anything—or everything—that he knew about Steve. That would probably backfire on Kyle, and even if it didn't, it would create even more unnecessary upheaval.

As it turned out, Amanda didn't talk to Steve that morning. He had made a hasty departure and could not be found. Glenn had done his best to assuage the others.

With slim hope that they might be able to trade on their presumably "dear" relationship with Steve, Amanda and Glenn contacted him the next day. Steve was receptive.

When they arrived at the church, he invited them into his sparsely furnished office and offered them a seat and some coffee, which they accepted. He carefully closed the door. He relaxed in his chair and sipped his coffee, prepared to listen.

Glenn began, "Thanks for meeting with us. We really personally care about what has happened, and we're also extremely concerned about the health of the church."

Steve responded, "I agree. Nothing is more important to me too. I hate for us to be at odds; you are both so dear to me. I count you among my friends. And you must know that Kyle represents a danger to the congregation."

"What makes you say that?" Amanda wanted to respond to specifics.

He scowled. "Amanda, you've seen how he attacks people. You know as well as I do that it's not just me. Look what he did to Leslie. That said, I've had enough, and I will not take it anymore. I can't do my job. And the board can't do its job. He is a complete distraction from the important issues we need to attend to. You know that."

"Steve, I see Kyle as being particular. Maybe people see it as overly so, though I also see some value in that. Not all of us have his ability to dive so deeply. As people say the devil is often in the details. What makes you say his memo constitutes harassment?"

"He was screaming at me! He capitalized whole words—and look at the bold print! He might have some value to the board, but I have to look after the overall health of this congregation. We can't have it. You are aware that he tried to punish me for an innocent mistake I made with expenses. That's harassment. Now this. Who's next?"

Amanda made a mental reminder to look at the e-mail again. Caps and bold—*this* was what he was upset about? And at a letter not even meant for him to read? As for the Leslie incident, she was tired of hearing that old trope. *Why does he keep bringing that up?* Having already rehashed the alleged punishment issue at the board meeting, she let it go.

Glenn said, "So you believe that Kyle randomly goes after people?"

"Yes. Leslie never hurt anyone. We're at the point where one of us has to go."

They were quite appalled by the threat.

Glenn said, "Steve, aside from Kyle, virtually everyone else loves you here. This fight isn't worth it. Are you suggesting we oust Kyle from the church? We don't do that here. Just by trying, you'd create a deep divide."

"I would *never* support ousting someone from the church, but he should not be on the board. If leaving the board prompts him to leave the church, then …" He shrugged.

Amanda pointed out, "Steve, according to the bylaws, the board cannot ax a member."

Glenn and Amanda exchanged glances.

Steve continued, "Glenn, with all due respect and love, you need to understand that if a large number of members had a complaint against me, that would be different, but it is only this one."

Neither Glenn nor Amanda knew what to make of the comment.

Amanda said, "Look, we know you are upset, and we understand how uncomfortable the meetings have been. Is it possible that you are inadvertently doing something that irritates Kyle—even if it doesn't bother other people?"

Steve looked up for a minute. "That's just it, Amanda. I can't think of a thing."

"So why don't you speak with Kyle about his behavior rather than taking it on the chin and complaining about it later?" She knew Steve would never do that, lest such a direct question opened the door for Kyle to let loose, but she had to see his response.

He smiled sadly and said, "I just don't handle bullies well. It's up to the board to do something to control the members. Since the board obviously isn't doing its job, I feel other leaders in the organization should be brought in. Kyle has a history of giving ministers a hard time."

Glenn said, "Don't you see how taking this conflict outside the board and involving others will create problems for the entire community?"

Steve took on a look of horror. "I would *never* do anything to hurt this church," he said with exaggerated sincerity and the pained expression of someone who had been accused wrongly.

Glenn continued, "But Steve, it *will* hurt the church. I guarantee it. If we were to have a referendum right now in which you pitted yourself against Kyle, you know you would come out the winner, but at what cost? Why would you do that? To what end?"

"I would never do such a thing. That's my point. I don't want this church harmed. But Kyle is doing that now, and he will continue to harm our church family if he goes unchecked. Just before you came, I had a talk with Marcela Perez and Martin Crump. People are worried that things have changed here in the last several months. Old-time members are sensing something is wrong. The loving feeling and joy has diminished."

Amanda tried a different approach. "Steve, you're the one with great interpersonal skills. You know how to deal with lots of different kinds of people. We have confidence that you can handle Kyle—you can be the bigger person and save the church from fracturing."

Still smiling, Steve reacted calmly and in an in-control manner. "I am not going to ignore this—and I shouldn't. Others agree with me. I can't continue with this pressure. It is taking a toll on me. I admire your loyalty to your friend, but let's just say we agree to disagree. I have another appointment."

Amanda and Glenn left. No longer in earshot, safely concealed in the car with doors shut, Glenn's face soured. His volume, though controlled, was louder than normal. "I think you might have been on to something when you said paranoid, Mandy. He's nuts. By the way, nice comment about the devil."

"Thanks. He really is afraid of Kyle, though I don't really know why. Other than being meticulous, Kyle really hasn't done anything."

"Well, that's just it. Steve is afraid he will."

"What? You think Kyle is going to attack him?"

"No, of course not. He's afraid Kyle will find out he lied about his degree."

"Well, it's a little late for that!"

"But he doesn't know it. And if he does, he thinks he can prevent him from saying anything—or from anyone believing him if he does. No wonder he feels pressure. He's scared."

"But he could so easily get out of it at this point. No one actually cares about the degree—only about the lie. It would blow over quickly. Did you catch that remark at the end about admiring our loyalty? As if that was our reason."

"Maybe that's what he expected of us. Complete fidelity."

They discussed what Steve said about Kyle's past history. Amanda admitted she had heard Steve say something like that before, but she had no idea what it meant. She began to have doubts about Kyle. *Is there something more to Kyle's enmity toward Steve than I knew about?*

---

Two days later, Will arrived for rehearsal early at Steve's behest. Before landing in one of the ubiquitous church chairs, Will put his big arms around Steve in a fatherly/best friend sort of hug. Steve reiterated how much he relied on Will's counsel. They sat close, whispering and hyper-alert to footsteps or voices.

"Steve, tell me what's going on. It's obvious you're under a lot of pressure. You know I am here to help you." Although Will liked and trusted many of the individuals on the board, he could not understand why this nonsense was still going on—and he was completely perplexed about why anyone would be at odds with Steve.

Steve seized the opening. He appealed to Will's good nature and desire to provide wisdom. Will, for his part, in addition to really liking the guy, saw the value in maintaining a good relationship with Steve since performing the musical interludes on Sundays offered him another venue for his music.

"Will, my dear friend, I wish I could tell you more. I hold you in such deep regard. You know I lost my father when I was young. I seek your guidance. I can't say too much because of church regulations. I love this amazing place and the people here. But, confidentially, I'm afraid I might lose my job."

"What? No way. That's not going to happen. Too many people love what you have done here. You are not going to lose your job if I have anything to say about it. And I will say plenty if it comes to that. I'll figure it out. But be wary of anything anyone asks you to do. Check with me first."

"Thank you, Will, for backing me. Please don't tell anyone how I'm feeling. It's just that I don't have the support of the full board anymore. Even the Corwells are deserting me. Let's keep this between us. Okay?"

Although he was disturbed by this revelation, Will knew the board would not fire Steve. They had no reason. Apparently, Whitman had turned some members against Steve. That's what bullies do. Whitman was malicious.

After rehearsal, just before going to the pub, Will cornered Amanda and Glenn, and both were circumspect. Neither said anything more than that some concerns were being worked out. Amanda attempted to reassure him that the board had not contemplated firing Steve. Will's trust in Amanda and Glenn was waning. Nevertheless, he left them on a positive note with an understanding that whatever was going on with Steve and the church had no bearing on the Minstrels. Amanda and Glenn begged off going out with the gang, claiming their daughter might call.

Will had insisted to Sheryl and others that he didn't want to get involved, but he became increasingly concerned about his own future at TLC. When he heard more from some other choir members about

Kyle's reputation as a bully, it lent even more credence to what he had learned from Steve.

Dinny called Will one afternoon a short time later, screaming, "Steve probably has his résumé out to send to other churches. We're going to lose him!"

Jonah asked Will to attend a gathering to discuss getting Kyle off the board. "Leslie will be there, and so will Patrick, Frank, Martin, Marcela, and three or four others."

Although he expressed his support for the idea, Will declined the invitation.

# Chapter 17

Not long after the e-mail incident, Sheila let the board know about another executive session. They met in a private room at the church with doors closed. She selected a night when nothing else was happening at the church.

"What's going on? Why are we having another executive session?" Dinny wailed prior to starting. "Does this have to do with Kyle *again*? Still? I'm sorry, Sheila, but we can't continue protecting him when he continues to harass Steve. Steve was very upset by Kyle's latest memo."

Sheila calmly explained that some things had come to light that the board needed to know.

After the incident with the memo, Kyle continued to press Sheila to tell the board what they knew about Steve's degree. The two of them, plus Amanda, finally agreed that the board needed to address it—and that it could still be contained within the board as a personnel matter.

In the meantime, Kyle's anger and deep hurt were surfacing more and more. He talked about defamation of character. He was not immune to the gossip and disdain to which he was subjected. Some people walked away from him or deliberately made a point of changing seats the moment he sat down. Others gave him nasty looks or grumbled. He was losing his grip.

Sheila, Amanda, and Glenn empathized, but had been afraid to take any action that might escalate the problem and cause a bigger rift. They had spent many hours trying to assure Kyle that revealing what they knew was not the right path, at least not yet. They were beginning to worry about Kyle's ability to restrain himself and contain the information. They were also concerned about the toll the stress was taking on his physical and emotional health.

Kyle arrived on time. That evening in November, the board waited and listened while he calmly told them what he had learned about Steve's degree, expecting to encounter at least a little disappointment, if not horror, at the breach of trust.

"So what?" Dinny challenged. "Who cares what his degree is in?"

"I don't care what degree he has, but if he misspoke, we have to ask ourselves why he wasn't forthcoming," Meg gently countered.

Dinny snapped back. "That's easy. He was scared. Kyle made him so anxious. It's perfectly understandable." She turned to Kyle, got right up in his face, said, "This is all your fault. You never liked Steve. Maybe you even hate him. You've been looking for something to get him on. First, you annoyed him with e-mails. Then it was all the stuff with policies and reimbursement. You put him on the spot, and embarrassed him. You never wanted him here. This is nothing more than a witch hunt."

Kyle did not respond.

Dinny continued in a high-pitched frenzy. "What is it that you want? You want him out, don't you?"

Kyle began his reply slowly by saying, "Yes, I do …"

Dinny turned a deaf ear to the rest of what Kyle said that night.

Kyle continued "But what *I* want isn't as important as what's right for the entire community. I'm willing to listen. I know people love Steve."

The board agreed that Sheila needed to discuss it with Steve.

Before Dinny stormed out and the others shuffled away in silence, Sheila made sure that everyone would operate with the understanding that the information discussed during the executive session was to remain confidential.

Only Sheila, Amanda, and Kyle knew about the fake diploma, but that information was withheld pending official verification—even though what had happened was obvious to them.

Later that week, Sheila met with Steve. She told him what they had discovered about the degree. "Steve, it appears the diploma you gave us is not legitimate." Sheila hesitated, allowing Steve time to absorb what she said. She hoped he would come forth with a solid and truthful explanation.

"Oh," he said. He shifted in his chair. Within seconds, his facial expression changed dramatically. His mouth formed into a half-smile, a slightly sardonic curve. "Actually, I'm glad we're having this meeting because I've been thinking and talking things over with my wife. I've been meaning to tell you that I'm stepping down as senior minister next year. I'm overworked, and it's been very hard on my family. I'm asking for my old position back—as minister of music."

Sheila did a double take, but she thought her prayers had been answered. She didn't challenge him, thinking the situation would resolve itself. No one would need to know about the diploma. She would work on the next step with Steve to find the best way to tell the congregation that their beloved minister would be stepping down but not necessarily leaving.

"I can't make any promises about getting back the old position. That's a board and a budget-dependent decision, but you can apply."

Once they decided it was better for Steve to make the announcement that leaving his present post was a personal decision, Sheila hoped conflicts would be put aside.

# Chapter 18

**Friday, April 13, 2012**

The church shooting had gone viral, although Kelly did not know how long it would be news. She was anxious to see church members' reactions to the arrest. News stations, including hers, would begin "viewer luring" with incessant speculations.

Before she left for the studio, she caught a glimpse of the note she left herself on her nightstand. She knew she would begin the research part of her day by scanning several other church websites, including Steve's former church.

At nine, she left the station, taking the back way after a restroom visit. She was not in the mood to chat with Zack. Actually, she often was not in a chatty mood, especially lately, but she knew she had to maintain appearances lest she get a bad rep. Everything, these days, was food for Twitter and local gossip. She didn't want to be known as a bitch, although sometimes she flaunted that side of her personality quite deliberately.

She pulled into a coffee shop, ordered a cup, and took off into cyberspace. There was no mention of Steve in any of the Ridgecrest Road Church's historical pieces. She checked her notes. Sheila said she had verified his employment and ordination. However, when Kelly called, she found no one who remembered Steve. If they did, they were keeping it to themselves.

Virtually everyone she had spoken with at TLC talked about what an excellent minister Steve was and drew attention to his background and how lucky they were to have secured his services. Several people had mentioned Ridgecrest Road Church. It carried prestige. She called Sheila to clarify what Kyle had told her about Steve being liar. Sheila revealed that Steve misrepresented his degree—and he had submitted a manufactured diploma. The diploma he submitted specified "summa cum laude." In regard to the degrees, Kelly verified that they had to have been forged. For one thing, the university did not use Latin nomenclature on its undergraduate honors citations and no honors at all—Latin or otherwise—for postgraduate degrees. Aside from that, the university had never conferred such a degree.

Kelly wanted to speak with people who knew him before he came to TLC, especially in Knoxville. She didn't know why she felt learning more about Steve Anderson was so important to her story. The police didn't consider him an eyewitness, although he was probably the only one facing the congregation at the moment the shooting occurred.

Online, she located contact information for ministers who might have been at the Knoxville church when Steve was there. She left a message with her e-mail address for one. Another was quite old and not well.

She talked briefly on the phone to Reverend Leon Morris. He listened and didn't say much when she told him who she was. She told him that she was looking for information on Reverend Steve Anderson but didn't mention the shooting, deliberately keeping her intent vague, saying only that she was doing a story on local clergy. She couldn't tell if he had heard about the event, though she hoped he hadn't. He told her he was busy and didn't wish to be involved. He was polite, but he told her he had nothing to say. At least he confirmed that he knew Steve. She left her contact information in case he changed his mind or thought of something he could share.

The first one sent her a cryptic message saying he would be contacting the UUA district representative. She didn't know what to make of that.

Looking up county public records online is not overly challenging. Kelly thoroughly enjoyed herself. Steve's records indicated dates of his marriages and divorce, number of children, court orders for child support, and several court orders for back pay and garnishing his paycheck. *A deadbeat dad? The minister?*

Kelly sent her mom a message and scheduled a Skype call over the weekend. That afternoon, she arranged a field trip to Knoxville. A quick tangle with Zack had yielded permission to go, though not with a cameraman. This would be a scouting expedition anyway, and she had to admit it might be better if she were not so obvious. A little incognito snooping might prove useful. In all likelihood, she would not be recognized in that part of the country.

The two-and-a-half-hour plane ride to Knoxville provided another opportunity to let things gel as her mind wandered. At first, she concentrated on the information she had and the questions it raised: Why would this guy say he had a degree that he didn't have? Why would he lie to a congregation that he seemed to cherish and who adored him? Why compound it with an ersatz diploma? Why not come clean when given the chance? Some other tangential questions emerged as well. Why tell people about the challenges of raising six children, when he clearly hadn't since Sue's children were in their late twenties and thirties?

She found herself thinking more generally about churches and church life. She tried to temper her judgments. She allowed that everyone—no matter how much they professed not to be—was judgmental about something. She let these thoughts go and forced herself back to what she had recently heard or read.

Several people felt that Steve had expressed a certain amount of vulnerability when he talked about being bullied as a child. Was it the whole picture? He certainly was smart. Was he shameless? Was he humble or arrogant? In any case, he certainly wasn't what he appeared to be and certainly not all he professed to be. Who and what was he?

She tried to force herself to assess all the information with a focus on Jonah and Kyle, vis-à-vis the actual incident. Jonah had lawyered up. Several people had described him physically but didn't offer much else. Amanda had mentioned he was very well read although not formally educated. Kelly had learned he didn't have sufficient money for the lawyer he had hired. She thought he would plead self-defense. Fancy lawyers surface for money, publicity, or an opportunity to set a precedent by arguing a new type of defense. *Was there an angle she hadn't anticipated?*

*Kyle was more than disgruntled and had been pushed to the edge, but had he gone over it?* As she put the pieces together, it seemed he had reason to be upset. But that was not an excuse for violence or a gun. He had set out to "set things straight" that day. *Had he been about to go postal until Jonah stopped him? What did the detectives know that she didn't?*

About thirty minutes into the trip, the week's frenzy caught up with her, and she started to nod off. Before she was fully asleep, thoughts of Ray entered her barely conscious mind. She had been so in love. They had plans. They had a life, if not completely mapped out, certainly an abiding commitment. Sure there were issues as to whose career took precedence, where they would live and the like, but what two-career couple didn't face that? They had an agreement! *If either one was unhappy, they would talk and work it out.* Kelly had thought all was well, and she was completely devastated when she learned otherwise. There was no room for forgiveness. She was not one to dwell on emotions. Of course she had them, even if she didn't want to talk or think about them. *If hearts are broken, they are meant to be bandaged or glued. There is no need for further examination or surgery. Why reopen the wound?*

One thought led to another, and soon she landed on thoughts about Zack. She liked Zack well enough, but she did not altogether trust him.

She had no reason not to, but he made her uneasy at times, as few people did. He threw her off guard on occasion, and she did not like that at all.

Later that evening, comfortably ensconced in her hotel room, cozy in her plush terry robe, she sipped a glass of red wine and scoured her notes, writing down questions as she went along. There were plenty of inconsistencies to ponder.

———

On Saturday morning, Kelly dressed in sweats and a baseball cap and took a long, brisk walk in the city. She felt optimistic about the day and looked forward to the next one, hoping to find people who might have known Reverend Steve. For once, she put her iPhone in her pocket, and it did not ring. Quite surprisingly, she did not feel compelled to text, search, call, or digitally connect in any other way.

She planned to attend church on Sunday for the first time in her life. She hoped she could engage folks in conversation. In truth, she had no idea what to expect. How had she become intrigued by *anything* that involved a church?

Back in her room after an enormous breakfast of curried deviled eggs and thick-cut smoked applewood bacon, two tiny ginger scones, and a brimming hot cup of coffee, Kelly felt nourished in her soul and stomach. She turned on her laptop for the obligatory Skype call with Mom and Dad.

"Hey, Mom, what's going on? Wait, I can't see you. Do you have your video on? Okay, that's better. What's up?" Her mother's face appeared, fixing her hair with her fingers, and then she saw Dad's hand waving before he sat behind Mom.

Her mom immediately asked about the shooting. Of course she would. Why hadn't she anticipated what she would say to her? She didn't want to tell her yet that she was investigating it. She didn't want anyone to know, especially Mom and Dad, that she was seriously considering quitting her on-air job so she could do investigative reporting. She knew quitting would be risky, and she didn't want to hear any admonitions or leave herself open to "I told you so" or a knowing sigh later on. Mom and Dad relished the idea that their daughter was quasi-famous and on TV. They were never thrilled when she took chances, although they were always encouraging about her career. When there were questions of physical danger, she tried to avoid letting them know. Those types of adventures had been rare recently, but years ago, she traveled occasionally to unsavory locations. There was a part of her that liked to live on the edge.

"I have information about the church shooting, but I'm not at liberty to share much now. You understand that. Here's what I can tell you that you haven't heard on national news. That church is a mess. Hah! Big surprise, right? There's a conflict having to do with the minister, but I don't know if it had anything to do with the shooting." Kelly could not read the uncharacteristic look she saw on her mother's face, and it was gone in a flash. Kelly's mom moved out of view of the screen. Dad, unreadable as usual, took her place. "Your mother went to get a cup of coffee. She'll be right back."

"On my time?" Kelly kidded. "Seriously, how are you guys?"

"We're fine, kiddo. Just worried about you, as always. Haven't heard much from you lately."

"Yeah, I know. Sorry about that. Can't be helped. I've been busy. But here I am in all my Saturday morning glory: no makeup, ponytail, sweaty, just back from a walk."

Kelly's mom wore a T-shirt, yoga pants, and no makeup. Her brown hair had gray roots that needed touching up, and an extra layer of fat had settled in around her belly and hips. However, she had not lost her animated smile, ever-moving hand motions, and propensity for fast-paced talking that helped keep her appearance lively and relatively youthful.

Dad looked a bit tired and strained, but otherwise, he was the same as always: gray, balding, protruding gut, and genuine, loving smile that complemented the twinkle in his shining brown eyes. "You're always gorgeous."

Kelly asked again about what they had been doing, and her dad listed the concerts and plays they attended, giving detailed reviews and recommendations should she ever get a chance to see any.

"Oh, here's Mom." Both parents came back into view. Mom filled in information that Dad had omitted when enumerating their exploits. And then she got right back to where she had left off. "You were talking about that church incident and the minister."

"You know that I think all religion is nuts and all ministers are nuts." At Mom's dismissive brush of the hand, Kelly retorted, "I mean it. Every one. Religion is at the root of all evil. They say it is the love of money ... well, that too. Sometimes they go hand in hand. But all wars ... religion. All bigotry ... religion."

"That's a little extreme, don't you think? To be fair, religious groups also do a lot of good things." Kelly's look of disgust was enough to stop Eliza from getting into it further. "So, Kelly, what's your take on the shooting?" Mom looked hopeful and worried.

"My take? Not sure. I'll let you know more when I can."

"Sweetie, if you find out any new information, we'd be real interested. Things like that have a way of getting very messy. Be careful."

Kelly thought that was a very odd comment, considering her parents didn't know about her project. She attributed the remark to a lack of knowledge of her job, which was to read a script with the proper inflections and facial expressions and ask the questions the writers told her to ask of a guest. Sure she did a little homework too, but they still didn't quite get that she was based in a studio.

"Well, I have a lot to do today. I better go."

"It's important to rest too and do some fun things. Get out of town, maybe meet some new people."

*If they only knew,* she thought.

"If you want to share anything that's going on, you know we are always here for you," Mom added.

Kelly sighed and moved out of view of the laptop video. *Here it goes*, she thought, *Mom wants me to talk about Ray or my social life or how I'm feeling.* Back on screen, she said, "I know, Mom. You're the best."

"Well, call us again or video or e-mail or whatever when you can." Dad came to the rescue. As intrusive as Mom could sometimes be, he was the opposite.

"Of course," Kelly said.

"We love you."

"I love you too."

Dad had hardly said anything. It was not unusual for Mom to chatter and ask more questions, but Dad was especially quiet. He disliked church almost as much as she did. Maybe he had no interest in the direction the conversation took. He wasn't one to get into drama. It was *facts* that mattered to Dad. Mom was different. She was into logic, but she also enjoyed a bit of gossip and a good mystery. She could get sucked into a story. She liked looking inside people. She could be horribly annoying, but Kelly appreciated her mom's mind. Eliza was a school psychologist.

Kelly knew she was a product of both of them: a fact-based person like Dad and the deep questioning/seeking person like Mom. Kelly liked things clear, accurate, and defined. She was working in a gray area, driven to push her way through the quagmire toward a conclusion: solving the problem, finding the answer, and seeking the truth. She liked closure and no loose ends. Occasionally, when it came to her personal life, she tied them off quickly, making sure she would not trip on them later.

She prepared for Sunday at Ridgecrest Road Church, laying out some clear objectives and a strategy for attending the service. She would be a seeker, someone who might be moving to town or shopping for a new church. She figured that someone would say hello. If not, she would have to be more proactive and pick someone to start a conversation with. Her primary goal was to make a friend, someone who would be receptive to a follow-up call. She'd start a conversation by mentioning

Littleton, optimistic that the person she spoke with would be watching the news and would make a connection with the shooting. From there, the conversation could go anywhere. She wasn't sure if anyone outside of Littleton would know the shooting occurred at "Steve Anderson's church." He wasn't a household name, even there. She knew she had to sidle up to someone who might have been at Ridgecrest Road Church fifteen or so years ago, someone older.

As she was plotting her course, she realized she had missed an opportunity to do the same at the True Liberal Church of Littleton. The best way to understand people and how they operate was to see them in action. Besides, Steve had not granted her an interview. Maybe it wasn't too late.

Reluctant to do so—she really did not want to ask for help—she pulled out her phone. Zack was the only person who knew what she was up to, and he was the only person she knew who had the capability to pull it off successfully. But would he help her? She had been so insistent about doing it all herself. Then again, he had a healthy ego. Why would he pass up an opportunity to do something of note that might add to the story and increase the chances of a good program in the end? She wasn't sure he believed in her story. She had an uneasy sense that she was being coddled. Was he merely allowing her to play to keep her happy? Would he really do that? She could not possibly be so invaluable that they would agree to spend money on her project just to keep her busy and interested.

She completed the phone call and made her case to Zack. Zack agreed, and he needed little convincing.

# Chapter 19

**Sunday, April 15**

Zack walked into the building with a feigned inquisitive look. He perused some pamphlets in the vestibule before a church greeter welcomed him and offered a program for the service. He dutifully put on his name tag, said he was looking for a church community where he'd feel comfortable, told the greeter he was new in town, and let it be known that he had just purchased a condo in the Lexington Towers, one of the most expensive buildings downtown. He took his seat after asking an innocuous question about the minister. The greeter told him he'd love Steve and quickly mentioned how everyone found his sermons and music inspiring. To Zack, the greeter sounded genuine, though he did think it was probably the standard spiel. He was surprised that there was such a sense of normalcy at the church since one of the congregants had been shot to death by another just a week prior.

Zack took in the architecture, portraits of former ministers, stained glass windows, and old wooden beams that held wrought iron chandeliers. He guessed the vintage to be from the 1920s, given the surrounding buildings, the historic registry label on the building, and what little he knew about Littleton's historical development. He decided on 1924. Out of curiosity, he would look for the cornerstone when he left to see how close his guess came. It was a little game he played with himself, testing his ability to deduce. He found the unembellished majesty of the place appealing. It reminding him, despite the Mediterranean design, of Scandinavian churches he had seen in his travels. The walls were bare, save the handmade tapestries of the four seasons and a couple of faded banners.

The sermon was "Ethics in an Age of Compromise," a title Zack thought was amusing, somewhat paradoxical. He looked at the program and found it astonishing that there was no mention of the shooting. He did not see any indication that the minister intended to bring it up.

Reverend Anderson took his place in the pulpit with no fanfare. He wore khakis and a plain-collared polo shirt. He looked perfectly normal, in control, and at ease. When the donation basket was passed, Zack was prepared with a good-sized check, an amount that would likely draw attention to him.

By the time the sermon was over, he had confirmed his presumption. Although one person mentioned the tragedy during his sharing time, the minister did not comment on it at all. Zack guessed the church had already held a private ceremony. Perhaps the congregation felt it was more important to show the community the health of the church.

After the service, Zack strolled into the social hall for coffee. He watched people for a while: older women in casual attire refilling the coffee urns, a few nattily dressed older men who did not say or do much at all, others, rather shabby in appearance, who might have been taken for homeless, and some scurrying around and chatting or making beelines to a particular person. There were many hugs, and while there were a few somber faces, the overall sense he got was one of good cheer, which seemed out of place. It all seemed like business as usual.

Several people approached him, asked a few questions, gathered a few facts, and then started conversations with someone else. A man approached—Patrick, according to his nametag. Zack introduced himself and subtly raised the issue of the shooting. Patrick told him that it was still traumatic for the congregation, but Steve's plan was to deal with it at selected moments and not all at once. They were planning a memorial service for Sam Winters for the following week. After another stroll to the coffee urn, just as Zack prepared to leave, Steve suddenly appeared at his side with a hearty hello, a ready smile, and a pat on the back. The conversation was brief, though enough was said so that either one of them could pick up where they left off or initiate a new conversation comfortably at another time. That had been the primary goal. Steve was affable and adept at small talk and weaving in compliments. When Zack thanked the reverend using his title, Steve smiled warmly, and put an arm around Zack. He said, "Just Steve is fine." Then he invited Zack back the following week.

---

In Knoxville, Kelly had a parallel experience. She had spoken with several people, including one longtime member. She casually asked how long the current minister had been there and who had been there before her. The chatterbox discussed the church history, the church's good works, and the value of being a member. In the course of her historical monologue, she mentioned several presumably well-known and much-admired ministers who had gone on to publish and/or serve elsewhere in larger churches. As Kelly had come to expect, Steve Anderson's name never came up.

As part of her fictionalized backstory, Kelly said that her mother had made her promise she would ask about an old friend from Knoxville. The fictitious friend was Sue Watson, and she married a Smith or a Jones.

The old woman concentrated for a moment, as if trying to remember. "Oh, yes. Is your mother Emily? You look like her."

Kelly cocked her head and looked at her quizzically. Seeing that the woman was confused, she quickly clarified that she was looking for someone named Sue Watson, a friend of her mother's, and then repeated that Sue had married someone named Smith or Jones.

The woman flinched before recovering and saying, "Oh, yes. I vaguely remember a Sue Jones, though that's such a common name … probably not the same person." She changed the subject and offered more coffee.

Kelly, having done her research, knew that Sue Watson-Jones had attended that church. She suspected the woman, if her memory could be trusted, might have more information than she admitted. Kelly knew that Sue Watson-Jones divorced in late 1998 and married Steve Anderson in 1999. She also knew that she gave birth to Claire Anderson about three months later.

Before catching her evening flight, she had some time to reflect. Questions were still bubbling up and floating around. She knew that fixing on Steve made little sense in a criminal investigation. Nevertheless, she had instinctively moved away from the shooting—no matter how many times she tried to force herself back to it. She began to accept that the angle of the story under construction spotlighted the church members and what happened before the shooting. Although the crime was the catalyst, it had become a backdrop.

Kelly knew Steve was devoted to his daughter. She speculated about what role he played with the other children. She made a note to find out more about his ex-wife, a lesbian given what Steve had told one or two people. She would cross that bridge later.

What about his current wife? Surely Sue must know something of his background, considering she met him at this church. Why would she go along with his deception about his degree? Kelly reminded herself that many of the church members did not think his field of study was important—and maybe it wasn't.

Switching gears, she made a mental note to find out what her makeup artist might know. Manny had referenced someone he knew who was a friend of Kyle's. Maybe there was more she could learn from someone outside the church community.

Just before boarding, Kelly glanced at her phone and saw that she had a new e-mail. Reverend Morris, ex-minister from Ridgecrest Road, asked her to call him on Monday morning.

# Chapter 20

## Late Fall, 2011

Chaos reigned once word got out that Steve would be stepping down as minister. Dinny took on a crusade to save Steve's job.

Amanda had gotten wind of Dinny's battle and tried to get her to calm down and see reason. With a huff and a sense of righteousness, Dinny said, "Amanda, I'm making phone calls. I don't know if I should. But I'm doing it because I have a right to do what I feel is right. I didn't tell anyone anything about the degree. That's confidential. It's not a big deal anyway. He made a mistake. He's human."

Despite Amanda's effort to clarify the facts and dissuade Dinny from doing more damage, Dinny folded her arms and tightened her lips. However, when they got up, she hugged Amanda to indicate they were still friends.

Dinny carefully selected who she called: influential people, large donors, longtime members, and the choir. They were Steve's people. She even contacted Paul and Linda Goldberg.

When Amanda saw that lies, deceptions, and half-truths were

circulating, her own sense of righteousness and need to set the record straight took over. But she was stymied without permission from the board.

The tension between Amanda and Dinny was thick. Dinny let everyone know that Amanda was against Steve.

Rumors continued to abound, and tempers flared. Some people were saddened, and others were furious. Letters poured in from people who had not been involved with church affairs for years. Sheila was inundated with letters in support of Steve.

Encountering Sheila in the office, Dinny reached out to explain her actions. "Sheila," she said, "I have lost two husbands. I am not going to lose Steve."

Sheila did not understand the connection, though having seen the two come out of the copy room, she guessed it was at least possible that something was going on, at least in Dinny's fantasy. She snickered inwardly, having heard twice from openly gay visitors that they sensed Steve was gay. Not one to give it much thought, at the time she had said, "Not as far as I know." Dinny went on with words Sheila didn't hear.

Feeling a need to flee from Dinny's nattering, Sheila responded, "I'm sorry you're distressed, Dinny. It was Steve's decision."

"Sure, that's the company line, but we all know he was pressured. Kyle even said he wants him out. That's what he has wanted all along, and he won't stop until it happens. You heard him. I know Steve still wants to be our minister—and we still want him."

Once again, Sheila thought she had bigger fish to fry, and the pond she had been forced into was murky enough. Not wanting to dive deeper, she did not bother to remind Dinny that Kyle had also said he didn't want to hurt the church.

But Dinny would not let it go. She followed Sheila when she picked up her mail, and she followed her into the office. "I'm worried that Amanda is going to turn people against Steve."

*Huh?* Sheila caught herself. "Why is Amanda a concern? As far as

I know, she and the rest of the board are keeping the issue with Steve a private matter. Aren't we?"

"People listen to her. She is just so *rational.*" Dinny's emphasis made it clear she thought being rational was a deficit, a moral outrage. Being rational precluded having feelings. "Well, I'm doing what *I* think is right."

Continuing with the tasks at hand, Sheila let Dinny have her say before she excused herself. After that particular conversation, Sheila concluded that Dinny had her head in the clouds and couldn't hear anything but the sound of her personal angels.

Remaining neutral for Sheila was difficult and painful, but she did her best to be reassuring. As agreed, Steve told people he would be leaving the ministry of his own volition; his family obligations were taking precedence. He stressed that music was his first love, and he would be honored to continue to serve through that medium. But a message is, as they say, all in the delivery. Steve made his official public announcement. While he had never been the least bit uneasy speaking, he appeared stiff—a child stuffed into a suit that was one size too small. People perceived his exhaustion. "I am depleted. I put in over sixty hours a week. With my family responsibilities and *all* that has been going on here, I can no longer bear this level of pressure. To ensure all of our well-being, I will devote my energy here to music as long as I am allowed."

His delivery was mostly flat, with a wince of pain and a trickle of a tear to evoke sympathy. His use of the word *pressure* could have been interpreted in different ways. His audience sensed his discomfort and the sacrifice he was making.

Several people approached Sheila afterward and asked her what was *really* going on. When they didn't get the answer they wanted, a new campaign began to get the board to at least let Steve know his old job was secure. Those behind this movement ignored the fact that there was a procedure to follow. No guarantees could be made—regardless of who was involved.

In the midst of all of this, after one of the Minstrels' rehearsals,

Jonah hung back with the Corwells. He said, "What's really going on with Steve, the board, and Kyle?"

Amanda and Glenn were grateful for the opportunity to talk to someone who was levelheaded. While Jonah had his faults, one of which was he never admitted to any, he was sweet and genuine. A bit naive in some ways, but for his age—he was considerably younger than the others in the singing group—he seemed pretty grounded.

Amanda said, "Tell us what you've heard."

"What I know is that Steve has been bullied by someone named Kyle, and the board isn't doing anything about it. In addition to putting in untenable hours, he was so upset and hurt that he had to step down as minister. I suspect there is more to it."

Glenn and Amanda gave each other a glance, hoping that Jonah would be able to get closer to the truth.

Realizing that Jonah knew nothing about Kyle firsthand—maybe not even what he looked like—Amanda asked, "Where did you get the idea Kyle bullied Steve?"

"From Steve, for heaven's sake. Obviously Steve has been told he can't talk about some things. But he wants to. You can tell he's holding back. Anyway, he confided in me that there is more to the story than he is allowed to talk about. He wants transparency. As a loving community, we deserve that, don't we?"

"Steve wants transparency?" Glenn asked.

"That's what he told me. I don't know what's going on with you people, but it's clear the board is dysfunctional and that Kyle is a big part of the dysfunction. He's on the board, right? Has he driven the bus over the cliff? We know he has it in for Steve, and Steve hasn't been his first target. I have it on good authority—two former school counselors—he is not mentally stable. We all know his history."

Amanda said, "They diagnosed him? First of all, I can say that what's going on is not about Kyle—"

"Well, it should be!" Jonah said. "Maybe that's the problem!" This outburst was even more startling coming from even-tempered, soft-spoken Jonah. Jonah was equally quick to suppress his anger and revert back to his former gentleness. "Look, I'm sorry about that. Steve is so adored. I love the guy. We need to protect him, look after him, and make sure he is treated well—or we'll lose him. He's sensitive."

Amanda sat still and said, "Pretty much everyone knows there have been some issues between Kyle and Steve. Glenn and another member of the minister's council have been working to help resolve them. All I can say now is there is more to it than what you know. It would be best to let the board do what it needs to and for the church members to trust us. We're working on behalf of the congregation."

"I understand, but I am not sure how much longer we can wait. We're going to lose Steve in the meantime. At least guarantee him his old job. And stop with the secret meetings."

"I would love to be completely transparent too. I do think people should know what's said during our meetings. But I have to respect Sheila's position, the legal advice we're getting, and the church bylaws."

"Oh, is there some sort of legal threat?"

"No, but we did need legal advice."

"I understand."

Glenn could not contain himself. "Jonah, you don't understand. You don't have all the information. Whatever it is you're guessing, it is probably not the truth."

Jonah seemed to accept that, said his thank-you and good-bye, and left on foot, hoping to hitch a ride home.

Later that evening, ignoring a repeat episode of *Law and Order*, Amanda and Glenn dissected the discussion with Jonah and tried to figure out what they could do to stop the hemorrhaging.

"Do you believe that Steve is *asking* for transparency?" Glenn asked.

"I guess he feels he has enough support, and it won't matter. I don't know. I'd like to believe our church friends would value what the church espouses."

"Oh, you mean question the answers?" Glenn asked.

"Yeah. That. That and the idea of the *whole* truth—that *truth* matters. Seek the truth—isn't that one of our mantras?" Amanda turned to Glenn and said, "I can't go to choir practice anymore. It feels hypocritical."

Glenn nodded.

Then she added, "Not only does it feel disingenuous and phony. It's like I am supporting a false hero. Isn't that a thing in the Ten Commandments?"

"You mean worshipping a false idol."

"Yeah, that works. Not gonna do it." She paused and then asked, "Do you think he would sue the board if the truth was revealed?"

"On what grounds? He doesn't have a case."

"We all know that, but it doesn't mean he wouldn't try to claim slander or some such. It would cost us to fight it."

"He hasn't got the resources to take on the church. Besides, it isn't slander if it's true."

"I know, but that doesn't mean he wouldn't try. And look at all the people who are backing him—even the Goldbergs are in the loop."

# Part 4
## Indictments

# Chapter 21

*Winter, 2012*

Will was at home with Sheryl venting, maybe fuming, while she listened patiently. They normally shared a quiet, conversational breakfast and coffee, but Will had awakened early, distraught, and he now paced up and down.

"It's that Whitman guy who's the real problem there, also Amanda. Boy, I never saw that coming. A year ago, I never would have thought she would be like this. We have to find out who the real leaders of the church are."

Sheryl was not as inclined as Will to get involved, but she also was not going to hold him back from doing what he thought needed to be done.

It didn't take long for Will to make a call to learn who the "influential others" might be. Although he didn't get a satisfactory answer from his first call, he decided he would talk to the Corwells in an attempt to get to the root of the problem and solve it. He was suspicious about why they had stopped singing with the choir.

Later, Will sat in the diner sipping his beer when Amanda and Glenn walked in. They exchanged friendly greetings and discussed some lighter topics, including what would be next on the agenda for The New Littleton Minstrels.

"You guys, I want you to know I'm serious about the group," Will said. "We have a big performance on the calendar for next fall, and I want to be sure you're in for the long haul."

Glenn answered first, without hesitation. "Of course we are! We love the group. We love singing. We've made this a priority. Why are you even asking?"

"It's just this stuff that's going on in the church. By the way, we've missed you in choir. What's up?"

Amanda and Glenn had agreed not to make a big deal about quitting the choir. Glenn simply said, "We wanted to take a break."

Although he suspected there was more to it, Will didn't press further. Instead, he worked up to getting their take on what was happening with Steve and Kyle.

"With Amanda on the board," Glenn said, "Not everything can be talked about. You understand that, right? In any case, we see church and Minstrels as separate. We know you love Steve and the choir ..."

"Yes. That's the issue. Sheryl and I have been talking. We don't want to get involved in church politics, but we also don't want to lose what we have. Steve is great. You have to agree. He has so much energy; we don't want to lose that momentum. We need him to be rehired next year, right?"

"Look, we don't know at this point whether he will be rehired as music minister. We don't know if there will be sufficient funds in the budget. But if *he* isn't, I'm sure there are other folks out there who can do the job."

"No! That's the point. There is no one else of his caliber. In any case, Steve has been doing such a fine job in both capacities. I simply don't understand why the board wouldn't rehire him. Sure, I know he *says* he wants to step down, but does he really? Look, I get that you have to toe the party line, but off the record … what's really going on? Let's have some transparency from the board."

Amanda felt uncomfortable that Will was using their friendship to mine information she wasn't in a position to provide. She felt heat rise on the back of her neck. "Will, there's a lot going on. If you knew the whole story, I'm sure you would understand why the board is doing what it's doing."

"Pssh. Whole story? Is this about that degree nonsense? I know all about that. So do others, and they don't care either. It's nothing. Tell me it's not *that* the board is making a big deal over. It's all so unnecessary."

Amanda knew that only a small group was aware of the falsified diploma. Steve would never have admitted that. But Steve—or someone else—had revealed something about the degree.

Glenn interjected, "We agree. It wasn't necessary at all. All of this could have been prevented."

Will missed Glenn's point, but he was certain he could win them over. "Sheryl and I have been thinking of moving because of this. She's even begun to look at houses elsewhere. If this isn't worked out, we don't think we can stay. If we're not here, I'm not sure how to continue with The New Littleton Minstrels. I might start another group." He laughed. He said it as though the conversation was all quite friendly and light.

Glenn thought that Will's veiled threat sounded manipulative, and he was crushed.

Amanda reacted. "Please don't do that! I'm sure this will get straightened out. But what do you know about the degree?"

"Bah. Steve told some of us that he has a degree in sacred music, but it's a degree in organ music. The organ is played in sacred places. Hence, sacred music. No biggie. Essentially it's the same thing. He built his career on it! So he misspoke. Happens all the time. Everyone fudges a little."

Amanda said, "You don't tell people your degree is in psychology if it's in teaching. You might say you have a background that includes psychology. You'd be breaking the law if you called yourself a therapist."

"Of course you would. This isn't the same. The degree isn't required. Anyway we shouldn't be acting like a business. A church isn't the same as a corporation. That Sheila with her MBA attitude! A little forgiveness is in order, don't you think?"

"Look Will, I can't say much more. But there are other things, too," Amanda continued.

"Pssh." Will waved her off and went on with his own train of thought. "The man doesn't need a degree to prove himself. How much schooling do you want him to have? He's ordained, for Chrissake! If he was good enough for Ridgecrest Road, why the heck isn't he good enough for TLC? You have to get rid of that guy Whitman. He's a bully."

Amanda, hearing the echoes of the parking-lot discussion from some time back, tightened her jaw and said, "He isn't a bully. There has been no bullying."

Glenn took over and said, "There is nothing in the bylaws that allows the board to kick Kyle out. Even if it were possible, there's no rationale for doing so."

Will said, "I've never mentioned this to anyone, but I saw him once. I didn't know who he was at the time. I've had no dealings with him, thankfully. I walked by when he was talking to Steve, and I heard him raise his voice. I think that was … well, maybe last spring. He was really mad. Then he stomped away and sat alone on a pew. He's crazy."

"No. He's not," Amanda asserted. "Our church welcomes all. That means diverse personalities, as well as diverse groups. People get angry sometimes. And Lord knows we have plenty of oddballs and people who act, talk, or think differently from what might be the norm. We don't kick them out."

Will said, "But we don't let them drive the bus. You can't let the crazies drive the bus."

Amanda said, "*He* is not the crazy one. Nor is *he* the one who is driving."

Will didn't comment. He wasn't convinced that Amanda and Glenn knew what they were doing, but he no longer had the energy to pursue it. The conversation made its way back to something light, funny, and neutral.

Toward the end of the hour and a half, after another round and a couple of burgers, Will confirmed that they were committed to the Minstrels and locked into a future together. None of them wanted anything to interfere with the fun.

Will felt confident that Amanda and Glenn would come around, and everything would be fine. After all, they wanted to sing with him!

# Chapter 22

Kyle knew he was targeted for expulsion from the board. He knew about the petitions being circulated. He knew he was a pariah. He hated the way people stared at him when he came to worship on Sundays. He felt humiliated and wronged. He was at his wit's end with no more options.

"I don't think I can take it anymore," Kyle said when he heard the "Sheila" ringtone. He adored Sheila, but he dreaded hearing what new barb was being aimed at him.

Answering the phone, he could barely contain his anger. With resignation he intoned, "What now?" He listened and said little.

"That was quick," Blake commented when Kyle put down the phone and breathed another big sigh.

"Steve wants to meet with the whole board tomorrow after service." He didn't say anything else. A long, suspenseful pause followed.

"About what?"

"He's been meeting with his supporters, including three board members," Kyle said with disgust. He sighed, paused again, and began to steam even more.

Blake knew better than to prompt him to continue, and he waited patiently in silence until Kyle was ready.

"That's just wrong. It's in violation of the ministers' professional code of ethics. Trouble is he never joined the professional organization, so there is no one to complain to."

Again Blake waited for Kyle to continue.

"Sheila says the meeting tomorrow is about the diploma. He finally confessed to her today, and now—after what, five months—he wants to apologize to the rest of us."

"She said that? He's going to apologize?"

"No, she didn't say that exactly. She said, 'Admit he did it.' I'm not sure what he's going to say. He didn't say anything when Sheila confronted him last November. Nothing. Now she says he had written his explanation in a letter to the district executive, supposedly last fall, and that he never sent it."

"So that's good, right? Maybe this will finally end."

"I don't think so."

Again Blake waited.

"Sheila told me I shouldn't say anything tomorrow because I'll be upset, and she's afraid I'll say something I shouldn't. I've been accused of saying all the wrong things even when I'm trying to get it right. I've been told I say things the wrong way even if they are the right things. I guess I have to say nothing. I've tried that before, and it doesn't seem to work either."

Blake nodded in commiseration.

"She gave me a heads-up about what's in the letter."

"Kyle, hon, I know this has been grueling and depressing for you ... but what could *he* say that would hurt more than you've been hurt already?"

"The letter references me by name and says I was the cause of Steve's mistake."

"Ugh, you caused it? Wait ... mistake?"

"That's what she said."

---

The board sat in the minister's office at the church. At the start, Sheila announced, "Since this is not an official board meeting, I'm free to act as a member and speak freely. I will also facilitate."

All board members knew something about the reason for this assembly—some because Steve had told them, and others because Sheila had.

Steve handed out copies of his letter, and everyone looked at it. Dinny scanned it briefly, at this point feeling secure because Steve had already spoken to her about the content. Others took more time to review every word. Tension mounted as key words were read, notably "lapse of judgment" and "given the extreme pressure Kyle Whitman put on me."

Meg turned white. She didn't speak first, but when she did, she said, "When you spoke to me just yesterday, you did not say you had submitted a *false diploma*. You *said* you had misspoken about your degree. To me, there's a big difference. I need to think about this. I don't know what to say other than I'm shocked and disappointed that you tried to minimize what you did." Steve stared across the room without focusing on anything or anyone.

Amanda took issue with the accusation against Kyle. "He didn't hold a gun to your head, did he? You *chose* to create the document, and it wasn't done in a rush. You waited and thought about it. That does not sound like a mistake or 'momentary lapse in judgment' to me. That's premeditated. I don't see how this constitutes anything but a conscious and deliberate act." She sounded like a lawyer in summation. In fact, she had begun to feel that a trial was exactly what was needed.

Steve directed his anger at Amanda in the form of the proverbial eye daggers. He spit out one word at a time, practically hissing, "With all due respect, Amanda, you do not understand the punitive atmosphere I was working under." Then he said nothing.

The least outspoken board member, Ruben, said, "I think Steve should resign."

Steve looked down and then focused on the ceiling.

Dinny threw the eye daggers at Ruben, but no one commented. Then she looked around solemnly and tried to make eye contact with the one or two people who she still expected were supportive of Steve. Now it had become one of those times when the lines on her upper lip were prominent as she assessed those around her. She didn't have much to say, but since reactions were being expressed around the circle, she added, "It's serious, but it seems to me, we should move on. Steve has admitted his mistake, and what's done is done."

When Amanda spoke again—out of turn because she just couldn't help it—she pointedly commented that there might be legal implications to consider; before the board discussed what to do, they needed advice.

Steve flinched and gulped. For the first time, he looked worried and not in control. The moment passed quickly. He said nothing. Amanda knew there was nothing they could do legally, but she wanted to see his reaction.

Sheila took a different tack. "I feel what Steve did represents not just a misdeed but a serious character flaw." She ran down the list of meetings during the last year, prior to submitting the diploma, where Steve would have had an opportunity to talk about his degree. He could have corrected what he had said and might have come out smelling like a rose. There were even several times when he could have admitted to the fake diploma without any serious consequence, at least to the church. "So," she concluded, "I have to ask why now? Why tell us now?"

She knew the answer. He had his support lined up. His confession had been made with his own spin to his cadre of friends, his loyal followers.

Steve simply replied, "I was scared. Intimidated."

Kyle, true to his promise to Sheila, didn't comment. However,

Sheila allowed him the opportunity to express his point of view. He asked two questions, which sounded out of place, picky, and somewhat beside the point, "You put it in writing, right here, even now, that you have the *equivalent* of a master's in sacred music. Why? Why did you write summa cum laude on the diploma? And I resent the use of my name in this document. I want that on the record." There was no record, however.

Sheila went home exhausted, having expended all her energy to remain civil. While the meeting might have seemed like a culmination of all that had come before it, it was actually only another beginning. Even though Sheila wanted to believe there was still a chance this business could end reasonably well, she had a strong feeling it wouldn't. She had no idea how to control the snowball that had taken on a life of its own, rolling down the hill and adding more layers. Deep inside, she sensed that there was a master puppeteer behind everything, and she was pretty sure it wasn't God.

———

Sheila had to schedule another executive session of the board to determine how it wanted to deal with the submission of the phony diploma and all the damage that Steve's actions had caused. It occurred to her that approximately five executive sessions had been held in the last two years, and all of them were about some problem with Steve, including two that were conducted with legal counsel.

It was clear that, despite how individuals felt about Steve personally, every single board member, even Dinny, agreed that the indiscretion could not be ignored. "I have spoken to each of you, and we are all in agreement that some action must be taken. Is that correct?" No one voiced an objection, and she got the nods she was looking for. "We have several options, ranging from firing Steve on the spot to doing nothing. Since we just agreed to do something, what do we want to consider?"

Amanda said, "Firing him would be an appropriate consequence, given the egregious act and the resulting damage. That's probably what most organizations would do. But I don't think anyone is recommending that. So—"

"Here is what I suggest," Sheila said. She put forth a proposal that called for Steve to make a formal apology to the congregation and create a plan to make amends and rebuild trust with the board and the congregation. In addition, she wanted him to take a course in ministerial ethics.

They hashed out the details and had a lengthy conversation about whether a written letter would be sufficient or if the apology should be spoken in a meeting as well. They agreed to both and established deadlines. They also agreed it would be important for people to be able to ask questions after hearing the full story. It had never been Sheila's intent to go public, but Steve had forced it. He had everyone crying for transparency. The congregation deserved to know why the problems and factions had emerged.

The board voted unanimously, and the plan was adopted. All Sheila had to do was present it to Steve. The entire board agreed that Sheila should not speak to Steve alone. Since no one on the board was neutral anyway, they recommended that Amanda, as VP, accompany her.

Sheila made the appointment with Steve for the following Tuesday. When she walked into the office, Leslie, Will, Jonah, and Steve were waiting to see where the meeting would take place. Amanda walked in a couple of minutes later with Glenn. He planned on doing some work in the church library.

A few seconds before they were to begin, Amanda whispered to Sheila, "I didn't know all these people would be here. What's going on?"

Sheila quickly said, "Neither did I. I guess Steve wants his team with him."

"Should I get Glenn?"

"I don't see why not at this point. It's not how I feel this should be handled, but I don't know what else to do." Sheila didn't see how she could tell those who had come that they couldn't sit in without creating an even bigger problem. These people were friends and fellow church members. Sheila and Amanda had been ambushed.

Amanda rushed off to grab Glenn and brief him on what was happening. They entered the shabby rehearsal room where everyone else was already seated. The discomfort of the chairs matched the awkwardness of the moment.

Sheila presented the plan with no emotion or embellishment.

Steve remained silent, alternately looking down at his feet and across at his cohort.

Jonah interrupted several times about how unloving and unfair it was.

Will harrumphed, "If he has to go public, it will ruin him. How can you destroy a man's career?" He gave the same argument he had given Amanda previously about the gray areas of college degrees. He tsk-tsked the board for overreacting to such trivial nonsense. The three of them knew nothing about the diploma; if they did, they were indifferent to the deliberate deceit.

Upset and prepared to protect Steve, the trio threw out obstacle after obstacle and defense after defense.

After a seemingly interminable amount of time, Amanda finally lashed out at Steve in an effort to prove that he had lied about the degree and deliberately falsified the diploma, including the summa cum laude part. She wanted to make a point that if he lied about that, he could lie about other things. But before she had a chance to finish, Will screamed, "Foul."

Steve asked, "Wanna bet?" He actually proposed his wife's annual pledge against the Corwells' pledge that his degree was summa cum laude.

Sheila called a halt, calmly stepped back, and reviewed the plan as a fait accompli, implying Steve had no choice but to follow the board's sanction. She noted that the board voted on this unanimously, and there was no negotiation. In fact, the board had also agreed that if he did not comply, then the option for dismissal would be on the table.

Steve, Jonah, and Will stormed out.

Amanda held back tears. A lump in her throat formed in anger and embarrassment for her inability to maintain a higher ground.

Leslie stayed on and asked, "What you're saying is he actually gave you a diploma that was a forgery? That's not what he led us to believe." She paused as she reflected. "Now I understand the board's decision."

They left with Leslie, believing they all had a common understanding. Nevertheless Leslie continued to work with Steve and his followers to figure out how they could, as quickly as possible, secure Steve's services for next year as music minister, and she never relinquished the idea that Kyle had it in for Steve.

Jonah circulated a petition in support of Steve that made references to the dysfunctional board and to Kyle.

Steve was charged with writing the letter to the congregation within a week. He was also supposed to tell the Minister's Council what he had done. Neither happened. Jonah pleaded for more time on Steve's behalf. Will continued to try to negotiate what the board was requiring of Steve. Sheila held firm.

When Amanda finally received her advance copy of Steve's letter, a day late, she hit the ceiling. The letter was completely skewed. Steve had omitted some of the most crucial pieces. Steve had skirted the essence of what he had done in his carefully penned epistle. It was an excellent example of his skill as a writer. At no time did he take responsibility for the damage he had done to the church. Nowhere did he admit to intentionally submitting a doctored diploma to cover up a lie. There was no apology.

Nevertheless, despite objections of no fewer than three of the board members, the letter was sent. The town hall meeting was set for the following Sunday.

---

Choosing not to use the microphone at the pulpit Steve, wearing his minister's garments, stood in front of the assembly, level with his congregants. The rules were simple. He had been granted the opportunity to bare his soul and make good with the congregation, prove his deep love for the community, and demonstrate his strength of character by accepting the consequences—whatever they might be—of his actions. He had to take responsibility. He was not allowed to mention Kyle.

Neither Sheila nor anyone else on the board had any recourse once Steve spoke; they had agreed that no board member could speak. This was Steve's meeting. Eyes were riveted, mouths were open, and compassionate sighs were heard as Steve wove his tale.

Steve knew he needed to show vulnerability and fallibility in order to get sympathy. His was a near-perfect performance. "My dear congregation, friends, I want you to know how much I love this amazing place. I beg your forgiveness. I want to tell my story. As you know, I have always objected to the phrase '*the* truth' as if there is only one. I ask you to hear and understand *my* truth." His face contorted to demonstrate his sincerity. Steve had his audience eating out of the palm of his hand.

After he spoke, he invited questions. A member who had some inkling of the real story raised the first question. "What is *really* going on? There is more to this than what you put in the letter and what you just said."

"Oh, *that* question right from the start." Steve laughed. "I'm so glad you asked. I wish I could tell you, but I'm not at liberty to discuss that. Suffice it to say, there were pressures placed on me that I could not endure. No one could have. So under the circumstances, I made a mistake, a lapse of judgment. It has never happened before in my career. I'm asking for your understanding."

The meeting went on. Steve adhered to the rules: He did not mention Kyle. He took responsibility for his "lapse in judgment." He asked for forgiveness. But he did not say he was sorry.

Only once did his serene, sad, contrived half-smile change abruptly—just for a moment—and then he recovered.

Sitting almost directly in front of Steve, Amanda could not contain herself as she listened to his answer to the first question. She muttered under her breath, loud enough to be challenging.

With his best schoolmarm impersonation, he bristled and glared at her insolence before regaining his composure and forming his mouth into a sweet, sorrowful, smile, projecting love for his audience. At the same time, he begged for mercy and compassion for being human.

Members ridiculed any member who said anything that even remotely questioned Steve's behavior. After many comments were made, one member announced, "I was a former law-enforcement officer. Steve is right about *truth*. There is always one side, and then there is another side. I say that we have heard enough. We need to move on and forgive."

After the meeting adjourned, Sheila, Amanda, and Glenn walked together to their cars. Amanda smoldered. "It's not the same. Asking for forgiveness places the burden on everyone else. If you say you're sorry authentically, meaning comes from within. I really don't think he's sorry for anything other than getting caught."

Sheila was weary and had reached her limit. "I'm pissed that Steve continued to implicate Kyle and the board as the reason for his 'lapse in judgment.'"

Glenn, who had been one of those ridiculed, had been silent up to that point. But now he seemed not to care if anyone overheard him. "What's with the crap about 'my' truth?" I mean, that's all well and good when you're talking about something that's subjective, like a piece of art, but there *are* some actual facts. Steve submitted a fake diploma. That's a fact. He did it after he lied. That's a fact. And it isn't the first time he has lied. I'm sick of him hiding facts behind *his* truth."

Kyle and Blake went off on their own. Kyle had fire and fury in his eyes. Several people heard him saying, "I just want to strangle someone."

# Chapter 23

*Monday, April 16, 2012*

After the 3:00 a.m. call to action from her beeping cell-phone alarm and the normal morning routine at the station, Kelly got back to her "real" work. She called Reverend Morris at ten.

He said, "I'm glad you called. I've been giving this some thought. At first, I admit, I did not want to get involved, but I talked it over with my wife. The more I thought about it, the more I realized I have an obligation."

Kelly worked to contain her elation, not wanting to sound too eager.

Reverend Morris had heard about the shooting, but he had not made the connection that it was the same Steve Anderson that he had known. He didn't know he was a minister there—or anywhere.

She confirmed that piece of information.

"So ... what you're saying is ... that ... he is in the pulpit ... giving sermons?"

"Yes."

"Performs weddings and other sacred ceremonies? He has full

responsibility for all church activities and ministerial duties?" He sounded incredulous. "Are his sermons any good? Do you think he might be plagiarizing them?"

*Whoa!* Kelly had not expected this reaction. She calmly reiterated that she did not attend the church and couldn't comment on the quality of his work. "Why are you asking?"

Reverend Morris replied, "He never did any of that at Ridgecrest Road."

As the story unfolded, Reverend Morris told Kelly that Steve was called the "minister of music" in much the same way someone would be given the title "finance minister." Steve took care of the music, "ministering" to the congregation through music, and he had never been given any responsibility for sacred ceremonies or preaching. Reverend Morris told her that Steve Anderson had been hired as an organist, but he asked for and led the choir after the choir director resigned. As far as he knew, he had never had any ministerial experience or training. He added, almost as an afterthought, that he believed the title of music minister was one that Steve had requested for status or tax purposes.

Kelly confirmed with Reverend Morris that Steve was not ordained—and was not made a minister—when he was working at Ridgecrest Road.

She thanked the reverend and put down the phone, stunned, as she reviewed what she had just been told. There was no educational credential, experience, or authentic ordination. Now it made sense that his name did not appear on their website or come up in conversation about the history of the church. He was not even a footnote, just an incidental past hire, a church organist who inherited the choir. He was not a revered reverend. In fact, he was a charlatan. A fraud. Bogus. *Did anyone else know?*

Kelly giggled at the notion of a dedicated vegan pushing hard-core ice cream on innocent children and thought *phony baloney* would be a good name for a flavor.

After the conversation with Reverend Morris, Kelly looked at her contact list and found the number and e-mail contact for a psychiatrist who had appeared on her show a couple of times when an expert was warranted. She would not consider Dr. Levinson a friend, but he was someone who would readily take her call.

She was drawn to learn about the psychological angle. What type of person would act the way Steve did? She was turning into her mom, a dig-deeper-into-people person. Mom might have some insight into Steve's personality type, but Kelly still had not told her what she was up to.

Dr. Levinson spoke with the authority that thirty years of clinical, academic, and research experience accorded. He had written books on pathology. Dr. Levinson, like any competent professional, couldn't assert unequivocally whether Steve was self-centered, a compulsive liar, or if there was pathology without firsthand observation. Given the extent of the cover-up and the fact that he had presented himself as a seasoned professional, he suspected the last one.

Armed with a list of possibilities, though no precise diagnosis, Kelly's heart beat just a tad faster as she considered the story's potential. Kelly thought that Dr. Levinson's professional comments were especially interesting in light of the fact that several of the people she had talked to had indisputably labeled Kyle as "emotionally disturbed," claiming that "professionals" had said so, though none had met with or interviewed Kyle. Then, there was also that other word—bully—that church members, plus Steve, had stuck on Kyle. *Was he?*

Indeed, for Kelly, this irrational behavior validated that church people were crazy. She knew it was not right to generalize. They weren't *all* crazy. She just had to figure out who was.

All of a sudden, she looked up. Why did Zack always look at her as though he were looking through her? It really irked her. Out came the TV anchor smile, not quite real, but not completely phony.

"Hey, what's up? Anything from your church visit yesterday?" she asked.

"You stole my question," he replied. "I need an update to take upstairs. Where's this story going? Now that an arrest has been made, most of the networks have lost interest. How can I justify that you're continuing your investigation? I need something, Kel."

Again she flinched. But she did need him on her side. She offered some of what she had learned. "I have some interesting and new information that promises my story will be a great human-interest piece. But you tell me—did you get anything yesterday?"

At this, he smiled his best Cheshire cat grin. "How about lunch someplace private to swap stories?"

Somewhat unwillingly, she agreed.

# Chapter 24

Two days after the town hall meeting with Steve, Amanda and Glenn were completely blindsided.

While the church consumed almost all of their waking, and sometimes sleeping, lives, they continued to sing with The New Littleton Minstrels. It was a welcome distraction. Since abdicating their place in the choir, singing with this group had taken on even more significance. They looked forward to every rehearsal and any opportunity to perform. It was a treasured social outlet.

Amanda and Glenn were straightening up their living room at five o'clock for Tuesday's scheduled practice. They had planned to offer beer and wine along with some snacks, something that they didn't always do, but they thought it might help everyone relax and loosen up. They were surprised when no one had rung the doorbell by 5:05 p.m. Will usually arrived early with a big grin, a big guitar, and some big idea to share.

They began to get edgy. After another five minutes, Amanda asked, "It is Tuesday, right? Was there a change that we forgot about?"

"I don't think so."

"Maybe we missed something. Let me check my e-mails." As she opened her laptop, conveniently sitting on the countertop, she added, "You better check yours too. Sometimes you get stuff that I don't get and vice versa. I've been on the computer on and off all day, but I didn't see anything. I'm going to go back a few days to see if I missed an e-mail from Will."

Glenn checked his e-mail too.

"The last thing I have," Amanda said, "is a list of songs he wanted to rehearse for the program next fall. That was last night at 7:41."

Feeling increasingly annoyed that the rehearsal—at their house—had been changed and they had not been notified, Amanda suggested calling Will to find out what was going on. Worry crept into her voice. "There might have been an accident."

"Let's wait another minute," Glenn said.

"Why? If they are not here by now, something is going on. What good will another minute do?"

"None. You're right. I'll call. Do you think this has anything to do with the church stuff?"

"We all agreed that whatever went on there was a separate matter."

When Glenn didn't get an answer on Will's line, he left a friendly message asking if there had been a change. This did not sit well with Amanda since Will always carried his cell phone. He didn't answer because he couldn't—or because he didn't want to. They waited to see if he would call back. He didn't. They tried again.

Sheryl answered Will's phone and said he was not there, but the rehearsal had been canceled. She seemed surprised that they didn't know, stating that Will sent an e-mail earlier. She gave no further explanation.

"We didn't get it," said Glenn flatly. He felt that not letting them know about the cancelation was intentional, and he was angry. Really, he was hurt as well.

Thirty minutes later, Will called. He was furious and yelled at

Glenn. He asked if he was calling him a liar and insisted that he had sent an e-mail about the rehearsal. When Glenn asked why he canceled, he ranted on about how angry he was with Amanda—so angry he couldn't be in the same room with her! Glenn tried to calm him down and make some sense of what Will said, but Will was unable and unwilling to listen. He ended the call with the modern-day equivalent of a slam.

Amanda put her hand to her head and reeled around once on the counter stool. She was unwilling to let things drop. What else could she do but send another e-mail? She asked Will to call her when things settled to explain why he was angry. She wanted to talk it out and get beyond it. She heard nothing back from him—ever.

The universe, or at least the God of Ethernet, sometimes conspires in unusual ways. About thirty minutes later, Glenn received a rush of e-mails, accumulated from late the night before, stored for some reason in cyberspace, only to come crashing in a torrential storm. One of the later ones, time stamped around four in the afternoon, was from Will, canceling the rehearsal with no explanation. Amanda never received a copy.

Pulling on their big boy and big girl pants, Glenn and Amanda faced a new reality—but not before they passed through disbelief, anger, and sadness.

# Chapter 25

*Tuesday, April 17, 2012*

On Tuesday morning, Kelly had an opportunity to chat with Manny again. She asked if he knew anything about the minister—or the nonminister. At first, Manny was confused about what she meant, but when she reminded him of his friends who knew Kyle, he put the question into context.

"Sweetheart," he teased, "what will you give me for all the juice?"

Always entertained by Manny, Kelly lightheartedly played along. "Well, I met this absolutely divine—by the way very good-looking— flight attendant the other day ... would you like an introduction?"

"Of course, darling. Anything else?"

"Hon, what do you know?"

"Kelly, I don't know about that minister, *personally*, if you know what I mean. But my friend Lanny did mention him ... and his gaydar is not usually off, though it could be, I suppose."

She pressed for more than a vague feeling. "What made you say that?"

"Well, Lanny thought he was cute, mentioned the minister's thick black hair. He happened to walk into the men's room when Stevie was in there." He winked dramatically.

"And?" She tapped her pen.

"Nothing. If a guy does not want to come out ... but Lanny said he had the look. We see it sometimes. Hard to describe if you're not us."

Satisfied that there was no hard evidence, Kelly dismissed the idea that Manny had anything significant to add. She asked about Kyle. No new information there either. Kyle was known to be a pain at times, but he was not known to be violent.

Kelly struggled with the want-to-have-it-all-figured-out part of her personality. There were too many conflicting pieces of information. Steve had been married twice. First wife left him for a lesbian lover. Second wife's husband coincidentally left *her* around the same time. When the two of them met, fireworks went off!

That story did not quite jibe with what the legal records had stated. The two divorces were roughly around the same time, but Steve Anderson and Sue Watson-Jones married quite quickly afterward. Then came baby Claire. Well, no crime there. It happens. She could understand why the actual timing and details of an illicit affair might be kept under wraps.

Kelly's discussions with Dr. Levinson and various Google searches opened the floodgates to interesting psychological profiles. She ran across an intriguing article about bullying and the shadow side of some bullies. Actually, she learned more about bullying than she ever thought she would want to know. She knew she could put this to use when the TV program finally ran. A few things struck a resounding chord: *Often bullies deny something in themselves. They project it onto other people. Vague claims can be levied against the victim. Bullies sometimes play the mental health card, implying that the target has issues.*

Another aspect of bullying behavior was the oft-used gang or group of allies. The bully typically did not do all the dirty work. By planting seeds in others, the bully was able to look quite innocent. From what she had heard thus far, Kyle did not have a huge following of supporters.

Kelly tried calling Steve again. She left her name and contact information. She had low expectations of a return call, but another thought occurred to her. She called him back and let him know she had heard much about him and how well regarded he was. She expressed her desire to meet him, personally, sounding less professional.

Several hours passed before her phone signaled. She recognized the number. After speaking briefly with Reverend Steve—in her mind she was now calling him the "very-not-Reverend Steve"—they made an appointment for the next day. She guessed that her altered line of attack had something to do with his returning her call, but maybe he just got less busy.

She gave this turn of events consideration. The police detectives had to have interviewed him for their investigation. Thus far, beyond that initial video, Mr. Anderson had hardly been mentioned in news stories other than incidentally. Given what she suspected about his personality, maybe that had something to do with his newfound enthusiasm.

Strange as she found him to be, she had to keep convincing herself that he hadn't done anything criminal. She had already learned that falsifying a degree was not prosecutable. She wished the church board had fired his sorry ass, and she didn't understand why they hadn't. It was fairly evident that they didn't know he hadn't been ordained. Even if they did, given the unbelievable level of tolerance of this group, the congregation might not have cared. Though one would think they would care that he was deliberately deceptive. Based on her own moral compass, it was just plain wrong for someone to misrepresent himself— even if he was terrific at his job. Water under the bridge, though, she guessed.

She assumed he knew she had been interviewing members. He might be curious about what they were saying. It's possible he thought he could learn something from Kelly.

She had Steve's initial—and only—public remarks from that fateful Sunday committed to memory. *The people of this community are deeply upset by what occurred here today. We are saddened at the loss of one of our own. But we will recover. Our church is an amazing place. Heaps of hugs to our blessed community.* She winced.

She listened to the audio. What he said was proper. It was also sterile. *Watching* the video, she saw a somber look. His gestures and ministerial garb reflected his authority and gravitas—almost. It was that "almost" that had gotten to her. It was *almost* as though he had prepared. All said, though, it was nothing more than a gut feeling. Someone else could easily see it another way. Someone else might say he was understandably strained given the circumstances, not accustomed to being in front of a TV camera, or something else.

She had to figure out what her strategy would be when they spoke tomorrow. She knew a lot about him. Direct confrontation could be interesting, but he might clam up or put on an act. It might be a good time for her on-air charm.

She had to think through her objectives and prepare questions; this might be her only shot. She wanted to come across as naïve, impartial, and curious about the church and its members. She wanted to get him talking. She thought it likely that she would need to provide some prompts.

Ultimately, she decided she would focus on Jonah, Kyle, and Sam. This would serve several purposes: *He would not think she had reason to suspect he might be lying. He'd create his persona as he wanted it defined. If he were the personality type that Dr. Levinson had intimated, it'd come off as a tad annoying—enough for him to want to turn some attention, if not a spotlight, on himself.*

She looked forward to seeing how it all panned out. Being neutral was essential for investigative interviewing. She knew she had a bias and a theory about what led up to the shooting, but she would remain open to changing her point of view. She was no closer to any answers.

She toyed with the idea that it might be useful to be slightly flirtatious, stroking his ego and conveying interest in him, as she had on her phone message. She detested this device, but it might lead to something revealing. She did not know if—or how—he would respond.

# Chapter 26

*Wednesday, April 18, 2012*

Not realizing the woman who had entered the coffee shop was Kelly Allen, Steve spent some time staring at her. He was struck by the young woman's beauty and style. His wife was not nearly as attractive; no one would ever accuse her of being chic. This woman, on the other hand, was stunning and elegant. Steve felt no sexual attraction, just pure visual admiration. He liked to look at and appreciate pretty things, aurally or pictorially. He considered himself a connoisseur of all art and all things beautiful. He regained control, though, quickly enough to seize the upper hand when he realized who this lovely thing was. It was important that this reporter understood the value of the church and his dedication to it.

Once Kelly introduced herself and thanked him for meeting with her, he said, "As you are no doubt aware, we are devastated by what occurred. I am sure you can appreciate that my time is limited, as I must put my energy, my heart, and soul where it is most needed."

Kelly politely, somewhat demurely, replied that she understood and would only take as much time as he was able to give.

Following the ordering of a latte for Kelly and regular coffee for Steve, they engaged in a comfortable conversation.

Despite having prepared questions about the three people involved in the incident, Kelly switched to an aikido strategy: let Steve make all the moves first. She could nicely step out of the way or change tactics if necessary. As it turned out, she hardly needed to have bothered to get ready at all.

Steve told Kelly that he had agreed to meet because it was important that he do so. He made it clear he was obligated to do the right thing. "I have to make time to arrange the memorial service. To be clear, I consider that service, as well as this meeting, a command performance. Also I believe Jonah needs my help."

"Of course."

"I'm sure by now a lot of things are being said about what happened here last week and what happened over the last year or so. I want you to understand that I am in shock, and I have nothing but sadness in my heart for all those involved. I have to conduct one more funeral, and no matter how many times I have to do these, I still grieve." He smiled, lips closed. "I much prefer the weddings. Weddings and birth ceremonies are so much easier on the soul. The first funeral I did here, as I recall, was for Carol … um … Vo … tari. I held that woman in my arms as she died. It was peaceful in the end, as it should be. Her family was very grateful for my presence. It was the least I could do."

Kelly noted that he stumbled over Carol's last name, but she gave a knowing nod, which was enough to encourage him to say more.

"The funeral was difficult due to the varied needs of her family members. They were not from this amazing church community. Matching their expectations with those of our beloved community was a challenge, but we did it. Everyone was pleased with the sermon, as well as my performance of Grieg's *Aase's Death* from the *Peer Gynt Suite*, something apart from my usual repertoire."

Kelly was bothered that he felt the need to give her so many details, but she made allowances that it might be his style. Still, she immediately concluded he was pompous.

When she asked for his take on what happened the day of the shooting, he answered gravely, "What I recall is that everything was going quite smoothly until Kyle stood up. After that, I have no idea. I tried hard to protect this congregation. Naturally, I don't believe in excommunication and would never advocate someone losing membership status. But I did not think he was a helpful board member; he was a roadblock, and I always thought he was dangerous."

Aha! Kelly pressed forward in her chair, thinking she might be on to something.

Steve took a quick gulp of his coffee. "What I mean by *dangerous*, of course, is damaging to the connections and congruence we have built here. I was right to fear he might blow up and lose control at some point, dampening morale even further. Frankly, his negativity had escalated to a level where it was undermining my own spirit and desire to be of service. I'm sure you can understand that."

Kelly gently confirmed that she understood and tried to get Steve to focus on what had been going on most recently within the congregation.

"I was aware of the discord when I announced I would step down as minister next year. People were upset, but I felt it was something the congregation needed to work out among themselves. I prefer to stay out of the fray unless I'm asked to intervene, which, unfortunately, has been the case all too often. So even though much of the discussion was about me and whether I would continue here, I thought it wise to encourage people to listen to each other—especially the elders—with a loving heart and take advantage of the benefit of their institutional knowledge and wisdom. I had spoken to several of them myself. I reminded them that they would need to hire a very experienced senior minister if I were to continue on as minister of music. I know how hard it would be for someone junior to step in with me still here. I'm not sure they'll be able to afford to hire a minister who's at that level. Anyway, hiring now is on hold. So we'll have to see what happens."

"Tell me more about the rift between you and Kyle Whitman."

"Admittedly, I became quite upset last year when Kyle continuously badgered me. Of course I knew his history. My predecessor told me. Kyle was annoying, but I felt my job was to accept our members as they are. I did my best to accommodate him. He invaded my office repeatedly or phoned or e-mailed. He pestered me, trying to push me to answer his questions, wasting my time. He got angry when I didn't respond to *one*! I filed a complaint with the board. It wasn't fair to the other members who needed my attention. I had hoped that the board would see that Kyle presented a problem to the entire congregation, but they chose to offer mediation instead of a stronger action. They needed to make it appear that they were being fair. I understood that. Since that's what they wanted, I agreed, but it didn't work. I didn't think it would. Kyle kept at it. Everyone observed his snarky comments and angry glares. He constantly plagued the board with his questions and examining of every detail. Nothing was ever good enough. Nothing was ever right with him. That fusspot kept the board from doing its important work. Imagine! He questioned my expense reports! He tried to humiliate me. Although I didn't mention this to anyone, I was very displeased when he started to refer to me as Mr. Anderson. It was insulting, to say the least."

That was the first time Kelly had heard about Kyle's lack of respect. That had to have rankled Steve Anderson. It probably tipped him off that Kyle distrusted his credentials. Maybe he even feared that Kyle suspected he was not actually ordained. About half way through his discourse, she became conscious of how fluent he was, so adept at telling his story.

Steve told her how happy he had been at TLC and that he had adopted it as his church home. She had certainly heard those words before. Then he spoke about his family: his "dear" wife and daughter, particularly gloating over Claire's talent with a father's pride. He mentioned how hard he worked, citing the number of hours. He noted that the increase in church membership proved his efforts were worth it.

He seemed to be concluding his talk. Kelly wanted to know more about Jonah since he was a key link in the whole affair. She was terribly curious about their connection, assuming there was one.

Steve seemed intent on ending the meeting, making the usual overtures about time and duty calling.

She leaned in, reached out her hand to pull him back, showed some teeth, and winked. "I was hoping you would have a little more time. This might be our only chance."

Steve could not resist. The very idea that a young, beautiful woman flirted with him stroked his ego, confirming his importance and his manliness. He capitulated. His comments about Jonah were also carefully articulated. "As for Jonah, he is the salt of the earth. He's an intelligent young man who cares a lot for the folks here. I don't know what got into him last week. Usually he's very serene. We are a peaceful, gentle people. I abhor violence. The only person I can think of who has been a problem is Kyle. I would suspect that Jonah was, in some way, provoked—as I was—by Kyle. It would not surprise me. Kyle has problems, and we must be understanding. But at the same time, we cannot allow it to injure us. A while back, he made one of the loveliest, sweetest people here cry. Leslie is well regarded by all. Picture that."

Kelly had heard this story before. She had hoped for new ground, new information, or new insights.

When asked about Jonah's defense attorney and strategy, Steve shrugged and said, "I don't know anything about Jonah's legal counsel— some bigwig, not local from what I understand. I know very little about Jonah's family. Maybe he has mentioned them once or twice. I don't recall. The congregation has taken up a collection, as I understand it. He probably could not afford much on his own. Like some of us, he has no money to speak of. I don't know about the conflict between Jonah and Kyle. Possibly, there was none. Maybe Jonah saw Kyle reach for his gun and tried to stop him. I never thought it would go this far."

Kelly gasped quietly as she resisted raising her eyebrows. Mr. Anderson apparently did not follow the news, or else he chose to ignore it, since his assumptions conflicted with the information that had most recently been reported. She carefully corrected him, "Perhaps you haven't heard. The bullets were fired from the gun Jonah brought."

"Oh."

She pursued another line of questioning to get Steve to talk about his past.

"I'm not sure why you would be interested in me." He paused, gesturing with his palms as if he were helpless. "I'm just a rather broke minister, originally from Tennessee. Humble beginnings. Played sports like most boys, had a short-lived baseball career in college until my hand injury." He raised his hand and looked at it as if remembering an old pain. "We came to Littleton because my lovely wife got transferred here. So we packed up and enrolled our Claire in school. I was prepared to look for a job, and/or to be a househusband and the primary caregiver for Claire. As it turned out, with good fortune smiling on us, a couple of people from this church heard about me and submitted my résumé to the board. I was hired as minister of music, and when the spot for senior minister opened up a few years ago, I accepted the call and continued to lead the music ministry as well. And there you have it."

"The members here speak very highly of you and your background. Do you mind if I ask why you left your previous church?"

"It happens quite frequently when a new minister comes in. Housecleaning is done. It was a large church, and several ministers left around the same time. The young man needed to make his own mark. I understood completely."

"Of course."

Steve shifted gears, apparently working through some train of thought. "The board kept insisting on private deliberations against my better judgment. I am very disappointed in them and how they handled everything. That wasn't the first time I was disappointed, but I trusted they'd do the right thing and take care of this beloved congregation. I really don't understand how they let it get so out of hand. It's a tragedy."

Kelly knew she only had a few minutes to get Steve to talk about Sam. So much of the conversation had been about Steve. "Tell me a little about Sam Winters. Did he know Jonah or Kyle?"

Steve looked startled by the question and stared blankly. He had no idea if they knew each other. Then, with renewed confidence, out came his answer. "Yes, dear Sam. A lovely person, so sad, heartbreaking."

Kelly asked about his wife and children.

"Rachel. And the children. The service will be challenging, which reminds me, I need to get back to prepare. I recommend that these good people put what happened behind them and move on. I suppose some will want to dwell in the past. As for me, I need to continue to be of service. Ha. That's why they pay me the big bucks! Thank you for coming. I have to get back to where I am needed."

She had never before been thanked for coming to her own interview.

It had gone reasonably well in that there were no ruffled feathers. There was no obvious reason for Steve to decline another meeting, and she got to hear directly from him. Nevertheless, Kelly was disappointed. He didn't reveal much that was new to her. Still, she did have a stronger sense of him. She had hoped he would say more about his early past and where he came from. She eased up on herself as she acknowledged that she'd have another meeting or find out more in some other way.

As she reconstructed the interview, she determined she had gotten a lot more than she had initially thought. First, he took control and shaped the conversation. He always contextualized, carefully positioning his responses rather than providing direct answers. He didn't appear to know much about Sam or Jonah. He should have at least known they were in the same singing group. Did he know more than he was willing to reveal—or did he simply not know the church members very well? There were moments when he seemed disconnected from his words. He detached when he spoke about the congregation, using *they* when others might have used *we*. He used some caring words, but in the end, they were just words. She wasn't feeling the love.

He made several references to money. When she reviewed the recording, she counted three times that he said he did not have much. Was she supposed to feel sorry for him? Was she supposed to see that he sacrificed his comfort?

Then there was the discourse on the funeral. That seemed self-aggrandizing, to say the least, even though he hid it under the guise of *humble service*. She knew it must have been the first funeral he had ever presided over, which was not what he made it out to be.

He had talked about long-term problems with Kyle and threw in information about being warned by the previous minister. She was unsure if that was significant—or if it were true. With regard to Kyle being a menace, he had specifically referred to the same incident she had heard from others.

What he said about why he left his previous position struck her as revisionist history. He left the impression that he was a minister there, but she knew he was not. He had not lied or told the truth.

It slowly dawned on her that when he explained why he came to Littleton, he mentioned his wife's job, a transfer, but he never said anything about her parents needing help or being ill. *Hadn't she heard that from someone?*

She shifted her focus to Jonah. A decision on whether to indict, and on what charges, would be likely by the end of the week. Kelly speculated about whether they thought it was premeditated. There was no state law against carrying a concealed weapon.

That evening, when Mom and Dad called, Kelly let the phone ring. She generally only answered the phone when she had a lot of time, which was almost never, or if she were expecting someone to call. She listened to her mother's rambling message.

She sensed that Mom really wanted to talk and called back with a reasonably cheery greeting. "What's up?"

"Kelly, have you heard anything more about the shooting?

Kelly took a deep breath before asking, "Why do you ask?"

Her mother said she was following up on their last conversation. Kelly chalked it up to her parents trying to take an interest in her work and let it go. She told them she was investigating the story from a human-interest perspective—not from a criminal angle. That was for law enforcement, lawyers, and all the TV talk show pundits, including the overly moralistic Mary Lovett with her never-ending legal gossip and righteous presuppositions that millions of viewers seemed to thrive on.

"You sound resentful of her, Kelly. Are you jealous?" Dad teased.

"Just tired of the crap."

"It's the business you're in."

"I know," she drawled painfully.

Her parents loved it when they perceived she might get a commendation, higher ratings, or a promotion. They were more intense than usual as they grilled her about this story. She hated to disappoint them. She had come to terms with the fact that a story has its own life and death and might not get aired. Nevertheless, she was enjoying watching it unfold. She enjoyed asking tough questions, catching people in their own lies, uncovering the truth, and calling attention to it. In her mind, the best was yet to come.

Mom asked, "What does Zack think about this story?"

Kelly had mentioned Zack to her parents a few times over the years, but the question surprised her. It was just like Mom to remember every tidbit of who's who. Since they were tiptoeing around any mention of Ray, Mom was likely to bring up other people.

"Zack's on board. He likes the idea, and he made the pitch to the execs. In fact, he even directly helped out the other day. It's all good. Don't worry."

Dad responded, "We're not worried. We trust you'll do a great job, as always. You have a good head on your shoulders. It's a plus that you don't have to battle with Zack on this."

Mom said, "It sounds like he really respects you. He listens, values, and considers what you have to say. That's good … in a boss."

"Yeah. Right. Zack. Well, I'm okay. I have a lot of work to do. I'll try to call next week if I get a break."

"Wait, before you rush off, do you have another minute?"

Kelly sighed inaudibly.

"Kelly, this story sounds very complicated. You might run into things that you never expect. I want you to be careful. If you need us, we're here."

She said, "Of course. Love you guys."

"Love you back—always."

Kelly was used to her mother worrying about her. Anything involving guns would worry her more. She wished her mother had more faith in her ability to handle herself.

Kelly was momentarily disturbed that they had called midweek and so soon after their last talk. What was so urgent? She worried that one of them might be sick. Then she dismissed those thoughts and turned to Zack. He had made a decent foray into the church on Sunday morning. Neither of them knew where that might lead.

She gradually became aware that she had enjoyed having lunch with him; her story was their point of connection. She had been reasonably relaxed around him for the first time she could recall. Even in college, she always felt tension around him. Though Zack seemed genuinely interested in this endeavor, she needed to be on guard—lest he try to steal her thunder or undermine her efforts in some way. She needed it to be *her* story and not *their* story.

For the first time in weeks, Kelly went to bed without thinking about Ray—and without needing to deliberately drive away a thought or swallow her feelings. She needed a good night's sleep.

# Chapter 27

*Late Winter/Early Spring, 2012*

Church members filled the meeting room. They were ostensibly there to observe, but several insisted on being allowed to make comments. Never before had so many people been interested in attending a board meeting. Sheila was resolute about having this meeting run smoothly and with decorum.

As they walked in, Kyle whispered, "Amanda, the cult is here." His joke did little to camouflage his fear. He and Steve sat on opposite sides of the table. Sheila called the meeting to order.

Steve had the floor first. He stood up. With unmistakable determination, a set jaw, and stiff, exaggerated movements, he handed out a printed copy of his plan to each board member and promptly sat down, confident that he had fulfilled the requirement. He fiddled with his pen while others read silently.

His plan to make amends was vague and said nothing about how he would handle any individuals, including Kyle. He said nothing about healing the divisiveness he had fomented.

Steve's direct insubordination in not enrolling in the ethics class was grounds for dismissal. However, prior to the meeting, Sheila made it clear that dismissal was not going to be discussed that evening—if ever.

Kyle was the first board member to speak. "Can Mr. Anderson please explain why he did not enroll in the ethics program as specified in the agreement?"

The board had been asked not to speak directly to Steve, presumably to lessen the tension. As soon as Kyle said two words, a moan spread through the crowd.

Someone shouted, "Leave him alone already."

Another one yelled, "Give him the respect he deserves."

Steve stepped in. "I have a church and a congregation to attend to. I did not have time."

This elicited some yeahs from the crowd and a nod from two board members.

Amanda wanted to continue on that track. "It feels like a deliberate slap in the face to the board." Before she could go on, murmurs from the crowd—along with laser-beam stares—stopped her.

Sheila intervened.

Amanda began again, moving to a different point. "Building trust doesn't come from reading a book or talking with a mentor as you have here." This time, she felt, more than saw, a burning glare from Steve, which was followed by boos from the audience and a smug look from Steve.

Undaunted, though constrained, she continued, "Trust occurs between people."

Steve said, "I will meet with Kyle as many times as he wants."

Amanda was not done. She said, "But Kyle is not the only one with whom trust was broken. There is an entire congregation—"

The crowd erupted with another round of muttering and booing.

Now reacting personally, she asked, "How about *me,* for example?"

Kyle, of all people, reprimanded her for speaking directly to Steve.

Steve fixed his face with a crooked smile. "Oh, Amanda dear, you and I can resolve things over a cup of coffee or a glass of wine."

Mouth agape and then tightly shut, Amanda went quiet. She perceived Steve's comment as belittling and phony. *The very idea that they could reconcile over a cup of coffee—in an hour ... or that such a small gesture could fix all the broken relationships he had fueled.*

Other board members did not ask questions. Meg read a well-prepared, thoughtful statement that indicated her grave concern about all that had transpired, which also implied she had shifted her view. She found it troubling how Steve and certain congregants had behaved, and she was distraught about how tarnished the church had become for her.

Dinny shared that, with Aurora's assistance, she had consulted her higher authority prior to the meeting. She read an original poem, receiving scattered applause. A few looked at one another with furrowed eyebrows, question marks all over their faces.

Sheila had cautioned the board ahead of time that they were bound by confidentiality not to reveal anything that had been said in executive session. So no board member mentioned the counterfeit diploma or any of the issues that had arisen as they related to personnel matters.

Before Sheila opened the meeting to comments from the attendees, Amanda made a plea to the crowd to "question the answers" they had heard—a phrase Steve often used in his sermons.

Several church members spoke, the majority with angry, visceral, pointed barbs at the board and loving words in support of Steve, who had been a victim. The one or two who quietly asked a question or made a statement in support of the board were completely drowned out by the noise of the others.

One angry woman stood up. She looked directly at Kyle and took aim with no evident qualms about what she was about to say. In a clear, loud and bitter tone, her vitriol spewed. "You have attacked this poor man, our minister. You have been out to get him for a long time, searching for anything, and when you finally found something, you harassed him. You bullied him. You do not belong here. You, sir, are *inhuman*."

Another woman called out, "We need to get rid of the bullies!"

As the excoriation went on, Kyle sat with eyes downward and red face, holding back tears and anger. His husband, sitting not too far away, was also close to tears. Then the audience erupted in applause, supporting the vicious verbal assault. The woman smirked and took her seat.

No one said anything else. Every cell in Amanda's body told her to say something or do something. She looked to Sheila who, no doubt, was feeling the same. Neither of them helped Kyle.

The meeting adjourned. Kyle bravely strode up to the woman and quietly asked to meet with her so he could share his point of view. She looked past him as if he were not there, though after a moment, she sneered and refused his request.

Amanda and Glenn walked out with Kyle and Blake in silence. They parted with hugs.

Amanda held herself in check as they approached the parking lot. The jeering echoed along with the reference that she and Kyle were bullies. The acrimony in the woman's diatribe followed by an ovation from so many, including Will, reverberated as well. These church members supported the contemptuous harangue.

Reaching their car, Amanda saw that they were parked next to Will. As he opened his car door, Amanda said, "I'm so sorry this has come between us and has affected our relationship with the Minstrels."

Will barely looked at her, said absolutely nothing, shut the door, and drove off.

Even before pulling her door closed, Amanda said, "Oh my God! That was the most junior-high moment I have ever experienced, including anything that might actually have happened in junior high. I was completely intimidated. I can't believe it. I don't know what happened to me, to my voice."

Glenn grabbed the steering wheel and fumed, "That's it. We're done. Or I am. We trusted these people. We thought they were friends. They're supposed to respect and care about others. For all their talk about love, they are not even nice people. We don't need them."

"Of course, we don't. We got along without them for years. It'll be a relief not to have to deal with this nonsense. I plan on resigning tonight. It's not worth my energy to try to help that place."

"They don't have a clue. They haven't heard anything other than Steve's spin, and they don't want to. They can't entertain the idea that they might have been fooled, that they could possibly be wrong."

"You know, Glenn, I still think they would understand if they were told about all the information and evidence we've seen. I actually think it's not all their fault. They've been used. I feel sorry for them."

"I don't."

"In a way, they are victims almost as much as Kyle is. Steve did them wrong and pulled apart the whole church while he was at it."

"What really burns me up is Will's silence and his self-satisfied grin."

"Well, he's one of those people. I *still* think if he had *all* the facts— and if he could get past his self-interests—he would have seen the truth and been—"

"Amanda, he didn't—and he won't. Let it go."

By midnight Amanda had written and rewritten her letter of resignation at least five times, all while debating whether to quit. Finally ready to click send, she stopped short and resigned herself to not resigning. She just couldn't let it go. Glenn, however, quit the minister's council without a second thought.

About a month later, fearing things were getting even worse for Kyle because of the ostracism and continued hostility, Amanda said, "Glenn, I'm really worried about Kyle. He's heartbroken, and I just don't know what he might do."

She had elicited a promise from Kyle not to do anything rash or anything that would get him into even more trouble. With second thoughts, Amanda eventually took it upon herself to call the police. She explained the tension at the church and how it had escalated. She told them she thought it was possible that violence could erupt. The officer didn't seem especially interested in her warning, but she said she'd make note of it.

# *Chapter 28*

*Thursday and Friday, April 19–20, 2012*

Kelly guessed the legal case was pretty clear. The state sought accidental manslaughter in the death of Sam Winters and attempted murder of Kyle Whitman.

She had a few interviews scheduled. One was with Will, who insisted on talking to her, and another was with Kyle. He had been released from the hospital on Monday. She also had a last-minute interview with someone who witnessed the shooting and contacted her.

Late that morning, Zack texted Kelly. He had gotten a call from Reverend Steve. She texted back: *want details*. So they went to lunch again. This time, they were even more relaxed. They shared a mocking snicker as Zack described how Steve fawned over him. Though church leaders tended to sidle up to folks with the big bucks, it fit so snugly with the picture of the unctuous Steve that both had been sketching.

Kelly told Zack that someone named Lance had called. He had talked briefly to Lara on the day of the shooting and made a statement to the detectives, but now he wanted to talk to her. She didn't expect anything of substance, just another congregant who thought he had the definitive answer to what happened.

Kelly liked puzzles, jigsaws, crosswords, and even the Rubik's Cube. She liked to play Scrabble too. With crossword puzzles, knowledge counts for something, but she also liked figuring out which letters went together to form words. She was especially fond of acrostic puzzles, going back and forth between clues to piece together a quote from a book. The first letter of each clue's answer revealed the author and title. It was about information, sentence structure, word formation, and good guessing. Sometimes, though, there was an ellipsis, a word with an apostrophe, or an abbreviation; in other words, something was missing from the expected. It was like solving a mystery; eventually, it all comes together.

What puzzled her most was that she couldn't tell if there were more to the crime than she knew about. What pieces were missing? Did she have all the facts she needed to solve the puzzle: an illegitimate minister, a shooter, a provocateur, lots of opinions, and different truths? Was there a single, objective truth? Was there a classically formed picture or an abstract hodgepodge that no one would ever agree on?

What satisfied her about most puzzles was that there was always a solution. But she had no idea if there was a solution to *her* puzzle, and her patience was wearing thin. She was frustrated and desperately wanted to throw in the towel, yet she had a hunch that she was crawling toward the light.

Thankfully, Kelly's conversation with Will was brief. It did not take long to see his blatant spin. Will was positive that Jonah was a good guy, a hero, and now a victim—not a perpetrator. He was absolutely convinced that Kyle was guilty of instigating and that he had brought a gun even if he hadn't used it.

He let Kelly know that he had seeded a fund for Jonah's defense, which partly explained how Jonah was able to hire a crackerjack lawyer. Others had also contributed, including the Goldbergs.

The missing piece, as far as Will was concerned, was getting public opinion to support Jonah.

Kelly thought Will was barking up the wrong tree. If there was one thing that irked her even more than softball questions and "he-said-she-said" false-equivalency reporting, it was trial by public opinion.

In the end, she left with something to think about. Will said, "There are those who think Kyle is innocent. They think they have inside information and the whole story, but they don't. Steve knows more than he's willing to say publicly. There is more to this than anyone is saying."

She believed that even tiny pieces of a puzzle, or one move, could prove significant so she agreed to speak with Lance on the phone. Lance happened to be visiting the church on the day of the shooting and had no connection to church politics. He told her—and he had told the detectives as well—that he saw Kyle reach for his bag immediately after he stood. Something must have disturbed or incensed him since he groaned at the same time. "He looked upset, maybe infuriated, or like he was in pain. How can you tell the difference?" It was a good question.

Lance thought there was something else that he saw; it gnawed at him. Reverend Steve had said or done something that looked odd. He made a gesture of some sort. Lance could not put his finger on what it was.

Lance went to the church because he had heard there was a gay minister there. It dawned on Kelly that Lance could be Manny's friend—Lanny.

After Kelly ended the call, she went home. The first priority was Jonah. She set to work making calls and surfing the Internet. She found college records, though there was not much there to work with. Jonah had enrolled and dropped out a number of times. He took courses in Sanskrit and Gregorian chants, but he never accumulated credits. He worked at ShopRite, and his fellow employees judged him to be a good worker and a nice guy. She had heard that he was a little erratic in terms of absences but was steady in terms of years; he had not switched employers in a decade.

*So, she thought, he is loyal. On the other hand, he hasn't risen in the job. Doesn't he want responsibility? Is he content with doing the minimum? Perhaps mundane work gives him time to contemplate more complex issues?*

Facebook had interesting, if not verifiable, information. Finding out about Jonah on Facebook was a lot easier than finding out about Steve since Steve limited his privacy settings. Kelly learned nothing *definitive* about either one, naturally, given the source, but she gained some interesting insights.

Jonah posted a great deal about himself and his life philosophy. He appeared to be untethered to any particular ideology, a free thinker. He was in a relationship with someone, but who or what sort of relationship was not clear. No name or gender. Along with friends—and occasionally even Steve—his parents and other family members commented on his posts. The family appeared to be close and loving. Some of what she read supported what people had said about him being supremely confident about his ideas. He was also compassionate. There were no red flags.

His father was a bit of an anarchist, or so it seemed from his posts. He was not necessarily a proponent of anarchy, but he was unhappy with government, a libertarian perhaps. He quoted the Bible, and there seemed to be a touch of a zealot embedded in many of his comments. With the back-and-forth comments on one or two posts, she surmised that Jonah and his dad did not always agree; perhaps Jonah had broken ranks with his family on some central issues.

Jonah and Steve were Facebook friends, but neither were "friends" with Kyle. *So,* Kelly thought, *I have become a Facebook stalker. Is there anything worse?* She laughed at herself and continued with her research. She began to put together a picture of Jonah, but it didn't explain why he had a gun and pulled the trigger.

She plowed forward to get clarity on how these disparate pieces of information and people fit together. Kelly began to write an outline for a script, and then she spent the rest of the evening reviewing the video that had been shot and her notes. She wanted to know if other networks had probed into some of the same areas she had. She watched the Mary Lovett program and other news reports. It did not appear that they had.

Much of her future work would have to be done in tandem with the legal teams. She prepared for the inevitable interviews with lawyers, which was not an activity she particularly relished.

---

The next morning with *What's Big in Littleton* over for the day, Kelly set to work once again. She couldn't stop thinking about Steve. While she saw he possessed the ability to charm—thus accounting for his devoted following—she couldn't appreciate how people could be so naïve and capable of being duped.

Steve was a pretender, but there wasn't much more that she could find on him. She had to figure out if the board knew he wasn't a for-real minister. If not, how would she let that cat out of the bag? He was still being venerated, and he was still in the pulpit. Did she have an obligation to out him? Was it none of her business? Was there a public responsibility angle she could play? She thought that might be interesting—a be-careful-out-there, word-to-the-wise tack.

Back in research mode, Kelly delved into the literature that Dr. Levinson had provided to explain conditions he believed would lend insight into Steve's personality. Starting again with "liar," and "pathological liar," she landed on pay dirt when she looked up "narcissist."

There were a ton of different checklists, but "narcissistic personality disorder" seemed to fit quite aptly. She was entertained by the idea that this "affliction" was often seen in ministers more than any other profession, even more than performers. She wondered about performers who posed as ministers.

She supposed she would need Levinson and at least one other shrink to appear on camera in the final production. They would provide gravitas, professional insight, and on-air testimony. She knew a bona fide professional would require direct observation of Steve to make an official diagnosis, and she hoped that would not be a problem by the time the show ran. She would encourage Levinson to attend the trial or review tapes, assuming Mr. Anderson made another appearance or two.

Her channel's news streamed all day as she worked. At four thirty, Kelly heard the familiar chime to announce breaking news. The TLC case had gone to a judge's hearing, and a ruling was imminent. Kelly was somewhat aware of the nuances of the legal system, and she knew it was not *de rigueur* to go directly to a judge and circumvent a grand jury indictment. Something was not as evident as she had assumed.

Lorraine Lewis, a colleague and friend on the afternoon news, stated that Jonah Spencer attempted to gain immunity by using the state's stand-your-ground law, fearing imminent danger. Lorraine reported that Mr. Spencer had a concealed weapons permit, had taken approved gun safety courses and lessons, and the gun had been acquired legally. Kelly assumed they had found out that Kyle was carrying too.

The state did not try to make a case for premeditation for the death of Sam, but they felt they had a good case for attempted murder when it came to the assault on Kyle. Kelly considered possible motives and didn't come up with much. No one, besides Steve, seemed to think that Kyle and Jonah had issues. From all other accounts, they barely knew each other.

The call from her contact downtown came later. Judge Marcia Renaud did not grant immunity based on the stand-your-ground law, but she allowed a variation on self-defense that the lawyers wanted to use. Jonah claimed that protecting his church family was tantamount to protecting his blood family and his own life. He regarded his church as "home." He also claimed they had been explicitly threatened.

The defense lawyer apparently tried for stand-your-ground as a ploy to set the stage for the public and for Jonah's defense strategy. The case proceeded to the grand jury. An indictment was imminent.

All week long, the press and church members had continued to speculate and make a lot of assumptions, which made for interesting copy. Kelly was always baffled by how often people *knew* something for sure without having all the information.

Assuming the grand jury returned an indictment, it would be an attention-grabbing trial, but its start date would be a long way off. She would have to set her project aside and pay more attention to *What's Big in Littleton*. She had been on autopilot with regard to her current responsibilities. Nevertheless, despite what her head told her, her instinct told her something else. She wanted to keep digging.

Zack's call interrupted her thoughts. As she explained everything to him, he listened thoughtfully. "Kelly, you don't have to wait for the trial. You can begin work on the video right now. With or without a verdict, with or without Jonah, you have a story. It's an interesting one. It's got the elements of a pretty good movie too. Keep in mind the shooting is the starting point from which you can go *backward*. All the information you gathered would have been there whether or not there was a crime committed that Sunday. We'll air after the trial, but a large chunk can be put in the can prior."

*Thank the forces for Zack after all. As much as he can be annoying, he is smart and incisive. He is more than competent. He is confident without being arrogant or cocky. Okay, sometimes he is cocky, but I can live with it. Zack really is a pretty cool guy. He divorced a few years ago, no kids—or maybe there is one. I wonder if he is dating.*

She had another appointment with Kyle that evening, and she looked forward to it. While she did not *think* Kyle was crazy, she had lost some confidence in her ability to judge people. If she had been wrong about Ray being right, then she could also be wrong about Kyle. Then again, she might also be right about Steve being so wrong.

---

In Kyle's living room, Kelly was struck by the framed prints on the wall and asked who had painted them.

Kyle responded, "I did. They're photographs."

"Gorgeous. And the framing is quite clever. Really enhances them."

"I did that as well. Took me a while to figure out how not to destroy the wall while I was hanging them."

Kelly was not surprised by this revelation.

Blake offered a snack and asked what she would like to drink. She declined anything other than water. Discretely, Blake left the house on an errand—to leave them alone and to seize the opportunity to get out while someone else sat with Kyle.

As she asked more questions, Kyle felt more at ease. She seemed genuinely interested in what he had to say. He let down his guard bit by bit.

His first statement sounded strange, though she had begun to get used to his brand of self-deprecating humor. He said, "Now that it seems I am not going to die, I suppose a lot of people are disappointed."

She tried to reassure him that most were grateful he was among the living.

As though a question had been asked, Kyle divulged, "I told the board members that I might file a lawsuit for both libel and slander. Steve and others were maligning me. He put my name in writing in his complaints and accusations. It's on record. Where was I protected in all of this? My reputation was trashed, and I needed to defend myself." His voice was calm and gentle as he talked to Kelly, but he described some very difficult-to-manage emotions and clenched his teeth as he thought back to how angry Steve had made him—and how hurt he was at not getting support from the church congregants. "I didn't want to damage the church or the church's reputation, but I had to do something to protect my own. I had to. So I planned to take action that Sunday. I needed it to be over."

"What action did you plan to take?"

"Well, everyone knows about my history with guns."

She couldn't tell if he was serious. She didn't smile.

A silence ensued before Kyle interjected another thought. "For the record, I have no objection to being included in your TV program. I want to be. I'm sick of speculation, rumors, and hearsay."

Kelly had heard from many others about what occurred before the shooting, but she wanted to hear Kyle's version.

Instead of talking about the shooting, he backtracked. "I remember one night when I was especially mad. Sheila, Amanda, and Glenn talked me out of doing anything that would upset others even more than they were. I know they had my best interests at heart, as well as the church's. I trusted them. I think they really believed it would all work out. But it didn't. I was so mad I could have killed him if he said just one more thing about me. Maybe I should have gone with my instincts then instead of waiting. At least Sam would still be here. Later on, Amanda asked me about my guns and made me promise …"

Kelly began questioning Kyle's emotional stability.

His eyes welled up, and he tenderly added, "I know that Sam's wife is completely distraught. I sent her flowers. The service is this weekend. I'll go if I'm up to it."

*He is bitter but caring and compassionate, gentle, and genuine. But he did have motive. And maybe he had a gun.* She wanted to hear what he had planned for that fateful Sunday, but she didn't want to press him if he wasn't ready to talk.

"Then there were the 'confession' meetings—the first one with the board and then the public one. Spinning *his* 'truth,' making me the scapegoat. I suppose I am the reason he isn't taller too! Why do the charming ones always get away with it? I'd really had it with being his whipping boy."

Again, she asked herself what he was telling her. *Had he started for his gun that day? Was he really capable of murder or murderous thoughts? Is he guilty of something? Or does he just feel guilty?* She changed the subject and asked whether he was surprised that Jonah had a gun.

"I didn't think anyone in that church had a gun—except me!"

She gently pushed for him to elaborate.

"I made no secret about the fact that I own guns. I inherited a large collection. I was taught to shoot when I was a kid."

Kelly asked, "So people knew you had guns. Had you ever threatened to use one?" She treaded lightly.

"You're kidding. I don't have my collection here. They're a couple of thousand miles away, locked in a vault in my hometown. I have a healthy respect for guns. I'm not inclined to use one."

"Do you have a license?"

"Yes, I do."

"Do you keep any weapons here at all?"

Apparently ready to talk about the shooting and thinking that question had already been answered, Kyle said, "I was as burnt up as I had ever been that day. I heard that some people were demanding that I be watched—and my satchel would be checked if I came to the church. I made up my mind to end it all right there, that day." He stopped talking.

Kelly wasn't sure if he was holding back or if Kyle figured *that* was the end of the story.

Just as she was about to ask another question, Kyle began again. He said, "I wrote it down: *repeating a lie often enough or loudly enough does not make it true.* I wanted them to know that what they said about me was a lie. The corollary is that if something is repeated enough, people *will* believe it. I was nervous, but I wanted the congregation to know how much I hurt. I hoped for some compassion as well as a little relief."

"What happened?"

"Nothing. Everything. I never got to speak. I got up. Steve turned red, and he glared at me. I went back to my seat and grabbed for my satchel. I was in pain. I don't remember much after that."

She was sure he had meant emotional pain, but for some reason she repeated the word. "Pain."

"I have reflux. That's what they would have found if my bag had been checked—my pills. And spare clothes. I had planned to go for a bike ride right after church."

"So when you were 'going to take action,' you were going to—"

"Speak *my* truth, *the* truth."

Part 5 Insights

# Chapter 29

*Spring and Summer, 2012*

As the shooting became old news, Kelly spent more time working on *What's Big in Littleton* as well as the morning news. She used her afternoons and evenings to research and write a script for the pretrial portion of the project. She had yet to settle on a title. Although the station execs were still receptive, they had not fully endorsed it. However, since there was minimal expense involved and she didn't request release time, they allowed it to simmer on the back burner.

In the course of her research, Kelly came across the name and address of Steve Anderson's ex-wife. It would be the next angle she investigated. She thought it would be interesting, and maybe even kind of delicious, to find out about Sue and Steve's grown children. No one seemed to know much about the Andersons, and there were some conflicting stories and recollections about the family. She had met one daughter briefly at Ridgecrest Road.

She itched to talk with Steve Anderson again, and she had never been granted any time with Jonah. However, she did have sources in the courthouse and connections to the DA and the law firm representing Jonah. She knew they explored everything too. Mary Lovett had been sure at first that the shooting had been the result of an accidental discharge as Jonah wrested the gun from Kyle. Now, she was confident that Jonah's was a clear case of self-defense, fearing imminent danger.

Kelly thought Jonah's actions opened the doors to premeditation although far from proving it. He had done everything by the books a few weeks before the incident. That also calibrated with what Kelly had heard about him. He took it upon himself to learn as much as he could about anything that interested him. Learning lots about random things was not so different from Kyle.

It was hard to know when the trial would begin. Jonah had been out on bail since the indictment. She hoped she would finally be granted an interview with him.

She needed to work more closely than ever with Zack since he had been ingratiating himself with some of the church members and Steve. Steve was especially attentive whenever he saw Zack, making sure to greet him by name and invite him to one program or another, most of which Zack avoided. It was not a comfortable assignment for Zack, and Kelly was impressed by his ability to commit and follow through.

Kelly made several more trips back to the Ridgecrest Road Church and kept in contact with some people she had met there. On one of her trips to Knoxville, she learned that Ellen Anderson had remarried, and one of her and Steve's sons lived with Ellen and her new *husband*. That son was in the reserves. Kelly had never heard anyone at TLC mention that Steve had a son in the service, and she speculated that Steve wanted that kept quiet. Maybe it didn't fit his preferred narrative. Craig—the son Amanda had met—lived near Littleton.

Sue's daughter, Sarah, was a little younger than Kelly and still attended Ridgecrest Road. After an initial introduction, they clicked and became Facebook friends. Kelly knew it was necessary to tell her Ridgecrest Road Church friends who she was. She needed to talk openly about the project before she brought the video crew from Littleton.

She believed that no one there would have any objection since no one had had an affiliation with TLC or cared much about Steve besides the children who might not want family issues and dirty linen aired. Nonetheless, they all knew about the shooting at Steve's church. She mulled over the possibility that they could know something else.

Being Facebook friends with Sarah made it easy to snoop a little more. Kelly used the same "identity" she had used when she initially visited Ridgecrest Road.

There were almost no pictures posted on Facebook of any of the sisters with Claire, their half-sister, or with Steve. The only pictures of them together were from when Claire was a baby. She also noted that the sisters never referenced a visit with their mother. There was no conversation with Steve, but Sue commented on various posts. Steve was not a big Facebook user, which was understandable. Kelly was somewhat surprised to observe that Sue looked considerably older than Steve, although she knew she wasn't. Sue's hair was gray and unstyled. In most pictures, she wore it pulled back or with a headband. She wore no makeup, was slightly overweight, and had a drawn, mousy appearance, but her commentary was upbeat and amusing. The sisters and Sue seemed to genuinely love one another.

Her own mom and dad continued to bug her about the project, always more Mom than Dad. She told them as much, or as little, as she felt like sharing. Yet each time she finished a conversation, she felt irritated. She didn't know why, but she mostly avoided conversations with them. Eventually, she would visit. It was not that she didn't love them. She did. They were her parents.

Kelly's thoughts returned less and less to Ray as time passed. She went out with friends and worked. There was no time for serious dating, and frankly, she had no desire for it.

One afternoon, after work, she read her script and her notes and decided it was time to come out—so to speak. She wanted to fill in the gaps as much as she could before the case came to trial.

Before scheduling the expedition to Knoxville, Kelly called Sarah. After their initial encounter in Knoxville, their relationship had begun to develop on Facebook. Kelly had grown to like and respect her from their exchanges, although she understood that while she "knew" some things about her, she didn't really know her at all. In her profile picture, Sarah was all dimples: a mischievous sprite sitting in a gigantic rocking chair. Her cover photo was a stunning shot of a flowering mountain in the Azores. Sarah was thrilled with the invitation to meet in person once again.

Kelly and Zack took the trip to Knoxville together. While they agreed the story was Kelly's, they also knew Zack played a key role in its development. Zack could provide balance and added insight. And Zack had a way of endearing himself to certain people, especially older women—and younger ones. Kelly couldn't deny that Zack's charm could work to everyone's advantage. During the last couple of months of working together, a lot of tension between them had fallen away. To be sure, there were inevitable clashes of style and a few inexplicable moments of discomfort.

On the plane to Knoxville, they found themselves sharing ideas on a variety of topics as the conversation flowed from Kelly's story to sports to religion.

Zack commented, "I understand the attraction of gathering to talk philosophy in the confines of a church setting. People naturally gravitate toward those with like views; it's a tribal instinct. And I like the UU concept that everyone is entitled to his and her individual beliefs."

"Yes! Just don't force them on me!"

"Well, that's the point of this faith—the church doesn't, at least in theory, tell you what to believe, but the group supposedly shares certain values and does service that's consistent with those values, both for itself and out in the world."

Kelly thought for a minute and then said, "Okay. But why do they call themselves a religion?"

"I don't know. Historic roots I guess. And, maybe, politically speaking, they want to be accepted. They want to have a seat at the table in the national discourse. It *is* a faith group, just not *blind* faith."

"Ha, and therein lies the rub. That openness might be true about some things, religiously speaking. But even in that church of tolerance—from what I have gathered—there is certainly a hierarchy. Also they, like every other religion, think theirs is better than anyone else's."

Zack said, "People are always judgmental—no matter how accepting they claim to be. People always see problems with someone who is different. Even if they aren't prejudiced regarding race, ethnicity, gender, and sexual orientation—even atheism and humanism are embraced—allowances are not always made for behavior that doesn't conform to expectations. Some people can get away with things that others can't. I'm not talking about anything harmful; mild aberrations like not saying good morning in a chipper voice could be scorned or questioned. People are inconsistent in their own behavior and application of the rules."

"Some more than others," Kelly added. "Where do you draw the line between being inconsistent and just plain lying?"

"It seems like that should be evident, Kel, but it isn't. Then there's also the middle ground of forgetting or misunderstanding—sometimes honestly and sometimes a convenient excuse. And what role does integrity play?"

"Good question."

They both fell silent as they thought about the trajectory of their careers and what role integrity played in them.

Zack and Kelly went to Starbucks to meet with Sarah. If Sarah got upset when she was told the truth, Kelly thought it might be easier to talk it through with Zack there. She would play bad cop against Zack's good. Kelly was annoyed with herself for getting attached to Sarah, not maintaining a professional distance.

When they greeted each other, Sarah was not surprised to see Zack. Kelly had told her that her boss would be joining them, though Sarah had no idea why. Sarah was taken by his rugged good looks, easy smile, and deep brown eyes. His dark complexion was striking next to his ashy blond hair. He was not classically handsome, though he was definitely appealing. She guessed roughly late thirties. *Perfect.* While instantly attracted, she also realized she had no idea who he was or even what he did for a living. Kelly had never mentioned what her job was.

Though she knew he could be married, Sarah couldn't help a little innocent flirting right from the start, something that did not escape Kelly or Zack. Zack was used to it and ignored or took advantage as needed. Kelly was put off at first, and then she decided it could help when Sarah learned the truth, but then she flipped back to being annoyed. She did not want to be a user—even if it might be a necessary part of the job at times.

Kelly bluntly announced who she really was and what she was working on.

"What?" Sarah reacted to Kelly's virtual slap in the face.

Sarah's initial incredulous comment was followed by a gulp, an apology, and explanation from Kelly. Sitting in a cozy nook with their lattes—a black coffee for Zack—Kelly reached out to touch Sarah's hand. "Sarah, I know it's no excuse that it's my job. I didn't mean to hurt you. And I'm really not being phony. I like you and have grown to respect you."

Sarah tried to regroup as she looked around at the eclectic group of coffee tasters, tablet readers, chatters, writers, and mommies. How did their little trio fit in? Not friends, not coworkers.

As Sarah recovered from her initial jolt and feelings of betrayal, the bitterness melted. She still liked Kelly. Kelly was not a sham; she could feel her authenticity.

Sarah's face relaxed as she exhaled and stretched her arms. The raised eyebrows and dropped jaw turned into a crinkle at the corners of her eyes and a couple of dimples on her cheeks, not at all what Kelly expected. Kelly had predicted that Sarah would probably shut down, maybe even walk out the door.

All of them sipped their hot beverages in silence.

After what seemed an hour, though was really two minutes, Sarah said, "You know, I'm really not altogether surprised by this. What I mean is, I'm not flabbergasted that the media is sniffing around. Ever since it became known that the Littleton shooting was at my mother's husband's church, I guess I expected someone to start asking questions. I just thought it would be lawyers or private investigators."

Kelly was perplexed. *What is she getting at? Is she babbling because she is uncomfortable? She must know more about Steve.*

Sarah said, "I'm actually relieved that you're doing this story."

"Help me understand why," Kelly said.

"Well, first, because I do trust you, Kelly. I know we haven't been real friends—and you deceived me about who you are, which doesn't feel great—but I think I understand why you did it. I feel a bond with you somehow anyway. I hope that's okay to say. I'm a little embarrassed."

Kelly shifted her position and mumbled, "Me too." She got up to use the restroom. She took her time going back to the table after washing her face and collecting herself. Kelly caught a flip of the hair, a girlish giggle, and a cutesy grin as Sarah lightly touched Zack's arm. *Crap.* She could not abide blatant flirting.

Sarah lifted her eyes to face Kelly and immediately suggested they go someplace more private. She invited them back to her apartment for an early cocktail.

Zack and Kelly followed behind in their rental. In the car, Kelly said, "We need to be careful and maintain our professional distance with Sarah." She meant to imply that he did. But in the end, they understood they both needed to maintain boundaries for themselves.

They speculated for the ten minutes it took to drive to her apartment about what Sarah might say, eagerly hoping it would be revealing. They were fully cognizant that she might have nothing interesting to add and only wanted to become better friends. They kept the possibility open that Sarah could say something that would actually blow apart their whole human-interest story, logically explaining Steve's behavior, and taking all the wind out of their sails. It would not necessarily be the kiss of death for the program, but it might present another point of view.

At Sarah's, the three climbed the stairs to her third-floor walk-up. It was not precisely Bohemian, but it was definitely eclectic casual. A small, pre-flat screen TV was precariously balanced on an orange ottoman by the overstuffed sofa. The sofa, covered by a tablecloth with an attractive blue and yellow Provencal print, took up residence under a window in the center of the room. A round wooden table with four mismatched colorful plastic chairs took up the bulk of one corner, while a mound of paisley floor pillows enjoyed occupancy in another, definitely a throwback to another decade. Aside from the furniture, there were some absolutely enchanting black-and-white photographs, a shadow box containing charming and colorful travel souvenirs, a few artsy candles, and a small collection of antique wooden pepper mills on a small side table. Even with so much stuff, the room did not seem crowded.

Zack and Kelly felt quite at home. This could be a problem since they didn't want to get too comfortable.

After the chitchat that accompanied the opening of a bottle of Apothic Red and arranging crackers, Brie, and smoked Gouda, Sarah sat and became subdued. "I don't know what you already know about my mother and Steve Anderson, and I am not sure if anything I might have to say would be of interest. I guess that since no detective has asked me or my sisters anything, Steve is not a suspect and had nothing to do with the shooting—other than happening to be there when it happened." She observed the glances exchanged between Zack and Kelly. "Here's the thing. As far as I know, he has never done anything illegal—unless it's illegal to break up two marriages. But my mother was complicit in that. I love my mother, but I think she was stupid to leave my father for that guy. My father might not have had the degrees Steve has, but he's smart. Though he's not as charming and handsome, he loved my mother. He was really hurt when she left him. I personally don't know what she sees in Steve, but I guess she liked the attention after having been married for nearly twenty-five years. You know, one of my church friends told me that Steve started to come on to him but immediately walked away. So he was even more surprised than the rest of us when Steve and my mom hooked up. Maybe it was the romance or the music. My mother had wanted to be a singer and a dancer. Maybe he offered that possibility, if not in actuality, in her imagination. Or maybe he really did make promises. I don't know."

Kelly and Zack didn't move an inch.

Sarah revealed even more, saying, "I will tell you this. We don't like him. We never did. Not just because of the divorce. We didn't like him before that. He was smug—and a tad creepy. He wasn't well liked in the church, though he was here quite a long time. He met my mother when he was the choir director. Oh, by the way, he was never a minister here. Mom told us that he became one in Littleton."

Sarah had assumed he got accreditation and training along the way, but she also was fixed on her assertion that he was not well suited to the role. "Did I tell you my sisters and I used to babysit his sons? The families sort of knew each other. That made their romance even worse."

Sarah's eyes began to well up. She stopped short of crying and stood to refill the glasses.

Zack and Kelly exchanged glances again.

Kelly said, "Sarah, I need you to know that what you're saying is on the record unless you tell us to take it off. I don't want you to say more than you're comfortable with."

"It's all right. Now. I think … I think it's time people knew about Steve Anderson and my mother."

"We know quite a bit already. We already knew about them hooking up before the divorces, and we know when they were married and when

Claire was born. While I'm sure your parents' divorce must have been upsetting to you and your sisters, these things do happen—"

"Kelly, I'm not a fool," Sarah said. "That's not what I'm talking about, and I expect any decent journalist would have puzzled that out already. I suppose it's one of the reasons my mom and Steve moved away, though. No, it's more that he emotionally cripples her. She does whatever he wants. I don't get it. It wasn't that way with Daddy. They were independent people, strong together and strong apart. With Steve, it's like she was entranced by him. I hated how she followed Steve around like a puppy. My mother loves children and is so good with them. I can't believe she let him call all the shots with Claire. My sisters and I have tried to talk with her, but she'll hear none of what we say. She says it's nonsense, and she loves him. They have an agreement: she works full time, and he takes care of Claire. But she always worked when we were little too, and that didn't stop her from making decisions and helping manage our lives. We don't like their relationship. We can't do anything about it, but we're sure as hell not going to condone it by going there and pretending we're one big, happy family." Sarah's rosy, sweet face turned sour. "Oh God, that's what Steve said when they announced their marriage. Made me want to puke. I don't think his boys were crazy about it either, but they probably didn't say anything. Of course, we had stopped babysitting by then. Maybe I shouldn't say anything else." She stopped suddenly.

Zack said, "It's okay. You can tell us as much as you want, and it will be your choice if you want us to leave anything out when—and if—the story airs. We'll have to return to record anyway, so by then, you'll be certain about what you want to say."

Kelly observed Zack's compassion and candor. He was direct, truthful, and gentle at the same time, which was not a skill she had yet mastered. *Mom is good at it too.* Kelly appreciated his kindness to Sarah on one level and even admired it, but on another level, she was not sure she liked the way this was going down.

Sarah subtly inched closer to Zack. With a slight smile, she said,

"I guess I'm into it now. Well, it was good that they moved away. I sometimes wish it had happened sooner. Steve does try—or he seemed to in the past. He said he wanted to be involved in our lives. I don't know. We found him to be too nosy and too syrupy, if you get my drift. He dotes on Claire ... for better ... or worse." She wrinkled her nose and shrugged, but after a moment's thought, her face contorted into a knitted brow. Her dimples disappeared. After a slight pause, she said, "One of the reasons we thought he was so...um...*icky* was because of something that happened during choir practice. It was not too long after he asked to be the music director—before the big promotion to minister of music."

Kelly leaned in as Sarah told them that she and her mother were in the choir when Steve was a new hire. He felt that some people were giving him a hard time. Sarah suggested that he might have been scared he would lose his job because he read a letter out loud to the whole choir from one of the older, more influential, more affluent church members that urged the rest of them to support him and his program.

"I was old enough to know something was weird about reading that letter. Other people looked at each other uneasily, embarrassed for him. But I guess it sort of did the trick, at least for a while. I heard later—and this *is* really bad—that the woman who wrote the letter, that is, who he *said* wrote the letter, hadn't. Some people knew—maybe everyone did—but no one said anything to him that I know of. If they did, nothing happened. I don't know if my mother knew. I wish I had said something to her."

Kelly and Zack breathed together and sighed.

Zack said, "Wow."

When Sarah excused herself to go to the bathroom, Zack and Kelly whispered, but they didn't want to say too much. They needed time to process what they had heard.

When Sarah returned, she talked about the family in a much more nonchalant manner, spouting information about her sisters, Steve's sons, and Steve's ice cream business. She hadn't kept close tabs with the boys, but she knew that one had moved closer to Steve and Sue. One still lived in the Knoxville area with his mother and stepfather. Sarah's older sister used to live outside of Atlanta, but she had moved from there to New York about three or four years back. She talked about her grandparents—both sets—still living in town and how nice it was that she still had all four grandparents, all reasonably healthy. Her mother, more often now without Claire, came once in a while to visit her parents. But none of them would travel to Littleton to visit Sue. Sarah wasn't sure how her grandparents felt about Steve since no one talked about it, but she didn't think they had been thrilled when he inserted himself into their lives.

After more cheese, crackers, wine, and a discussion about a new movie and who should run for president, they were quite enjoying themselves. Bonding over sarcasm and common interests, they spent the rest of the evening in mostly light conversation.

Kelly and Zack left at a reasonable hour in a burst of laughter. Walking to the car, Kelly stumbled, perhaps the effect of too much wine, and Zack caught her arm. She didn't resist the help.

In the car, she teased him about not being professional enough to resist Sarah's obvious flirting.

He bucked and said, "And you, Miss Trippy, were completely professional?"

"She wasn't coming on to me." Kelly heard the slightly acid tone in her voice and knew she had gone too far.

Zack raised his eyebrows and grinned, which irritated the heck out of her.

Kelly was on the phone with her parents on a Sunday morning in September when her father said, "So how is the story going? Have you found out anything more? Or have you lost interest with the trial still pending?"

"Dad, it's still on the stove, and I stir the soup and taste it every so often, but I have other projects and stuff to work on. I haven't forgotten it, but there's nothing much new."

Mom asked, "Have you learned anything more about all the people involved?"

*That* question again. "Yeah, there've been some interesting developments. I'm not completely sure how it's all going to fit together or if it ever will."

"Sounds complicated," Mom began.

Dad added, "That minister sounded interesting … from what you'd been saying."

*Why did Dad mention Mr. Anderson?* Kelly said, "Yes, very."

"Have you been able to speak with the guy who was arrested? Has he given an interview?" Dad asked.

"No luck there. His lawyer has kept him on a tight leash and is sworn to silence. The only statement he made was something about doing what he needed to do, that his actions were entirely appropriate."

"Really? A man was killed. Another injured. A church disrupted."

"Hell, that church was disrupted long before the shooting. But when he made his statement, Jonah Spencer appeared genuinely sad, terribly upset, and remorseful that he had *accidentally* killed someone. He seemed to be beating himself up for that—though not for having a gun there in the first place. He thought the gun was justified and necessary."

Mom said, "If I know you—and I think I do—you'll find a way to meet him and get more. But what else is going on in your life?"

Kelly did not want to discuss her social life with her parents as much as she knew they wanted her to have one and to be happy. She didn't think she would ever be happy enough for them. It was better not to say much rather than to disappoint them. "Oh, you know, dinners with friends, a party or two, movies, business and charity events. I go out quite a lot if that's what you're worried about. I keep busy."

"Good. We want to know you're getting out. You've been through a lot."

Kelly appreciated her mother's empathy, but she really didn't want to listen to it. "I've got another call. I love you." She hit the end-call key and breathed deeply.

Coincidentally, her phone did ring an instant later. Jonah's attorney told her that Jonah wanted to talk to her—and only to her. He insisted on being present himself. She would be allowed an interview as long as it didn't go public until she was given authorization. Though the lawyer knew Kelly was working on a human-interest story that was related to the shooting and trial, he was certain that she could not have uncovered anything relevant that he didn't already know. Allowing Jonah to speak had only to do with him wanting his truth to be known.

She made no promise about the content of her report, but she signed an agreement that she would wait for permission to air anything. They met in a private, windowless conference room well after working hours to avoid any chance of rumors circulating.

As Kelly entered the conference room, she saw a large, clean-shaven young man, sitting with his head bowed. When he looked up, she caught an expression that seemed to signal self-assurance. He was dressed neatly in jeans and a jacket with a T-shirt underneath and sported a new pair of Adidas sneakers.

As she reached to shake hands, Jonah stood and gave her a big bear hug. "I have nothing to hide and have always been willing to talk with the press—or anyone for that matter. But my lawyer has advised me against it. I've been without my church family, and I miss them. I have my parents and sisters and brothers and my significant other and some other friends, but I don't—and can't—talk to them about everything that happened at the church."

Kelly said, "What can you share with me?"

"I'm so grateful to be alive, but I'm in deep distress about Sam and his family. I never meant for anyone to get hurt—not even Kyle—if I had a choice. I never hurt anyone in my life before."

"But you had a gun. Why?"

"I had to protect my family, my church family. I needed to watch out for them. Steve was so scared. We were warned that something terrible could happen, might very well happen, on that Sunday. I knew that Kyle was dangerous. I knew he had guns, and I knew he had anger-management issues. He was obviously angry that day."

As Kelly suspected, Jonah was one of Steve Anderson's worshipers who trusted and believed in him. She thought there was more to it, though.

Jonah said, "My parents are good Christians, devout. I respect everyone. I was brought up with love and devotion. I don't have an unkind bone in my body. I harbor no negative judgments or grudges. Ask anyone who knows me. Ask anyone at church. I sometimes ask for help through prayer when things aren't going well: when my truck breaks down, when I have no money, or when I get sick. I accept whatever help I get from wherever it comes. People have been good to me; they lend me money sometimes or buy me dinner on occasion. I have no complaints."

Kelly wanted to know more about his relationship with Steve. Was he just a choir member, a devotee, or was there more to it? Why did he feel the need to protect Steve? Part of the agreement had been no *grilling*—just allow Jonah to talk—and talk he did. Kelly was anxious to get more details. She sat patiently and waited.

Jonah appeared serene and said, "I know Steve loves me and will testify on my behalf, and then this nightmare will be over. I've tried to attend church on and off this past year, but I'm not allowed to talk about what happened. It's very difficult to be there. It's been frustrating to listen to speculation and not be able to comment. Also, they don't want me upsetting the new members. So mostly I've stayed away."

Kelly made a consoling noise.

Jonah said, "I hear that the court of public opinion is not really against me. If anything, it seems people are upset that something like this could happen in a church. I am too. At least no one is calling me a lunatic. I heard a few theories about a right-wing fringe element. That's just nonsense. Anyone who knows me knows that's not the case. That's just extrapolating because I went to that Christian mission boarding school in Texas. Though I disagree with their philosophy and methodology now, they're nice people who mean well. I don't happen to like proselytizing. I believe people should be able to think and decide for themselves what they want to believe—or don't believe. All that I'm allowed to say about *that* Sunday is I believe in my heart of hearts I did the right thing, the best thing, the only thing that I could have done to protect Steve and the church. When you have knowledge that something terrible is about to happen, it's your responsibility to do everything you can to stop it, right? When you love someone, you have an obligation and a desire to protect the ones you love. I believe in taking personal responsibility."

She gleaned that Jonah had more than an inkling that something bad would happen on the day he fired his gun. *What had he heard that led him to believe his family was in imminent danger? Family? How close did he really feel to people there? And to Steve? Fear is a powerful motivator.*

"I'll take the stand in my own defense if I have anything to say about it." He looked directly at his attorney with determination. "You know how lawyers are. They never think that's a good idea, but I'm not hiding anything. I believe in the goodness of people. The jury will see that I'm not a menace to society. I acted in accord with my conscience, within my rights to defend. I took precautions well within my legal rights. Kyle had threatened Steve, and by virtue of that, he threatened the church as well. He had posted something on Facebook that implied his crazy intentions."

Kelly raised her brows in surprise.

He continued, "There was a cartoon of a man saying, 'Enough is enough,' and he was pointing a popgun at his boss. The caption read, 'This is how I feel after a day at work.' Kyle posted a comment comparing that to how he felt about church meetings. Joke? Maybe, but George Bernard Shaw said, 'When a thing is funny, search it carefully for a hidden truth.' Steve was terrified. Kyle was an angry man with guns who had made implicit threats, and there was no telling when he'd erupt."

Kelly wanted to ask Jonah what prompted him to choose that particular moment to pull out his gun—and why he was so frightened right then—but the lawyer put an end to the discussion. She didn't know what to make of it all.

# Chapter 30

## February and March 2013

Working out some details before the trial, Kelly gave Will Marlborough a call. He was surprised, but thought there was nothing to lose by speaking with her again, given that her show might be interesting. The most important things, he believed, was for justice to be done and the truth to be known.

He and Sheryl were relieved when *some* people stopped attending Steve's services, including Amanda, Glenn, and Kyle. In the meantime, the church had grown again. People who knew nothing about the incident arrived each week to partake of the love and musical entertainment. Will remained in the thick of it.

When Will saw Amanda or Glenn in town, he crossed the street or ducked into a store to avoid them. Once, at a concert he watched them walk in, stared long enough for them to see him, and then turned to talk with the others in his party. Another time, he made a hasty exit from a wedding they all attended at the church, staying only to turn pages for Steve while he played the piano during the service. Dinny was the only other remaining singer of the original Minstrels, but Will had found some replacements for the defectors.

Kelly assured Will she would not ask about the trial per se, having heard he would probably be called as a witness, but she wanted to know how he felt about everything nearly a year after the shooting.

Will was pleased that his voice would be heard on a TV program. He said, "I really don't want to see Whitman in court. I can't stand the idea of being in the same room with him. There is no doubt in my mind that Jonah was defending Steve and the rest of us. I sure hope they don't drag Steve through the mud, though. I don't know how he could endure any more."

Kelly asked Will to elaborate on his view of guns and gun violence.

He replied, "I'm completely against guns. I think SCOTUS was dead wrong in the last interpretation of the second amendment. It happens. Someday it will be revisited. Regardless of the law, the research and evidence suggest very few are any safer with a gun. They only *think* they are. In actuality, the gun they own is more likely to be stolen, used accidentally, used impulsively, or never used. Imagine running to your locked gun cabinet when an intruder comes in your house: 'Excuse me, sir, while I get my gun.'" He laughed heartily at his own sarcasm. "Or if you had one loaded and the intruder was your son ... or the intruder sees you with it and shoots first. It's unpredictable. Look at what happened here."

Kelly couldn't resist the challenge. "But you seemed to be all right with the idea that Jonah had a right to defend Steve and the community. He had a gun."

"I can't put it together. I wish he hadn't chosen to use a gun. But he *was* trying to defend us from a lunatic, and there was no telling what that lunatic could have done. It's true. That's why I called the police a few days earlier, but it didn't do any good."

Kelly had also hoped to meet with Sue Anderson prior to the trial. Sarah said she would try to introduce them, but it didn't happen—not that she hadn't tried. Everyone seemed to accept that Steve needed to shield Sue and Claire, but no one said from what.

A year after the shooting, Steve was still the minister at TLC. During the maelstrom that had followed the incident, the new board felt they needed Steve's steady presence and didn't have the wherewithal to engage in a search for a new minister. He, somewhat modestly, had agreed to one more year of double duty for the sake of the community, sacrificing his own work-life balance. He also had admitted that since there was a new board of trustees, and Kyle was no longer on it, the pressures he had felt a year before had substantially dissipated.

Steve agreed to another meeting with Kelly, albeit a brief one. This was shortly after he made a "no comment" comment when asked about Jonah's defense by Kelly's colleagues in the press. She was invited to come to the church.

Steve greeted Kelly cordially. He ushered her to a chair and remained standing, pale lips tight, arms crossed. "I'm not getting involved in the trial. As I told the attorney, there is nothing I have to say." He sat down and sadly uttered, "I wish the best for Jonah. I hope he survives this ordeal. I will counsel him as his pastor if requested, but our new church board suggested I stay away. We have to think about the church itself. After the incident last year, we lost a number of members, and new ones were scared to attend service. But recently numbers are up, and the joy has returned."

Kelly was stunned by what Steve said, given that just a few months back Jonah had been completely confident that Steve loved him and would surely testify on his behalf.

Steve said, "They said Jonah is claiming he was defending his family—me, specifically. Of course we are all family here. It could be a good defense. I hope so for his sake. But I will not be on the witness stand, unless they subpoena me, which they won't. No reason to. I have nothing to say that will help him. It's such a shame, what happened. A tragedy. But we do need to move on."

Kelly's shock factor doubled. *Is he completely distancing himself? He could be a hero if he testified for Jonah. Jonah adored him. He knew that. He cultivated it. Wouldn't the church community want that as well? Had they all forsaken Jonah?* Then she recalled the psychological abstracts she had read. "What happened just before the shooting? Why do you think Jonah brought a gun that day?"

Steve's arched eyebrows suggested surprise, and his normally fixed half-grin instantly changed to a frown. "I can't say. I've always maintained that Kyle is a bully. I'm not going to say I'm sorry that Kyle is no longer attending this church. But as for Jonah, he surprised me. I guess you never know if someone will blow something out of proportion or misconstrue what they hear. I'm not going to elaborate. I need to keep good counsel. I don't want to say anything that could hurt Jonah."

"What could you possibly say that would jeopardize Jonah's case? Aren't you worried that without your corroborating statements, he could be seen as having made up the whole story?"

"I agreed to talk to you so we could be clear about my role and obligations. I said no comment the other day, and I won't make a comment publicly, though I want you to understand—for your article or book or TV show, whatever it is you're working on—that *I still* take responsibility for this beloved church community. It is my top priority, aside from my family, of course. I'm doing my best to stay out of the limelight and continue doing good work to develop this amazing place."

Kelly said, "I heard so much about your wife and daughter. I was wondering how they have weathered this storm? How are they doing now?"

Steve sat up straight, making sure he enunciated every word. His condescending half-grin was still plastered on his face. "I understand that some people are questioning why my sweet wife hasn't been at church lately. To be clear, she doesn't have any information about the shooting. She has a full-time job and is very busy. Claire is occupied with her dance performances and her friends. Before you ask, let me tell you that Sue will not be talking to anyone. There is no reason for her to. She wasn't there at the church that day, and she has nothing to do with what happened."

---

After putting that distasteful conversation aside, Kelly was determined, more than ever, to have that long-delayed meeting with the *ex*-Mrs. Anderson. She had checked into Steve's undergraduate school records and sought information about his life before college. Other than some scant school reports, nothing much emerged. She knew he had married Ellen Fields during grad school. She presumed that Ellen knew more about Steve's early life, and she might be willing to talk candidly.

Kelly called her, and they agreed to get together rather than having an extended phone conversation. Since they'd meet over the weekend, Zack was free to make the trip as well.

On the flight to Knoxville, Kelly and Zack had time to discuss the initial phone conversation with Ellen and how they would proceed. They also talked about the trial and agreed that if Jonah were claiming stand-your-ground and protection of family, he would likely benefit from corroboration. If Steve would not testify that he told Jonah he was in harm's way, then who would?

In Knoxville, they freshened up and waited in the hotel lobby for Ellen. They had agreed it would be better to meet at a hotel than in her home with potentially nosy neighbors. Ellen would tell her sons more about their father when the time was right. Up to this point, the boys still thought of Steve as a good dad. They had no idea Ellen had to fight for child support, and they had no idea about the rest of it.

Ellen was a chunky, muscular woman with a plain face marked by bad skin, a wide nose, and small eyes. Her thick lenses were set in old-fashioned granny glasses. She appeared resigned to telling the truth, circumspect yet frank. Kelly asked Zack to remain in the room to mitigate bias and provide perspective. He sat quietly in the corner. Ellen did not seem to be bothered by the video camera.

Steve and Ellen had met in college as undergrads. They were in the same music program and then went to grad school together. They got married the year after they got their master's degrees and were married for almost twenty years, but their marriage had never been smooth.

One of their first major fights had occurred about a year after graduation when Ellen, Steve, and another friend were applying for jobs. They had all majored in performance with organ music as a specialty. Other than in churches, there were few job opportunities for organists. They had trained to be concert performers, and working on Sundays seemed beneath them, not to mention the poor pay. Ellen believed she needed teaching credentials to become gainfully employed and started taking courses in choral and instrumental education. She continued to write music and perform when she could, but Steve insisted that he was better than that and deserved more. He didn't want to be *just* a teacher. He enrolled in a doctoral program, confident that he would be a world-renowned composer and a solo artist. She was never sure why he thought the organ would be a better solo instrument than piano, but he was set on the organ, citing his history of playing in churches.

Ellen had picked up his résumé one day and saw that he had changed his degree title. Instead of writing, "MA in music performance, specialty organ and composition," he had added "liturgical." It was not a big change, but she wondered why he did it. In addition, he had inflated his precollege accompaniment experience and made his work sound more like he was a professional performer and an expert in religious music. They fought over the minor lies but, in the end, it didn't matter to Ellen since nothing came of it. Steve tried to convince her that their friend had done the same thing and that it was fine since everyone "adjusted" credentials to look more attractive to employers. In any case, he said he *was* an expert in church music.

"The previous summer, we traveled to Europe with a professor and some other music students. A few of us had been told that we could sit for a minute and play the beautiful ancient instruments in some of the cathedrals we were visiting." She snorted as she recalled that time in her past. "After that, Steve started telling people that 'they'—and then later just 'he'—had been invited to play the most celebrated church organs of Europe. It actually was a bit of an inside joke at the time, and I didn't think a whole lot more about it."

Kelly asked, "How did Steve pay for school?"

"As an undergrad, he had a partial academic scholarship—he was very smart—but not a music scholarship. He had a work-study opportunity and opted for a library job. He read a lot and researched a lot, and it was perfect for him. But grad school required a small loan and working on the side. Steve had a few odd jobs—he was even on a cleaning crew at one point—but mostly he played the organ in churches on Sundays and holidays and whenever else he could. He was a hired accompanist, taking direction from choir directors and ministers."

"What about synagogues?" Some interviewees had specifically said that Steve played in them, presumably verifying his broad religious worldview.

Ellen chortled and replied, "No, that wouldn't have been likely. First of all, there were hardly any synagogues where we lived or where he grew up. Second, most Jewish services do not use instrumentalists— certainly not an organist and rarely a pianist." Kelly knocked herself on the forehead with the heel of her hand. Ellen continued, "Steve was always resentful of the guys who had sports scholarships. He liked to think of himself as a talented quarterback, and he often talked about his younger days playing football and baseball. But with hands meant to play piano and organ, he could not indulge. I barely ever saw him toss a ball with friends or the boys."

Ellen did not know a good deal about Steve's life prior to college. While she had asked questions like any young woman in love would, he was reticent to talk about it. She had met his mother only once, at their wedding. She died shortly after that. Ellen had not gone to the funeral at Steve's insistence. Steve had some difficult times early on, and his father died young. She had reasoned that their relationship was not good since Steve never waxed nostalgic or claimed to miss his parents.

"All conversation about family was truncated. He had only a couple of pictures of himself as a boy, which he brought back after his mother's funeral." He had told her he cleaned up his mother's house, made a few donations, and threw just about everything else away. She added, "The only thing I saw him bring back was a small box that he said contained his childhood memories. He hid it somewhere. I never saw it again.

"Steve had an older sister, but they had little in common. His sister had moved away from their hometown when he was twelve or so, shortly after his father died. I never learned what caused his father's death. I thought it was a heart attack since it was unexpected, but it might have been an accident. It was one of those open-ended issues that never seemed worth upsetting Steve about. Once, I asked Steve about his father's health after a congenital heart murmur was heard in a routine exam of one of our sons. Steve was a little evasive, but he conceded his father might have had one. However, since the doctors didn't seem concerned about it, I didn't pursue it. What would it matter if Craig had inherited it from Steve's father?"

Ellen elaborated on her growing distrust of Steve. Over the years, she contemplated divorcing him several times. She even filed once a couple of years before their actual divorce, but he had convinced her to stay together for the kids. In actuality, she thought he needed her more than she or the boys needed him. She was the one with the steady income and health insurance. But since he did contribute something to the household income, it would have been harder for her to manage financially without him. She also felt it would be better for her relationship with her sons not to abandon their father. She never wanted to make him look bad in their eyes. When she withdrew the divorce petition, they reconciled in the eyes of the law. But their relationship was unhealthy. They fought a lot. The more independent she became, the angrier he got. They never had a satisfactory sex life, although Steve liked to think they did.

"Steve always made major decisions about the boys and how they would live, in spite of my financial contributions. At first, I assumed it was a sign of his devotion, but he got more persnickety about the boys as time went on. He insisted that their room had to be cleaned by ten on Saturday mornings. They had to practice their piano lesson before leaving the house with no negotiable options. They were not allowed to talk to friends—male or female—on weeknights. As my confidence, self-esteem, and income grew, I became less and less tolerant of living the way he dictated. Even so, it was not until his affair with Sue that we actually separated. It was embarrassing that he was having an affair with a member the church where he was employed."

Kelly said, "I heard that you left Steve for a woman."

Ellen sighed heavily. "That sounds like Steve. Doesn't surprise me at all. It's hard for him to see his own culpability. He likes to evoke pity when he's not being the hero. Truth be told, I was ultimately relieved of the burden of having to deal with his control issues. Trying to figure him out was exhausting. Then came the problem of child support. He paid at first and then gradually less and less and finally nothing."

His delinquency had gotten Ellen's dander up not only because of the financial pressure she felt but also because of the hypocrisy. She said, "All the claims he made about fatherhood being sacred, all the accolades he sought for being a perfect father."

Kelly asked, "Wasn't he a good father?"

"To the public, Steve looked fatherly. He coached Little League, gave his kids piano lessons, and was there for every performance. What people didn't see was that he was constantly frustrated that his sons weren't chosen MVP. He resented that they didn't seek, nor were they asked, to be in the school talent shows. When he tutored them, they balked. Steve gritted his teeth and pushed harder. Although he appeared to be a man who treasured all young people, he really wasn't. It took a lot out of him to be around kids. He was a bad teacher in general, and he lacked the patience required to teach his own children. Though he stressed the importance of kids having fun all the time—and most of the parents believed he was sincere—quite a few observed his scowl when he perceived a bad call, when a kid made an error, or someone didn't come through in the clutch. He sure didn't like it when they didn't win. Only one mother called Steve on it as far as I know."

Kelly asked, "What was his reaction to that?"

"Not good. He stared at her and clenched and then unclenched his fists."

"Did anything else happen?"

Ellen said, "He recovered and didn't do anything, but his facial expression didn't soften for quite a while. I believe the children loved their father, but they were not especially close with him—even as young adults. I saw a difference between how they were with their stepdad versus their father. They were so much more genuine and relaxed. When I first heard about the shooting in Littleton, I had no idea that Steve had acquired the credentials to be a minister. It's not inconceivable that he exaggerated his earlier church experiences in the same way he joked about playing all the cathedrals of Europe. In his mind, it could have morphed into the truth."

In the next moment, Ellen became conscious of the possibility that Steve was closer to the shooting than it appeared to everyone. She began to shake and cry.

Kelly said, "You are the ex-wife who was wronged. It wouldn't be unusual for you to think the worst."

Ellen nodded, sniffled, and gulped back a sob. "What if Steve has a bad gene and passed it along to my sons?"

Off the record, Kelly suggested that Ellen talk to some psychologists and doctors about the risk of passing along a bad gene. She shared that in her research about narcissistic personality disorder, she had found that more often than genetics, there had been pathology; that is, trauma was the source. But she also had to acknowledge that both could be contributing factors. Not much was known.

The videotaping ended comfortably enough, and Zack and Kelly went to the hotel bar to celebrate a successful day.

Sitting next to Zack, Kelly thought about her own heart murmur.

***

Jonah fervently believed Steve would be there for him right up until a week before the trial. When his lawyers told him that Steve would not be called to the stand since he would not corroborate the story, Jonah insisted on speaking directly to Steve.

He called upon his minister for a confidential talk. Jonah had assumed the lawyers were not savvy enough to present the request in the right context. He knew that they didn't have the personal relationship he had. Jonah understood Steve. He grasped the magnitude of Steve's sense of privacy and respected it. He also knew Steve felt a noble calling to protect the church and his family from negative publicity. Nevertheless, he knew that Steve loved him, and since he held the key to his defense, he would ultimately do the right thing.

Jonah was wrong. When they met, Steve looked him in the eye, brought forth a tear, and said, "You must have misunderstood. I am so sorry, so very sorry you interpreted what I said in the wrong way. Yes, I was upset. But I never meant to imply that I needed physical protection."

Jonah protested patiently, softly, and sincerely. "Steve, I did it for you. You were so worried. You said you needed to watch your back. Those were your words. You reminded me that Kyle had guns. Remember the joke Kyle posted on Facebook? It worried you."

Steve only shook his head and said, "I'm sorry. I don't remember any joke."

"The cartoon! I showed it to Will and to you. The one with a gun?"

"Oh. That."

"You asked us to 'stay vigilant.' You told us—and me when we were alone—that he was dangerous. Steve, I was scared for you. I wanted to protect you. You know that."

Steve shifted his position, looked down, and thought for a moment. "I was worried about my job and was talking about watching my back in that regard. Oh, Jonah, my friend, I believe what I said was 'some people advised me to watch my back.' I admit I did think my job was in jeopardy with good reason. I meant for you to be vigilant in terms of faith."

Steve offered Jonah moral support, but he could not take the stand and swear on a Bible that he said he was in "physical danger." He had to be honest. He didn't want to damage Jonah's defense.

Jonah was devastated. He was hurt, and he was angry. He was angry with himself for misinterpreting what Steve had said. He wept minutes after Steve left, feeling shame and incredible remorse for the havoc he wreaked—and the lives he destroyed.

But he was certain there was something else that he could not have made up.

# Chapter 31

**April 2013**

Kelly and Zack attended the trial together. No one denied that Jonah had the gun and fired it. The question was whether he had the right to—whether there was clear and present danger or a legitimate reason to believe there was.

There were several character witnesses for the defense, a couple of psychologists to discuss state of mind, and legal experts there to interpret the law. It was left to Will to support Jonah's interpretation of "imminent danger." And there was Jonah himself. His lawyers had agreed to put him on the stand.

The two journalists took copious notes on what was said and wrote detailed observations of the reactions. Many of the TLC folks were there the first day. The next day, the "church crowd" had dwindled to Amanda and Kyle, their spouses, and Rachel, Sam's widow. Sheila came in whenever she could get away from work. Dinny attended the opening statements but didn't return until the last day.

The prosecution presented its case. In addition to the testimony of the technical and forensic experts and the detectives, Kyle gave his testimony, answering questions concisely, as he had been prepped to do. While somber and terse, he made a fairly sympathetic victim. He could not say what prompted Jonah to fear him or attack him at that particular moment. He remembered being in pain just after he rose to speak.

The defense was able to bring out the fact that Kyle was a registered gun owner and owned guns. However, when the detective had been called to the stand, he made it clear that the only fingerprints on the weapon used were Jonah's and his brother-in-law's. The prosecutor made sure the jury heard that at least twice. There was no tussle. It was also indisputable that at no time did Kyle reach for a gun of his own and with good reason: he did not have one there.

Kelly processed the facts quickly. Kyle had never touched the gun. Jonah did not wrest it back from him. Kyle had not posed an imminent threat by virtue of a weapon, so it was up to the defense to mount a case for self-defense, showing that Jonah had reason to have feared for his or Steve's life for some other reason. Then again, the burden to prove intent was on the prosecution. They presented facts about Jonah's gun lessons and borrowing the gun just prior to the shooting.

Although flushed and bothered when the defense attorney tried to badger Kyle into admitting how much he hated Steve and how angry he was, Kyle made it clear that at no time did he threaten or consider physically hurting anyone.

Will's testimony for the defense reasonably supported Jonah's case. He adequately reinforced Jonah's interpretation that Kyle was dangerous. He was able to mention Kyle's "thinly veiled threats" on Facebook and elsewhere. He also swore that he interpreted Steve's comments the same way Jonah did. However, upon cross-examination, his testimony lost strength when he could not say for sure that Jonah's and his interpretations of Steve's comments were the *only* way they could have been understood. He had to admit that what was seen on Facebook was a cartoon—and Kyle's comment didn't mention Steve or anyone else. He was also compelled to say he was biased because of the way he felt about Kyle and Steve. He ended up saying it was possible that Steve had not meant to imply he felt physically threatened and that perhaps Jonah had literally jumped the gun.

Experts on, and supporters of, the stand-your-ground law made it clear that Jonah did everything by the book. The gun was legal. There had been a background check when the purchase was made. He had not stolen the gun. While this testimony spoke to the legitimacy of the gun and supplied some evidence of the degree to which Jonah was afraid and also acting responsibly, it also served to remind the jury of premeditation, something the prosecution again elicited.

Trying to make the case for imminent danger, the defense team introduced information about Kyle's behavior prior to the shooting. Witnesses had reported seeing Kyle get up, knowing he was angry, and hearing him groan. Several said they saw him reach toward his bag, corroborating Jonah's view of what occurred moments before he fired. They tried to suggest that this extreme agitation was out of the ordinary and that Jonah would have had reason to believe Kyle was going for a weapon. The DA had them admitting anything could have been in his satchel, even a cough drop. Of course, it had already been stated that there was only one gun on the premises: the one Jonah carried.

Jonah made a good, honest witness for himself. He came across as sincere and repentant about what had happened, but he held firm to his conviction that he was protecting his church family and had a right to do so. In cross-examination, he had to admit that he *could* have misinterpreted the extent to which Steve was scared or what he was scared about. Jonah's attorney created a scenario that had Kyle manipulating it from the start, goading Steve into fearing for his life and asking for protection. The argument was rather sketchy at best, but it was accepted into the transcript. Doubt.

When Kyle was called back to the stand it was revealed that he had been having trouble with acid reflux, which caused him both angst and pain. He testified that he carried medicine all the time and that a flare-up caused him to start for his satchel. The DA established that Kyle was an innocent victim.

The sad thing, Zack and Kelly both agreed, was that Jonah appeared rather benign as well.

It would be up to the jury to decide. From Kelly's point of view, it did not look promising for Jonah. She still ruminated about the gun. He had not owned and presumably never used one before, given the timing of his lessons. He hadn't appeared irrational or desperate. In fact, the defense team had done a very good job of demonstrating his gentle nature. It always came down to guns. If there hadn't been one, no one would be dead. Hurt maybe. Maybe there would have been a scuffle—but probably no more than a shouting match.

After the break, the defense attorney took advantage of his right to recall Jonah to the witness stand. Between sessions, Jonah had told his attorney something new.

On the stand, as his attorney carefully put the questions to him, Jonah said, "I only had in mind to protect Steve."

"Please tell the court what you told me during the break."

The attorneys for both sides had already met in the judge's chambers about the new information being presented, and Judge Renaud allowed this addition to Jonah's previous testimony with no objection from the DA.

The lawyer repeated his request, and Jonah continued, "On the day of the shooting, Steve, our minister, said to me that he would signal me if he saw anything unusual, anything that suggested that Kyle was about to do something dangerous—if he saw Kyle's weapon. Steve had panicked the minute he saw Kyle enter the church that day. That's why he called me aside before the service."

"Please continue, Jonah. What happened after the service began?"

"Everyone saw Kyle rise when the invitation for sharing was announced. I had my eyes on him and on Steve. I was sitting close to him. I needed to know that Steve felt safe. Kyle turned back toward his seat and reached for his bag. Steve's face was beet red. He put his hand up to his forehead and rubbed the corner of his left eye. It was very deliberate."

"What did that signify to you, Jonah?"

"I understood, at that moment, that Steve *knew* Kyle was going for his gun."

"Objection!"

"Sustained."

The lawyer said, "We have already established that Kyle did not have a gun. But did you believe that Reverend Anderson had seen a gun either then or earlier?"

"Yes, sir. I did think that."

"Tell the court why."

"Sir, he told me that Kyle owned guns. Steve said someone would check his bag when he entered the church."

"Do you know who checked the bag?"

"I do not."

"But you believed it was checked?"

"Yes."

"Whether or not it was, you assumed there was a gun in the bag since no one told you otherwise."

Jonah nodded.

"What made you so certain that Kyle was a dangerous individual?"

"We knew Kyle had a license and permit to carry—and that he could not be trusted. We knew he had threatened and intimidated Steve. We *knew* Kyle is not balanced emotionally."

"How did you know all that?"

"Steve told us."

"Your trusted minister."

"Yes, sir."

"You also believed that Reverend Anderson, the very popular—some might say 'adored' minister at TLC, *your* minister, was sending you a signal of imminent danger?"

"Yes, sir. That's when I pulled my gun out. I was certain at that moment that Kyle had one in his bag. Steve had verified it with his signal."

"Was there a predetermined signal?"

"No, sir. He just said, 'Watch me. You'll know.'"

"By *he*, you mean the Reverend Steve Anderson?"

"Yes, sir."

"Were there other church members who had been privy to this warning, this conversation?"

"I don't believe so. But there were others who knew how frightened Steve was."

"Yes, we have heard their testimony. Why do you think he confided only in you about the gun?"

"Objection! Asking for opinion," the DA interjected.

Judge Renaud answered, "Sustained. Rephrase, counselor."

"Were you specifically selected to protect him?"

"I believe so. I was close to him. He told me that he trusted me above all others."

"Did Steve know you had a gun?"

"I told him I could get one if he thought I should."

"One more question. Do you know why Reverend Anderson has not testified on your behalf?

"No, sir. I don't. Not for sure."

During the brief recross, the DA worked in a comment that suggested Reverend Anderson was not there because it never happened the way Jonah described. He was able to get Jonah to admit that he acted alone and no one else knew about his plan.

Kelly and Zack looked at each other. By the line of questioning, they figured the defense was either desperate—or Steve had decided to testify after all.

But it wasn't Steve who walked into the courtroom.

"You may step down," Jonah's attorney said.

"I call Susan Anderson to the stand." There was no objection from the DA, having already accepted the new witness.

When asked why she waited so long to come forward, Sue replied, "I knew Steve would be upset if I testified, but I realized Jonah needs help. I think my husband will understand that although I'm disregarding his wishes, I'm trying to do the right thing. He's a minister. I hope he will forgive me."

The murmur from the crowd grew, and the judge's gavel echoed.

Sue said, "Steve is not as strong as he likes people to believe."

"Why didn't the minister testify on Jonah's behalf?"

"It's my belief that he's afraid he might not do it exactly right. He might say one wrong thing or his words might be misinterpreted. He's afraid he might do more harm than good, afraid the lawyers might twist his words. But *I'm* not."

As the story unfolded, all in attendance learned that Sue knew about what was happening at the church. Steve was very anxious about it all. He insisted that she and Claire keep a distance from the goings-on at the church, so they wouldn't get hurt. Sue did not say a word about Kyle. She said she didn't know him at all.

To illustrate how upset Steve was, she told the jury that his routines had changed. He had curtailed practicing; he got sloppy when performing the few last times she heard him. He repeated the same pieces. That wasn't like him. He stopped rehearsing his sermons at home on Saturday evenings. Instead, he recycled old ones with slight variations and new titles. He had a good formula.

She admitted she hadn't been there when Steve told Jonah and others that they needed to "watch his back." However, she said that he had used those words at home.

The DA said, "I find your statement peculiar."

Sue said, "I am not actually sure Steve was talking to me at the time or if he was just muttering, but I heard him say those exact words. I asked him what was wrong—and he told me not to worry, that he would deal with it. I believed Jonah had a legitimate reason to trust that Steve was scared for his life."

"Why wouldn't Steve come forth?"

She answered, "Steve is a proud man. He has an image and a reputation to uphold. He needs to show he's strong—for the church, for Claire, and for me."

The DA asked, "What do you know about your husband telling Jonah Spencer and others that he felt threatened?"

"I believe he could have told others that."

"*Could have.* But you do not know for sure that he did?"

"No." She looked down, embarrassed. Before she could be stopped, however, she said, "Steve meant for that to be understood. I can't imagine that he was only scared about losing his job. It had to be more than that. He has lost jobs before, and we have managed."

That last part was stricken from the record, but everyone present had heard it.

Sue was very supportive of Steve and said nothing incriminating or even negative, unless being scared was considered negative.

Kelly was glad Sue had come forward of her own accord. It revealed some character. She might have used an even stronger word than character—maybe *fortitude* or *courage*—had Sue not been so obviously protecting her husband's weaknesses. She made Steve sound caring and vulnerable. She put a positive spin on behaviors that might be seen by someone else as self-serving, callous, or worse. Even if it pained Kelly to admit it, she didn't blame the woman. Lots of people would defend the ones they chose to spend their lives with.

From the defense's point of view, Sue's testimony might have helped Jonah a little. Unfortunately, Sue did not witness any conversation between Jonah and Steve. Nevertheless, it left room for doubt, or in this case, validating the argument for the defense.

---

Late that afternoon, Kelly managed to secure an interview with Sue— another exclusive for her program that was scheduled to air in just a few weeks.

In her office, Sue glanced about quickly, looking anywhere but directly at Kelly. Like a small, anxious child, she kicked her legs under the table.

Kelly quickly gained Sue's confidence.

Sue gradually disclosed more information. "You need to know that Steve is a peace-loving man. He has worked his whole life for peace." However, when pressed for examples, all she could offer was a peace march or two that he attended. But Sue added, "He's a vegan for moral reasons—not just health."

Kelly thought Sue seemed defensive, preemptive perhaps. *The lady doth protest too much.*

Sue began, "A few weeks before that Sunday, Steve told me to stop coming to church with Claire. I've learned not to question Steve. When he makes up his mind, it's best to accept what he says. Claire didn't like going anyway. She was becoming a little rebellious, typical teen stuff. She was irritable and ornery in her father's presence, and she resisted when she was asked to bring him his coffee. He did not like that. I understand we have to convey a proper image as the minister's family. I can do it, but Claire is finding it difficult. Steve didn't want any slipups. I'm sure people would understand and be patient if Claire behaved like a teenager—that's the way UUs are—but Steve insists on not taking any chances. It's important to him that we all look good."

Kelly asked, "What can you tell me about his early life?"

Sue relaxed, stilled her feet, and sighed. "I know him as well as anyone, but I don't know everything about him. We met later in life. Steve and I missed the early years together, and it seemed pointless at our ages to review every detail of our past lives. So we haven't. Of course I've asked him a few questions, and occasionally something's mentioned, but given the circumstances of how we met, we agreed not to dwell on or probe into the past. We leave well enough alone."

Kelly asked, "Do you know anything at all about his family?"

Sue said, "I never met his parents. They died long ago. Steve has no other family. Oh, maybe there was a sister. He lost contact with her years ago. She might not even be alive for all I know—or all he knows. He never talks about her. As far as he's concerned, she deserted him and left him with his mother. I think his father had died by then. She was several years older."

Kelly felt an inner pang at the mention of *desertion*.

Not wanting to go too far astray, Kelly worked the conversation back to the shooting and the church.

Sue said, "I could tell something was really bothering him. He's better when he has a set routine, when he can count on things being the way he plans them. He likes to act spontaneous, especially when he tells jokes, but he isn't. He likes a clean house, everything in its place. Claire and I are the sloppy ones. He's not happy with that, but he cleans up after us. In church, it doesn't look like he cares. He leaves coffee cups all over, but I guess he does that to fit in. They're more casual there."

Kelly wanted to know how much Sue knew about the degree and the diploma, having considered the possibility that Sue had helped him create the imitation. "Why did he request his old position and step down as minister?"

"Oh, he said he was tired, overworked, and under too much pressure. He did get his résumé out, but I don't think he ever sent it anywhere. I saw it around the same time I saw his old diploma. I had never seen that before, but as I said, I am not the organizer or cleaner."

"When was that? Approximately?"

"It was in the summer, I remember that. Probably eight or nine months before the shooting." Sue spoke naturally and without guile.

Kelly surmised that Sue was not aware of any of the details of the forgery. *Blinders,* she thought.

With no prompting, Sue began to talk freely about Steve, kind of dreamily. "He's sensitive, an artist who needs the freedom and time to create. He's a good husband and father. He and Claire have always been very close. It's fine that he's Claire's primary caretaker." Her tone changed only slightly when she added, "The only thing that bothers me about it—just a little—is that because he plans her life down to the minute, I have to ask him if it's okay when I want to do something that's not part of his plan. But it's not a big deal. Once I came home later than expected, and he let me know that wasn't acceptable." Realizing how that might sound, she added, "He was worried. I haven't done that again. No need to cause Steve concern. I'm not sure what's going to happen if Jonah is convicted. I think Steve is praying a lot. He prays when he feels that he's not able to control something. I guess he was brought up in a formal, traditional church. It's okay. He can pray if he wants." She looked down and twisted her ring. "He doesn't know I agreed to testify or speak with you. I didn't tell him. I'm not sure how he'll react."

Kelly reassured Sue that she could review the statements for the TV program. However, Sue didn't agree to be videotaped, saying she would have to think about that.

Kelly urged her to take care of herself, and they parted company.

Later that afternoon, Kelly summarized what happened with Sue and reviewed the trial with Zack. They could not comprehend how Sue didn't know Steve was not an ordained minister. She had been an active member of Ridgecrest Road Church. It seemed to them she was in denial. They concluded that Sue and Steve had an unhealthy relationship. Of course, they already knew how controlling he was, what it had been like for his first wife, and a lot more. They thought Sue was afraid of him but now considered what he might be capable of. No one had hinted—not even Sarah—at abuse.

*But he was so tightly wound,* Kelly thought.

The assumption was that there would be a verdict by noon the next day. The statisticians and legal pundits lined up the data to be used as content for TV shows like Mary Lovett's and to fill space. They would consider the number of witnesses, how long the trial took, how long it had taken to select the jury, who comprised the jury, the actual defense used, etc. They rolled it all into some statistical analysis that would predict how fast the jury would decide.

Kelly understood this was entertainment and not important news. She objected to the mash-up. Her new program would not be labeled "news," "entertainment," or "reality show," but that would actually have been apt had the term not already been so badly abused. She was not sure what the genre would be, but she insisted that no ad would say, "You won't believe…"

The legal teams for both sides had established that Kelly did not have anything of evidentiary value that could be used to defend or prosecute Jonah, and she had recorded no testimony that directly related to the incident itself. Having heard Jonah's surprise testimony about the signal, she remembered her short phone chat with Manny's friend and wondered if that signal was the nagging detail Lance had been trying to recall. The detective and the attorneys ascertained that he was not decisive enough to give testimony in the court of law. He had not been subpoenaed.

Kelly knew it was entirely possible—and probable—that what Jonah said was true. He had acted on Steve's behalf, and Steve had asked him to protect him, but there had been no evidence that Kyle posed any real danger.

The phone rang. *Zack? How interesting*, Kelly thought. *We already spent some time rehashing this before we went our separate ways. He never calls to just talk. In fact, we rarely just talk. We work together.* She took the call.

"Hey. What's going on? Have you heard something?" she asked him.

"Nope."

There was an impatient pause.

Then she asked, "So?"

"Kelly, have you eaten yet?

"No. Why?"

"Will you have dinner with me?"

"Is there something going on? What's up?"

"Kelly, I'm asking you to dinner."

"A date? You're asking me for a date? Who *does* that anymore? Tonight? Really?"

"You do not make a guy's life easy, do you?"

"Never have. Never will." Pause. Chuckle. "Okay. Where? What time?"

After putting the phone down, she changed into a smart black dress. It was simple, classy, and flattering. It had been her go-to dress for a while, and she felt sexy and glamorous whenever she wore it. She added a new necklace—made in Peru, chunky, and red—and did her makeup. Kelly felt excited, which she had not felt in a long time.

As she put on her heels, adding three and a half inches to her already long legs, she looked in the mirror. She hesitated. *What am I doing? We finally have a good working relationship, and I better not mess it up. He's my boss! Workplace romance is dangerous, even if consensual. Slow down, girl.* Kelly waited for her date to pick her up. Inside, she was eager and anxious. Externally, she adopted the "everything as usual, nothing different, no biggie" attitude.

When Kelly opened her door for Zack, he was nothing short of wowed.

For his part, he had vowed not to date anyone—and certainly not Kelly—for a host of reasons. He respected their work relationship too much. He wasn't quite sure what had compelled him to ask her out. His thoughts turned to his son. He never felt like he had enough time with Justin since the divorce but he was not with him now, having lost a custody battle last year. He had promised himself he would try again. He knew his ex was not evil and would not harm Justin, but he also knew she and her family were flaky. He wanted Justin to have a firm footing. He had asked Kelly to dinner on impulse. He had no ideas at all about their long-term potential, but despite her hardened exterior, he did think she was sensitive and balanced. *And, really, wow, look at her. Looks alone don't suffice, though they don't hurt either. When she isn't on guard, she is a hell of a lot of fun. She has a wicked sense of humor! We've had many good laughs during the last year. And she is so smart. What's her story? Maybe their date would reveal more of it. At the very least, some fun and good conversation would be had—and maybe more.*

---

The next morning, they learned that the jury had finished deliberations and would be announcing a verdict within the hour. Zack and Kelly rushed to the courthouse.

As they entered the courtroom, they were caught off guard when they saw Steve Anderson. He also saw them together. After an initial lift of the eyebrows, his grin transformed into a concerned frown as it dawned on him that the rich prospective church member was somehow connected with the beautiful, snoopy reporter. Kelly saw the look change and tried to fathom what he might be thinking. She didn't really care whether Steve put two and two together. Nevertheless, she strode over and boldly greeted him with her special on-air smile. She introduced Zack by name but not by profession, wanting to keep Steve guessing and uncomfortable.

Zack immediately picked up the cue and said, "The good reverend and I have met. I've attended Steve's church a couple of times. How are you, Steve?"

"Just fine, Zack. Ms. Allen, good to see you. Zack, what brings you here?"

Kelly, quick on the uptake, said, "I was just going to ask you that. I mean, today in particular."

Steve's smarmy smile reappeared. He was back in control. "I wanted to be here for Jonah, of course. I understand that my wife tried her best to help him out. She is a good soul. She meant well, I'm sure."

Kelly said, "Well, it looks like they are about to call to order. The bailiff just walked in. We better sit down."

As Kelly and Zack went toward the bench where they had been sitting each day, Steve walked in a different direction.

*Guilty on all counts!*

The gallery gasped, and a few people shouted, "No!"

Jonah broke down in tears as he scanned the room for Steve, presumably beseeching him for help.

Steve walked over and put his arms around Jonah in a stiff embrace. His expression conveyed his condolences. Kelly could not hear what they said to each other. But when they parted, Steve looked satisfied and Jonah stopped crying. He was led off to await sentencing.

Everyone knew that Jonah would file an appeal, but it was unclear what evidence could be brought to form the basis of a new trial with a different verdict. The state had effectively made the case that Jonah had created the dangerous situation by bringing the weapon to church. Sam's widow and children deserved some satisfaction.

The judge's perceptions and biases might come into play for sentencing. The judge could go lighter on Jonah if she believed there was just cause to have brought the gun to church to protect his family—despite the guilty verdict. On the other hand, if she thought he had no legitimate reason for that particular defense and was taking undue advantage of the stand-your-ground law, she might come down hard. If she did not approve of the law or had an anti-handgun bias, she might be especially tough on Jonah.

As the crowd started down the courthouse steps, a woman stepped forward. A shot rang out.

Steve Anderson hit the ground and wailed, "Why?"

She sank to her knees, tossing the gun aside as the guards surrounded her. "You can't get away with *everything*! It's just not right."

# Chapter 32

Sue was arrested, taken to the local police station and placed on suicide watch. Kelly Allen was the only person aside from her attorney who Sue would talk to.

Kelly asked, "Why did you do it?"

"I had to do something if Jonah was found guilty. I know it wasn't all his fault." Sue seemed in control and aware of what she was saying.

"Where did you get the gun?"

"It's Steve's. He keeps it in a basement cabinet, in a little box marked 'mementos.' He moved it from the old house. Had it forever. He had no idea I knew about it. I'm not as stupid as he thinks."

Kelly's face contorted slightly. "Sue, what did you think shooting him would accomplish?"

"I don't know. I didn't think. I didn't even know he was planning on going to court today. I followed him."

"But you took the gun?"

"I wasn't sure what he might do to me the next time he came home … or to Claire."

"I'm not following."

Sue mechanically rolled up her shirt so Kelly could see the bruises. For the first time, Kelly noticed a cut above Sue's left eye. Her lip was slightly swollen.

"What happened?"

Sue did not answer.

"This isn't the first time?" Kelly asked.

"He always held back. He would clench his fists and walk away. Sometimes a midair slap was held in check. Claire disappointed him last weekend." She swallowed hard, imagining what she thought could have happened. "He's always been careful, but it was getting worse in the last two years with all of this pressure. He never did this before."

*Even now*, Kelly thought, *Sue is defending him*. "Sue, he was losing control?"

"Jonah needed help. Steve wasn't going to help him. He does exactly what he wants to do. He always has. He was so romantic. He swept me off my feet. And then there was Claire." Sue's face shifted from a vapid smile to a sneer. "My daughters knew. They always knew. I should have listened to them, but I wanted my marriage to work. He was coming undone last year and did a number of things he shouldn't have done. He knew it, but he didn't apologize. He never apologizes." Sue was drifting in and out of lucidness.

Kelly tried to bring her back to reality. "Did you suspect him … of anything?"

Sue snapped, "Like what? Oh, an affair? No. Well, he could have, I suppose. After all, if you do it once, it could happen again. Truthfully, I didn't care what he did with anyone else in that way."

Kelly raised her eyes and shifted in her seat.

Sue's eyes went blank, and she tilted her head back, dreamily. "I really thought he loved us."

"I'm sure he did … does."

Another sneer crawled across Sue's face. "No. Steve loves himself."

Kelly scratched her head. "Why the testimony? And what you just told me? Why didn't you tell the truth when you were testifying?"

She grinned, "I didn't *lie*. I have learned a lot from Steve."

Kelly realized that Sue had carefully constructed her story to be truthful in a way that would help Jonah without damaging Steve. Steve's image was so important to him, and Sue knew she had better not hurt it in the public eye—or he would hurt her. She thought she had done a good job on the stand—that he would be satisfied—but he had not been pleased. "I loved him so much. I only wanted to see the best in him. I only wanted to be perfect for him. Claire felt the same way." Sue hardened and said, "He drove her hard. He tried to make it seem like he was an old softy. But he wasn't. He never yelled at her, but the pressure to perform was constant. That look ... she could see when he was disappointed. She's a teenager. She wanted to spend more time with her friends. That irritated him. She knew it."

Kelly asked, "Did you and Steve talk about this?"

"He is so sure of what he's doing all the time." She sighed, and tears ran down her cheeks. "He had to be stopped. God only knows what else he has done. Jonah does not deserve to go to prison for what he did."

Kelly was not sure which *he* she was referring to.

---

A week later, Judge Marcia Renaud gave the maximum prison time allowed by law. She delivered her message with a grave lecture about thinking through the potential consequences of one's actions, jumping to conclusions, and not thoroughly investigating allegations and other options before bringing a gun to a public place, especially a place where people expected peace and to be safe and sheltered. It didn't matter if, presumably, it was for protection.

Jonah bowed his head and nodded.

# Chapter 33

Kelly had gotten endorsement for a series called *Insights*, and advertising space had already begun to be sold. With the dramatic ending to the trial, material for the first show was timely.

Kelly visited Sue several times. After pleading guilty, she had been transferred to a psychiatric prison. She was deeply troubled, and her mental state was precarious.

Jonah's appeal was being planned.

Still, despite the drama and allure of a real court case, Kelly insisted that *Insights* was about people—on an individual level and a group level. The series would investigate the complexities of human dynamics and individual behaviors to help people better understand one another. This first program, "At the Heart of the Matter," would explore the potentially dangerous behavior of a narcissist of the caliber of Steve. She also envisioned it being a vehicle for shining a light on spin versus truth.

Nevertheless, Kelly was still plagued by a feeling that there were pieces of the story missing—not about who Steve Anderson was but about why he was that way. She pursued another source of information.

After her interviews with both wives, it continued to vex her that there was nothing known about Steve prior to college. He had no longtime friends. A sister had been mentioned, but no one knew anything about her. The sister could very well have been one if his inventions, a prop for some story to add a degree of legitimacy or color.

Kelly had taken Zack up on his offer to hire a private investigator, who reported finding a woman named Amelia Lake, née Anderson. Steve's sister was still living in Tennessee, although not in Knoxville and not in Clinton, their hometown.

Zack briefly summarized the report for Kelly: Amelia Lake was a very private person with few friends. Although she had married twice, she had also divorced twice and lived by herself with her three cats. No family visited. She did not belong to any organizations. She appeared not to socialize with coworkers, other than an occasional after-work drink: one glass of wine or a Coke. She was a social worker, a rather nonsocial one. From all reports, her work was beyond reproach, and she had helped many children, which was her focus. This had been her career for more than thirty years, and she was nearing retirement. Interpreting the PI report, it appeared that she was reasonably content with her life. All photos showed her with a genuine smile, especially when she was with her clients and cats. She had no police record, but she appeared in court many times on behalf of "her children."

Kelly went to Nashville alone. She and Zack hadn't gone out socially since the first date. They were gradually relinquishing some of their inhibitions, but they both worried about chemistry overtaking common sense. So they kept a certain distance. Their working relationship was productive and without the tensions that were once there. When he said it was *her* story, he had meant it. It continued to be her story, and she wanted to fill it in by herself. He trusted her to do just that.

In Nashville, Kelly picked up her rental car. On the way to the suburb where Amelia lived and worked, Kelly had time to think about how to approach this woman. She had not called ahead, not wanting to risk rejection.

She played with the idea of accidentally bumping into her and starting a conversation. She pondered the notion of finding some way to get a third-party introduction, much as she had with Sarah. In the end, she felt being straightforward and honest might be best. If they were going to talk, Kelly wanted it to be a frank discussion—no beating around the bush or trying to hide information.

She waited until Amelia was leaving work around six. Kelly eyed the sixty-something woman, willowy and pale. Her steps were secure; her stride was long and almost athletic. Introducing herself by name and TV status, Kelly stated her business and quickly summarized why she wanted to talk. To be able to do that in under a minute was testament to a skill that Kelly had acquired and honed over the years.

After collecting her thoughts, Amelia sighed. "I'm not surprised you're here. I heard about what happened. I guess it *is* time to talk."

To Kelly's astonishment, rather than talking at the diner that Kelly had scouted, Amelia told her they would go back to her house. Her small bungalow was not far away. Directness, sincerity, sensitivity, and a degree of warmth suited both women, and they formed an immediate bond.

Amelia lived in a brick-red-trimmed house with numerous potted plants and flowers on and around the entrance. There was an old wicker rocker with a tattered pillow and cat toys on the porch. Although Kelly had initially felt sorry for the woman, presuming she was lonely, that thought vanished. This was a woman who seemed to have found inner and outer peace. Kelly felt in harmony when entering this home.

The living room had wood floors covered with homemade, hooked area rugs. The sofa was small, cozy, and red. Though it was a plain room with little in the way of décor, it was anything but sterile. Not surprisingly, the only photos were of her cats, past and present. There were small sprays of flowers around the room and one large stunning bouquet of hydrangea in the center of the small oak dining table. There was also a beautiful, hand-painted wooden fireplace screen. Kelly noted initials, A. L., written in a flowery script, in the lower right part of the screen.

Amelia put together a tiny, but sufficient, supper consisting of a fresh vegetable omelet and homemade biscuits. She offered a glass of supermarket wine. Kelly graciously accepted the food, and the conversation proceeded cautiously from both sides. Reluctant to probe into anything personal, Kelly had prepared to ask Amelia only about Steve.

Eventually, Amelia wanted to talk about everything. Tears welled in Amelia's eyes as she spoke of those long-ago memories. She had not thought about Steve in many years since he had been dead to her for a very long time. She described Steve as an intellectually gifted child. His musical talents, however, were developed and refined over time. He had not been what someone might have called a prodigy, but he was a really good student. He learned everything he needed to learn.

Steve was the baby of the family, the second child and a boy, which was especially important to his father. He was a tough, hard-driving man who wanted the best and the most for his family. He had not gone to college, but he was adamant that his son would get ahead. He gradually worked less and less and relied more and more on making it through Steve. While Steve's mother provided piano lessons and musical encouragement for the children, his father planned on Steve getting an athletic scholarship. He thought becoming a professional ballplayer was the quickest way to money.

Amelia explained that she felt she was merely added baggage in the family. Their father rode Steve hard, trained him, and pushed him, but most of the time he discounted Amelia. He scoffed at Steve's interest in music, yet he applied pressure on Steve to be the best at it—and be the best at everything. Amelia wanted to be close to Steve and felt sorry for him. She also felt a huge sense of responsibility, but he never seemed to appreciate anything she did for him.

Kelly asked about his sports activities, again remembering the conflicting comments between Steve and his ex-wife.

"Steve played a little sports throughout childhood, but he was not big enough or talented enough to be outstanding. He had slender fingers and a small frame, although he was average height. I could not imagine he would have ever been on the A-team. Truthfully, he didn't aspire to play, despite his pretense otherwise. Our mother stayed in the background for the most part. She was caring enough, but she never tangled with Father. She never wanted to make waves."

The story brought on fresh tears as Amelia described their father's alcoholism and progressive nastiness. He had hit her only once—a bloody lip from a hard slap—when he called her a slut. She had been eleven or twelve. "It wasn't so much the slap as the venom that spewed with it. For the most part, I managed to keep out of harm's way and out of sight. Staying invisible was the safest strategy, and I've continued to employ it throughout my life. As far as I knew, it was the only time Father was physically abusive. I never saw him touch Steve in any way, but Steve was always afraid of him."

Kelly hardly needed to ask any questions as the words streamed forth from Amelia, but when Amelia got up to offer chamomile tea and a mini-donut straight from the package, Kelly asked, "Would you describe Steve as a peace-loving and gentle man? Was it a result of his father's roughness?" She added, "Sue described him that way, and so had others. Of course, I know this is not the case. Maybe Steve saw himself that way, and it was how he wanted to be perceived."

The teacup rattled in Amelia's hands as she poured the tea. Her countenance changed drastically from sad to hard and scared. "We were at our aunt and uncle's chicken farm for several weeks one summer. I was sent back home before Steve. I found it disgusting watching how the chickens were kept and killed, and when I spoke up, my aunt and uncle explained how it worked on the farm. They tried to make me feel better about it, but I didn't feel better—and they sent me home."

Kelly didn't have a chance to ask how Steve fared.

Amelia said, "Steve seemed especially disturbed by what occurred on the farm—but in a different way. At first, I was annoyed by Steve's reaction. He was maybe seven or eight. I even got angry with him. He became obsessed with watching the heads of the chickens being chopped off. I tried to get him to stop looking, but he wouldn't. It was like he was excited and repulsed at the same time. He was intrigued, but it appeared to be more than that. He seemed almost possessed, certainly preoccupied. The look on his face was unsettling. He was sent home a week after me. I guess they were angry with him. He never said a nice word about Aunt Fran and Uncle Mitchell after that. Actually, he never said anything at all about them. I never saw them again. I have no idea whether Steve did. Mitchell died around the time Mother did. I heard Fran passed a short time ago; maybe it's been two years now. Steve had always loved fried chicken, but he refused to eat any chicken after that. There was something more to it than empathy for the chickens or mere disgust. It was more like an act of self-discipline, a deprivation, a way of controlling his desire. It was like anorexia in some way. He had always been as tight as a drum for a little kid, but it got worse after the farm."

Kelly listened without saying a word.

"In my first six years as an only child, Father barely said anything to me. He came home only for dinner, yelled at mother, and pretty much ignored me. Steve was a different story. He craved Father's attention. He was a pleaser. He did everything he could to please Father and Mother. He would change his behavior, depending on who was around. If both of our parents were there, Father was the one he'd try to please most—or displease least. However, Father never seemed to be happy no matter what Steve did. He continued to ride Steve about being 'a nancy.' He started calling Steve that when he was three or four."

Amelia described the development of Steve's fears. "First it was monsters under the bed, and then, it was the big kids at school—or at least that's what he said. There might have been some teasing, but in Steve's mind, everyone was picking on him. No officials from school ever reported anything as far as I know, and I never heard any rumors from the other kids that he was a target. We grew up in a small town. I would have heard if Steve was being hassled."

Kelly listened intently to Amelia's description of Steve's lack of ability to stick up for himself. Without judgment or disdain, Amelia used the term *crybaby*. His sniveling annoyed their father. Amelia attempted to intervene on Steve's behalf without their father knowing. "I tried to help him with his confidence, and there were many times Steve *acted* like he was strong, but he continued blaming others for everything. He seemed terrified of doing anything wrong. Father was probably the cause of that, though I don't know for sure. Maybe it just became a habit. Maybe it was inborn. Maybe it was all of that." Amelia poured a second cup of tea. "There was a strange, scary relationship between Father and Steve. Several years after we went to the farm, Steve found Father in a pool of blood. He was worried about what Father would do if the house wasn't clean, and he scrubbed up the blood. Without knowing any better, he destroyed the evidence. Father died of a gunshot wound to the head. The gun was in Father's hand.

"The police questioned Steve. At first, they laid it on thick with him, especially about cleaning up. There had been speculation that it might have been a murder made to look like a suicide, and we were all probed about possible enemies. Father, as you can imagine, certainly had his share of bar fights. Plus he owed people money. But we didn't offer much information.

"Not one of us would admit that we didn't have a lot of regret about his being gone. Mother was visibly shaken but also relieved. I cried despite my hatred of Father. Ironically, Steve didn't cry. At that point, he toughened up. Father would have been proud. Sometimes behavior can't be explained. I always wondered why Steve was home that afternoon since we both made a point of staying out as late as possible when Father was there.

"I had no idea why he would clean up, but the police accepted his explanation. I never saw Steve as irrational. He always had a plausible answer and wriggled out of everything. Steve *knew* the man was dead— or at least badly injured. Why didn't he call an ambulance or the police? He was twelve—not five. I wasn't about to call attention to it. I wanted out of that house as fast as possible, but I do regret that I didn't do more to help my troubled brother."

Kelly asked, "What about the final police report?"

"I guess the police presumed Father was drunk, and in his drunkenness, he killed himself. No one pushed for any other determination. I lost all sense of responsibility for my family at that point. I only wanted to take care of myself. I had little to nothing to do with Steve after I left. I maintained contact with Mother, but the relationship was strained. When I phoned, Mother let me know Steve wasn't interested in talking.

"Mother was always quite proud of Steve. *She* thought Steve blamed himself for Father's death. She thought he believed Father killed himself because Steve was a disappointment. *I* doubt Steve ever felt any guilt or thought of himself as a disappointment. I was estranged from him, and I can't really say. Honestly, I couldn't tell you for sure what happened or why.

"Steve was always the center of attention. Even when he complained or cried, he would somehow extol his achievements. I wanted Mother to get counseling for herself and Steve, but she didn't. She believed people should take personal responsibility for coping with whatever came their way. She never had been one to whine or make excuses, which was funny considering how Steve behaved. Psychology and counseling were mysterious to her, and she was not going to have her son labeled. She'd heard of misfits being sent to institutions for the insane. That terrified her. There was no money for it anyway. She told me Steve was fine. He never got into trouble. Mother continued to rely on Steve to provide. Instead of feeding into a sports fantasy, she had him take jobs at local churches, playing the piano and organ on Sundays.

"I suppose he liked the attention; it probably made him feel important. And he was more suited to music than baseball or football. He made the rounds of various churches over the next few years, but he mostly played in their church. Occasionally, he was part of a talent show or performed in a local concert. Mother told me he wanted to be a concert musician.

"Mother fell ill ten years after Father's death. Steve had been away at school, but he came back for her funeral. We only spoke as needed to make arrangements and divide family possessions. Steve went through the attic and came down with a small box. On his way out the door, he took one or two pictures of himself. I was able to look at him with fresh eyes. He was no longer a boy. We were no longer under Father's control or Mother's obligations. He and I hadn't spoken in years. He showed no regret about that. With the benefit of distance and my studies in psychology, I was increasingly convinced that there was something wrong with him. Neither of us had been there for Mother, but everyone assumed Steve had been the devoted son—and I was the irresponsible, unloving, and unappreciative daughter.

"He didn't seem sad at her funeral. I didn't show a lot of grief either. I loved her, but I needed to break away. When she died, I was married to my first husband. I had a whole new life. I left our town for the last time. Steve and Mother hadn't known how nearby I lived. I moved only two hours away. I moved to Knoxville for a little while, but then I came back here."

Kelly had not been taking notes as Amelia spoke, but she was absorbing everything Amelia communicated. She was close to tears. She excused herself for a restroom break to compose herself, considering that Amelia might need a moment. When she returned, Amelia picked right up where she had left off.

"After Mother's funeral, I became terrified that there was something genetically wrong with him. Although he'd say the right things at the right moment, he seemed mechanical and hollow. He looked sad on cue, and he grinned winningly when he or someone else told a joke.

"I was pregnant at the time. It scared me that I might be passing on bad genes to my child. What if I had the same tendencies as Steve but had somehow managed to suppress them? Maybe I was irrational because of the hormones. I was really scared. After I gave birth, I became increasingly despondent. They said it was postpartum depression. It didn't feel normal to me. I did my best with my little girl, at first, but eventually my fears intensified. I drove my husband away. I made him take my little girl with him. I couldn't bear the thought that I might injure her, even psychologically." Amelia stopped speaking and looked at Kelly. "We divorced. He remarried a lovely woman, and his new wife raised her as her own. I knew my baby would have a good life. I hoped it would be a fulfilling and happy one. I never tried to contact her, even though I really wanted to." She choked back tears. "I was so ashamed. I did manage to follow your life from a distance."

Kelly saw her own blue eyes reflected in Amelia's. She breathed in deeply and asked, "Have you ever gone to the Ridgecrest Road Church in Knoxville?"

Kelly thought of the older woman she had spoken with there. The woman had mentioned a resemblance to Emily. *Amelia.*

Amelia took a deep breath. "Yes, I was a member for a period of time, but when I heard that Steve had interviewed for a position as organist, I left. I had no desire to run into him."

At that moment, Kelly confirmed what Amelia already knew.

Tears streaming, Amelia reached out to hug her daughter. Kelly softened in her arms. On a completely primitive level, she knew why this story had been *her* story from the start. She had completed the puzzle.

She thought of Steve, and a chill ran down her spine. She made the final connection.

"People routinely buy into outlandish claims that calm particular anxieties, fill given needs or affirm preferred worldviews. Religions and wrinkle-cream purveyors alike depend on that."

—Frank Bruni, *The New York Times*
August 25, 2012

# *Epilogue*

## *Kyle*

I didn't even know he wasn't ordained. I really didn't say enough. I should have been more direct. I regret everything and am deeply saddened.

Sam. Rachel. Their children, Tommy and Lena. Jonah. Sue. Too much pain. I have no pity for Steve—though, knowing he can't help himself, maybe I should.

## *Amanda*

Steve is still working at that place. He returned to TLC after he recovered from being shot. Unbelievable. Even after "At the Heart of the Matter" aired, even after learning from that program that Steve had not even been ordained, nothing changed. People can't cope with reality. Apparently, Steve fills a bizarre need, and church members are not willing to let go of him.

Before the trial, even before the shooting, I tried—and so did Kyle—to provide the facts and set the record straight. No one wanted to hear it. I believe in my heart of hearts that Steve goaded Kyle … because he needed to discredit him to save himself. In some ways, he's easier to forgive than the others. Even though he knows right from wrong, he can't ever see himself as wrong. He's scary.

In retrospect, there are a lot of things I would have done differently. I think what held me back was I didn't want to do anything that wouldn't be well received or in the range of acceptable behavior for those people. But I'm not sure anything I did would have made a difference in how things ended.

I had hoped to reclaim a caring community. I gave it a try. I wish more people would take the time to *really* try to understand others and not make assumptions. It takes courage and work to ask questions. If only at least some people had apologized or even acknowledged their part in creating the horror.

Dinny pretends all is well, and Will won't even look at us. Maybe Littleton isn't big enough for all of us. Sometimes I think in terms of music when I think of Dinny and Will. For Dinny, it's the fairy godmother singing "Bibbidi-Bobbidi-Boo" in the Disney version of *Cinderella*. For Will, the refrain from Paul Simon's "The Boxer" runs through my head: "All lies and jests, still a man hears what he wants to hear and disregards the rest."

Sue's solution was the worst. It is astounding to me, though, that even after everything that happened, so few are able to understand it from her point of view. Poor Sue. And Claire is still with Steve—what will become of her?

## Sheila

I believe Steve was capable of seeding the idea that Kyle was a physical threat and could have given the go-ahead signal to Jonah.

It's also possible that Steve was terrified for his job, his life, or both. Or even that one was a subset of the other. It's clear to me that he was afraid of Kyle—that Kyle would or could expose him. Kyle was an easy target, a perfect scapegoat. But does that make Steve guilty of anything other than being deceitful and spiteful?

Whatever he did or didn't do, he did not suffer any consequences—other than a superficial gunshot wound. I suppose the new board will have some troubles with him eventually.

Here at TLC, like at most churches, we talk a lot about love. But we don't seem to *do* much of it. People think it is an automatic emotion that doesn't require work, but there's a lot of thinking that goes into a relationship. The thinking part, the asking part, the understanding, and putting it all together part was missing at TLC. That said, even if you don't love a person, you should respect him or her.

I have questions, lots of them. I don't have many answers. I'll tell you one thing for sure, though. I'm very happy that the church is no longer my problem.

Sue is a mess. She worries constantly about what she did and what will happen to Claire. I've visited her a couple of times. She still maintains that the man had to be stopped, and she regrets having failed to stop him. Poor Sue.

### Dinny

I don't know what to think anymore. I went to the trial for a bit on the first day. I couldn't take it. It was too upsetting. When I went back, I looked to my higher angels for strength and guidance. The trial turned out all wrong. I'm sure everything will get ironed out during the appeal. Jonah is innocent. He did what any of us would have done. Well, not any of us, but some of us. I couldn't have done that, of course, but I understand why he did it, and I forgive him. I miss Sam and Jonah, but I'm moving on. Whenever I see Amanda, I smile and give her a hug to let her know I forgive her too.

Steve is a good person. I refused to watch that TV program. It's too painful. Steve was terrified—that's all. He didn't deserve the treatment he got. He and I go out for wine every once in a while. I don't blame him for not taking Claire to that place where her mother is.

I don't want to hear any more about it. People who insist on rehashing everything are not doing themselves any favors. I love my church, and I love Steve. I listen to what Steve has to say each week, and I allow his music to permeate. It makes me happy. If everyone behaves in a loving fashion, people will eventually forget and move on.

The whole episode with Sue confused me. I knew her. She was a peace-loving person. I never thought she could find a gun, let alone use one. Well, we're not always right about people. I'm angry with her, and I guess she belongs where she is, but I don't like to think of her being confined. No one deserves that. They say the gun was Steve's and traced back to his father. I guess it was an inheritance, but I don't know. I don't believe he would have a gun. Steve struggled for a while, but he's a survivor. Thank goodness. I'm not sure about Sue. Poor Steve.

## Will

I did not like the way they treated Steve at TLC back then, and it started again recently. Sheryl wanted to find a new church. We left TLC and went back to our old church, but it was not because of Steve. One day, I saw Whitman at *my* church. He has balls, that guy. He's unwelcome at Steve's church, and then he comes to mine? I was so mad I had to leave. Sheryl wasn't pleased about that, but we walked right out before the service started.

I'm not going to let him intimidate me, but I won't tolerate his presence. Maybe we'll move to another town. Steve made everyone feel so good. I miss that. Damn it. I'll go back to *my* church and ignore Whitman. He can't bully me!

I don't get Sue. She seemed so sweet and so devoted to Steve and Claire. Those cute pecks on the cheek she would give Steve—always with a grin. Why would she shoot him? It just doesn't make any sense. I don't believe anything that was said on that Kelly Allen TV show.

I gave her permission to use some of the video and interviews, but I didn't like how Steve was portrayed. It really irked me. And I have to say Amanda Corwell doesn't know what the heck she's talking about. She's dead wrong. What a disappointment. Well, lessons learned. Poor Steve.

# *Afterword*

## *Sue*

Sue remains under psychiatric care, having pled guilty to attempted murder by reason of insanity. She took responsibility for what she had done to Steve, although she never said she regretted it. However, her ever-present sense of guilt regarding Jonah and Sam is overwhelming. She can't stop crying unless she's heavily medicated, which she is most of the time.

Once Kelly's TV program aired, sympathy for Sue's situation increased. Her family is hopeful that someday she can return to some semblance of a normal life.

Her older daughters and her ex-husband visit regularly, but Steve does not allow Claire to see her mother. He has sole custody.

## *Jonah*

Jonah was sent to an upstate prison and is working on his appeal. He has been writing a book and is hoping it earns enough to sustain Sam's family forever. Steve has not visited him or made any contact.

## Kelly

Kelly's story is not finished. In a way, it has just begun. The show aired and was a success. She continues to work in a niche of investigative journalism that focuses on the human side, the psychological side, relationships, and behavior. She is currently in postgraduate school, in a PhD program, working closely with Dr. Levinson. She is deepening her relationships with her parents—all of them—and she is working with Zack on many things.

# *Acknowledgments*

When I first thought of the idea for this novel, I desperately wanted to give it away to someone who was an accomplished writer. I even had a specific author in mind. However, when I discussed it with a dear friend, he suggested that I do it myself. There were many times I regretted Robb's challenge, but I have never regretted his encouragement. Without that initial impetus, this book would never have been started.

My husband and life partner was a source of continuous support throughout the process. Early on, Dave maintained an appropriate distance, but he was always close enough to provide words when I drew a blank or offer perspective when I was too close. At a point when I was just about ready to call it quits, he spurred me on with his willingness to plow through. He worked with me on the details and was my "word caddy." Without his help, the book might never have been finished.

Thanks to Martine Bellen, my first editor, who patiently plodded through several iterations and offered numerous suggestions that were inordinately helpful in getting me beyond some rather poorly written initial drafts.

Paul Greenfield, a New York writer, offered the first objective review.

I appreciate his courage. I was mortified to find out I did not have a novel at all at that time. His general suggestions seemed overwhelming, and I shut down for a while. However, he was right—and I am grateful for his professionalism and candor.

Teresa—my friend, ally, and the epitome of diplomacy—read my first effort. I now know that it was simply awful. I am so thankful that she didn't tell me that and instead suggested it would make a good play. Maybe someday I—or someone else—will do a conversion.

I told the story to numerous family members and friends, and I want to thank them for listening and not telling me to shut up, although I knew they probably wanted to.

I would be remiss if I did not at least mention the person without whom the concept for this book would not exist. I am remiss.

# About the Author

This is Tina Spangler's first attempt at writing and publishing a novel. With an educational background in counseling and psychology, she pursued a career as an organization development consultant and coach. Her decades of experience observing human behavior, along with her natural analytical instincts, compel her to question the answers and dig beneath the surface. She can handle the truth and is amazed at the number of people who can't. She lives in Saint Petersburg, Florida, with her husband.

Printed in the United States
By Bookmasters